Black Ops

by

Jess Parker

PublishAmerica
Baltimore

First printing

ISBN: 1-4137-5511-9
PUBLISHED BY PUBLISHAMERICA, LLLP
www.publishamerica.com
Baltimore

Printed in the United States of America

Dedication

Judy
My wife since 09/03/54
She told many years ago that I could be a successful author.
I finally took her advice at 70 years of age; *Black Ops* is my third book.

Acknowledgments

Judy Parker, my wife, my number one fan, and a great editor. Victoria Allen, MD, my doctor. I gave her the title: "The Best Doctor in the World."

My children: Tom Parker; Clay Parker; Sheila Stone; Karen and Mike Pruett; Erin and John Sackman. They have offered encouragement all along the way. Mary Ann Smith, photographer.

My cheer squad at the Rowdy Table, Kitsap Mall, Silverdale, Washington: Joe McManus, Ralph Strickland, Blaise Sweet, Amy Sweet, Linda Tecson, Mel Tecson, Wes Morton, Charlie Davis, Bill Probst, Patricia Thorsted, and many others who drop by for a visit.

Other books by Jess Parker:

Detachment X-Ray
Covert Avengers

Foreword

The river boat coasted up and smoothly came alongside the community pier in Venture, Washington. The helmsman was Jake Green, who was known in the area as The Fisherman. Three other men left the boat with Green, and most people of Venture could identify them as United States Senator Sam Martin, Dean Andrew Pilkusski of Central State University, and Vice President Victor Slawson of the United States of America. The Fisherman had been offered a number of political positions, but he had answered all offers, "The position I am interested in is my seat on the boat as we troll down the river for prize salmon."

The fishermen off loaded some nice prizes. There were four fish over 25 pounds and five more coming in between 8 and 10 pounds. One of the larger salmon became dinner for the evening and the others were sent to food bank stores. Green had started the act of giving his extra fish and game to people in need after he had returned to the community from a stint in Washington, D.C. as an aide of Senator Martin. (*Covert Avengers*). The three visitors were not only visiting a friend, they were trying to enlist his aid. Senator Martin had accompanied Vice President Slawson, and both of the politicians were trying to persuade Green to return to Washington, D.C., to head up the Committee to Elect the President.

Senator Martin was a long-time friend of Jake Green and was acting as an agent for the President of the United States. Vice President Slawson had been introduced as the strongest Vice President in history. The political plans in his future included winning the election after President William Farmer had completed his second term. Senator Martin was trying to convince Jake to take the political appointment and argued, "Jake, this is important because we are trying for the best possible candidate, not because we want to elect the first black president. Victor is the one we want. He is a brilliant man and will be a great president."

Martin tried to ignore Green, who said, "Sam, I will be truthful. I don't want to go to Washington in any position. From what I have seen in the past few hours—and knowing Victor Slawson's history, I agree that he probably would make a fine president. But Sam, you have to remember how I left your office amid the rumors about the assassination of Dong Ping. If those rumors resurfaced, it would be a detriment to the Vice President and the President."

Sam Martin chuckled and whispered, "Yeah, tell me whut happen with the big Chinee. It weren't you or your three buddies 'cuz all of you wuz surrounded by agents and policemen."

Martin had dropped into his good ole boy style conversation and let out a whoop of laughter when Jake whispered a reply, "Sam, I will tell you one truth. I am not discussing Dong Ping any more."

The vice president joined the conversation and said, "Jake, it would be an honor for both the president and me if you would join us in Washington."

Everyone laughed when Green retorted, "Mr. Vice President, we are already in the great state of Washington. I am glad that you are honored to be here. Believe me, sir, we are honored to have you visit, but look around—Where had you rather be, in Venture, Washington, or Washington, D.C.?"

The politician kept the humor going by declaring, "As Victor Slawson, I would pick Venture, but as vice president, the Pennsylvania Avenue address fits me very well." He continued in a more sober vein, "Seriously, Jake, we need people like you, and Sam Martin guarantees us a win if you are on board."

Dean Andrew Pilkusski broke in with an agreement and suggested that the present and hopefully the next administration would be very good for Central State University. "Jake, where do you think we get enough money to pay for the work you do?" This got a chuckle from everyone.

Green backed away from all suggestions about going with his visitors. He even discussed the rumors about the assassination of the Chinese leader. Vice-President Slawson suggested that all it would take to quell the rumor would be for Jake to go publicly and deny all of the rumors. Jake chuckled to himself and noticed that Sam Martin was looking at him with raised eyebrows. The Senator offered a slight smile when Jake said a final no—he would not be going back to D.C. for any position. He was tempted, though, just see what the reaction would be from the FBI and CIA. Both agencies had done their best to tie the assassination of the Chinese leader to Jake and his friends.

Green had recognized Hsu Dong Ping as a Chinese Army Major who had tortured captured Marines during the Korean War. Green had accidentally become involved in a frontline advance and was with the survivors of a marine battalion that had been captured by a contingent of the North Korean army. Captain John Silvers, officer in charge of the front line spotting party, recognized the Chinese officer as Long Ball Kwong. During a march to the north Silvers, Green and three other marines escaped, and years later, Jake Green and his friends had planned to assassinate Dong Ping, who was in line for the Premier of the Chinese government (*Detachment X-Ray* and *Covert Avengers*).

After the escape from North Korea, Green and his friends were immediately split up and officially, their adventures never happened. A few days after Jake returned to his ship, orders arrived for him to report to the transportation office at the Yokosuka Naval Base. He was met by a Navy Commander and escorted, with others, to the Norfolk, Virginia, Navy Base. This started a series of training exercises and undercover operations that led to *Detachment X-Ray*. Jake's career with *Detachment X-Ray* ended abruptly and he was advised to go to deep cover in civilian life.

He stayed in deep cover in his adopted town, Venture, Washington. Years later, his friend Senator Sam Martin persuaded him to take a position in the senate office. The story told in *Covert Avengers* commenced when Jake discovered Long Ball Kwong and then accidentally rediscovered marine comrades from North Korea. The five old soldiers decided to assassinate their wartime enemy. They received on-the-job training with local operations against personal or common enemies.

Chapter 1

When the Washington visitors left Venture, Jake returned to his normal routine, fishing for himself, and occasionally acting as guide for out-of-town fishermen. He came home one afternoon and a message was on the telephone answering service. A female voice calmly said, "The leeches are in Porter Lake." Jake sat down and listened to the message a couple of times. Then he smiled and leaned back in his chair. A memory from a few years ago came flooding in concerning a training exercise on a beach along the Virginia shoreline. A young female Navy seaman had come out of the Great Dismal Swamp covered with leeches. Jake forced her to remove all clothing so that he could rid her of the bloodsuckers with salt water. His memory continued when, years later, he had the occasion to once again work with Darlene (Seaman) Coppage. They had parted after a very dangerous operation and Jake had slipped her his unlisted telephone number with a message, "In case the leeches arrive again."

It was evident that Darlene Coppage was in need of special help because she wouldn't have sent the message without dire need. Jake used an atlas to locate Porter Lake in the mountains of Idaho. He did not hesitate: the house was closed, a bag was packed and a telephone message to a friend noting the abrupt departure. Within an hour after the message, he was heading east on Interstate Highway I-90. After moving into Idaho, he turned south toward the high mountains. During the run south, he spotted a direction sign for Porter Lake at an intersection, which afforded a small motel where he would spend the night.

Jake was on the road again at 0500 and at 0615 he crested a hill and Porter Lake was spread before him. The small town was on the western shore of the lake and Jake started dreaming about trout fishing. A small restaurant appeared at the head of the community pier. He went in for breakfast and was served in a back booth. Jake took a seat facing the door. It opened and Police Chief Darlene Coppage entered with two men. A big grin spread across her face when she saw Jake and headed for his booth. The chief introduced the Mayor of Porter Lake and editor of the local newspaper. Darlene said, "Jake, what a surprise to see you. What are you doing in Porter Lake?"

They all laughed at his reply, "Well, I was heading down the interstate and realized that I needed to stop. So I checked in at the motel and this morning I saw the road to Porter Lake. I started smelling trout and just followed my nose." Jake continued, "How in the world did you become chief of police? I knew you when you were Seaman Coppage."

He felt the pressure of her knee against his as she said, "Good, I will be your fishing guide. I know a hole where the big ones live. Meet me at the boathouse about five o'clock tomorrow morning. Oh, and I became chief when no one would take the job."

Green decided to get to the pier early. He wanted the chance to observe the surrounding area without being obvious. When he arrived, some fishermen were ready to make their first cast at sunrise. The boat people were preparing for launch, some were already moving to their favorite locations where the big one would bite. Jake was relieved to see the early risers, because he could blend into the scenery with his fishing gear in hand. Darlene Coppage arrived and they lowered her boat into the water. She moved out and was staying clear of the other fishermen. They didn't try to talk over the engine noise, and when it was cut to trolling speed they rigged their lines and put them over the side.

Jake said, "O.K., Seaman. Tell me about the leeches."

She replied, " I have three schools of the bloodsuckers in my town. The narcotic smugglers offer most of the problems because they bring in the buyers and distributors. Then we have the skinheads trying to hold up both sides. The supremacists have a lot of support from some of the natives—even our favorite mayor is willing to look the other way because of the money he gets from the three groups."

Jake did not respond for a few minutes and then he asked, "Can I do what I think is best to salt the leeches?" She nodded her head and started to reply, Jake held up his hand before she could speak. He continued, "Darlene, your are chief of police. Consider what I just implied. Think about it for a while, but now, let's get that big one."

They hauled in the trolling gear and rigged for casting. Darlene pulled the boat closer to shore. She pointed out a spot for Jake to cast and as he did, he received a heavy strike. The trout jumped and Jake saw that he had caught his trout. He told Darlene that this was the big one until a bigger one was caught. He saw the flash in her eyes and grin that accepted the implied challenge. The fish were striking fast and most of the big ones were being released. Jake glanced around and found their boat entirely surrounded by other fishermen. Darlene yelled at a couple of them bragging that the big ones had been caught and released and would not be biting again. Two limits had been taken and kept for dinner. All of these were just pan-sized that Darlene had promised to cook if Jake would clean.

Neither of them had mentioned their previous conversation and did not until they were clear of the surrounding boats. She left the group at trolling speed, out of respect for her fellow anglers. When they were about half a mile from the marina she stopped the engine and said, "Jake, you take care of things the way you want to. Don't tell me, but if you need help I will be there."

"Thanks pal," Jake replied, "I know I can count on you, but I will attempt to stay clear of your town. If I get into a problem and need help, I know whom to call and that includes you."

Chapter 2

Jake commenced his investigation by following the mayor of Porter Lake as he played his game of offering protection to all groups. It turned out that Mayor Bruce Willingham was a Grand Wizard of the local chapter of the Ku Klux Klan. One night Jake was led to an abandoned school where the combined supremacist movements met. While the meeting was going on, Jake toured the outside of the building and was relieved that no children were in evidence. He made his way back to his automobile and dodged a security patrol. Jake mused, “Better watch what I am doing. I should have figured that there would be security employed for the meetings.” He noticed that the guards were wearing neo-nazi uniforms and were armed with automatic assault weapons. It became apparent that it would take planning and careful movements for this group to be stopped. Some of the planning would have to answer the question whether or not he could carry out a mission without support.

Darlene Coppage was not considered for the mission because, as chief of police, she would be invaluable as a source of information about the coming and goings of all her enemies. A plethora of names came to Jake’s mind, Carpenter, the sniper, was always there, as other names were discarded. Yet there was hesitation of involving any of his friends. On one of his patrols he found an ideal spot for a sniper that would cover the entire area. His thoughts were, “Carpenter and I could control anyone within sight, but how could we take the building? I wonder if Colonel Tolliver can still handle explosives.” The names Tolliver and Carpenter brought back many memories.

One morning at breakfast, Darlene passed a note that Jake pocketed. She said, ”You should think about leaving. I don’t see how this situation can be solved.”

"Let me take care of such events," he answered. After leaving the restaurant, Jake moved out to the end of the pier. The note stated that a planeload of drugs could be expected on Sunday of the following week. Information also indicated that the leaders of both groups would be in attendance for a strategy meeting. This surprised Jake because of the blatant disregard for the local authorities. He also read that the Klan and Nazi groups were schedule to parade on the same day. In the note, Darlene explained that this situation had never occurred before and she speculated that all of the leeches were coming together in a joint effort to operate the different enterprises as one operation.

Jake drove out to the interstate and checked into the motel that he had visited before going to Porter Lake. After getting settled, he left the room and located a pay telephone. He dialed a number and was pleasantly surprised when Lydia Carpenter answered. Without identification he asked, "Is this the most beautiful woman in the world."

She immediately answered, "Only if you are my personal coffee maker." She was referring to Jake's visits where he was an early riser and would have coffee ready when she and the sniper arrived in the kitchen. Lydia continued, "Where are you? We would like you to visit if possible."

Jake responded, "I can't come to your place, but tell that ugly husband that the trout are biting in Porter Lake, Idaho, and I might need help landing them. A week from Sunday is the tournament." He made a similar call to Washington, D.C., and asked for Colonel Tolliver. His old friend was no longer a colonel—somewhere along the line Tolliver had become Brigadier General, U.S. Marine Corps. Jake left the basically the same message that he had delivered to the Carpenters. He added, "Tell the General that I will certainly understand if he does not want to go to the tobacco market at Porter Lake, Idaho."

At the mention of tobacco markets Tolliver would know the caller. He and Green made history in the days of the formation of Detachment X-Ray. They disappeared for almost a month during a survival training exercise. While their comrades were crossing the Green Swamp and becoming prisoners in an exercise prison camp, they had a great time at two of the best North Carolina tobacco market towns. In both calls, Jake suggested meeting at the Lake Front Motel in Coeur d'Alene, Idaho.

Chapter 3

At breakfast on Friday morning, Jake told Darlene that he would be leaving after the morning fishing trip. She looked surprised but didn't question him. He was secretive for her benefit because he didn't want her to be anxious until the mission was completely planned. The noon departure was for the benefit of the citizens who had seen him in and around town and most times with Chief Coppage. Jake made sure that as many people as possible were aware of his leaving after having lunch with Mayor Willingham and George Strong, editor of the Porter Lake newspaper, the *Idaho Sun Times.* He waved at Darlene and called, "See you another day, Seaman Coppage. Keep your boat clean. I might be back this way soon. I haven't finished using Porter Lake. I think the "big one" is still out there." She grinned and waved.

Jake checked in at the Lake Front Motel in Coeur d'Alene at 1800 and reserved other units to be available for his visitors on Monday. He settled in and started mapping Porter Lake from drawings he had made and pictures he had taken while visiting the area. The drawings were of the airplane landing area, the surface loading area, and the meeting place for the supremacist groups. His notations were clearly printed in the margins. Actual photographs taken from surrounding locations backed the entire drawing. Darlene Coppage had furnished pictures taken of the characters involved with the different organizations. Jake was relieved that the mayor was the only local official involved with any of the outlaw organizations. The information was thin as it concerned the smugglers, but Chief Coppage had put together a good packet on those receiving the contraband. The leadership was out of Boise and the laborers were from Porter Lake—most struggling to support their families. A note was made that the local people, if possible, would be segregated from the others. Jake made a point not to allow that concern to jeopardize the mission and/or safety of the individuals carrying out the mission.

A helicopter was hired on Sunday and Jake spent most of the day criss-crossing the Porter Lake area comparing his drawing with actual airborne observations. One thing stood out, which wasn't expected. The aircraft-landing ramp was hidden from the projected vantage point he had selected from the surface observations. Extra passes were made and pictures taken until the pilot became interested in Jake's story about an "airborne survey of all the mountain lakes." Upon arriving at the Lake Front Motel, he immediately commenced making new plans based on the new information concerning the Porter Lake aircraft-landing ramp.

Sunday morning he looked once again at the survey drawings and pictures and was satisfied that the most likely problems had been addressed. He smiled as he thought of the visitors he was expecting and was sure other problems and ideas would be noted. The restaurant next to the motel was lighted and it appeared that their day had begun. The visitors he was expecting waved as he came through the door. There were visitors he had not expected at the same table. "Old home week!" he exclaimed. Carpenter brusquely told him to sit down so "brefas" could be served. The unexpected pluses were John and Samantha Silvers along with Sarg and Darlene Jacobs. After greetings were over and everyone settled down for "brefas," Jake told them that another person might join them. The mid-westerners occupied the reserved rooms, so he would have to make arrangements for Tolliver in case he showed.

Tolliver showed up with a great surprise for Jake. He introduced his wife as Marie, but Jake laughed and grabbed her for a hug and kiss, then he said, "Marie hell, her name is George," (*Detachment X-Ray*). After the Tollivers were settled in, Jake invited them to a meeting in his suite at 1100. As they parted he said, "Tolliver, I know about your star. So think about what you are willing to join today"

The general laughed and asked how Jake knew he was a flag officer. Then he said, "Hell, Jake, if I turned you down, I would be killed by my wife. She says that she is going, also. You might say there are two ready and willing operatives, so lead on, lead on, oh, master." They all laughed because of the stories about the trip to the tobacco markets.

Jake was working on the displays when the knock on the door sounded. His friends were waiting to enter. When all settled he introduced the Tollivers and with everyone discussed backgrounds and how they related to each other. Tolliver did not indicate his Marine affiliation, and Jake said, "You guys listen up. You are ex-Marines and Mr. Tolliver here is also Brigadier General Tolliver, U.S. Marine Corps."

Sarg Jacobs got a laugh when he complained, "Oh rats, you mean to tell me I have to stand at attention again?"

The general spoke up, "You bet your ass, Sarg. If you don't, I will tell my wife and her name use to be George. Wait until you hear her story." It wasn't long before the group was relaxed and having a good time. They really got a kick when Jake related how George would get them out of trouble with the pace she would set.

Darlene Jacobs spoke up, "O.K., Jake, what is going on? Have you got another premier in your sights?"

Jake laughed and responded, "No, nothing like that Darlene. A friend of mine is in trouble. She is chief of police of a small town here in Idaho. It has become a haven for the drug traffic and other contraband to the northwest. Then, to top off that situation, it is also the hometown of the local KKK and the neo-Nazis. The mayor of Porter Lake is the Grand Dragon, or grand something, of the KKK."

George spoke up and asked, "Jake, are you talking about Darlene Coppage?" When he nodded, Tolliver spoke up. "We know Darlene, and I say let's do what Jake is planning. I have been sitting on my ass for a long time."

Darlene Jacobs received a chuckle when she declared, "With a name like Darlene, I am ready to help."

John Silvers spoke for the first time, "What are you planning, Jake?"

Green unrolled his drawings and pictures of the Porter Lake area. He explained all of the situations and timing. His information was that a planeload of drugs would come in on Sunday morning of the following week. Jake noted that there would be a full week to complete the planning and surveying the situation. He also pointed out the perceived problem of the aircraft landing area; it wouldn't be visible from the most prominent hillside. This problem was being discussed when Carpenter suggested that instead of the hillside position, he would stay on the lakeshore where a stand of trees met the waterline. Jake asked the sniper if he could keep the plane from taking off after unloading.

Carpenter did not hesitate, he said, "Yep."

There was no explanation of how he could do the job and no one asked.

Jake said, “Wait a minute, now. I plan to take out all of these people, so it might—and probably will turn bloody. Does anyone want to back out before we go any further?”

There was a long silence then John Silvers quietly said, “You can’t live forever. Samantha and I are in for the duration.” There were unanimous nods around the room. Jake said, “O.K. Lets memorize these pictures and formulate a plan. On Monday I recommend a camping trip up toward Porter Lake. This will give you guys a chance to become familiar with the area.”

The weekend was taken up with studying, talking, arguing, and planning. All of the participants were stubborn with their ideas and desires. By Sunday afternoon, Jake was satisfied that the mission could be carried out successfully and all of his forces were in agreement. The plans called for a coordinated attack on all sites, with attempts to take the three leaders alive. But everyone stressed the point that this would not be carried out at the expense of anyone’s life. The local labor force came under discussion and all agreed that as many as possible would be left alive but restrained for the local authorities.

Chapter 4

The camping trip was initiated at noon on Monday. Three vans were rented from three different companies—two in Spokane and one in Coeur d' Alene. It was decided that Jake and Samantha Silvers would take the supremacists headquarters. Carpenter, Jacobs, and George would be after the aircraft and crew while Tolliver and Darlene would go for the unloading crew. Silvers and Lydia were assigned the drug transport personnel. If the leaders could be captured, they were to be brought along with any contraband and money to the Klan/Nazi headquarters. The local laborers would be forced into a beachfront storehouse. Jake emphasized that no one was to take any unnecessary chances to make the capture. He also instructed that the hits wouldn't go until the contraband had been unloaded and reloaded to the transport vehicles. He said, "I don't think we should involve the chief of police. If we get into trouble, she would be invaluable to have as an insider. She said that she would be available for anything I would need. I told her to stay away and she doesn't know where we are or what we are planning. I made a big deal out of leaving and Darlene appeared a little disappointed. She may think that nothing is going to happen."

After the camp was made up and all provisions stored, Jake said, "O.K. Let's go take a look. Because of our number, maybe we should travel separately. Does anyone have any questions about how to get there?"

Sarg said in a complaining voice, "You mean I have to walk?"

The others laughed and Jake went to Samantha and said, "Here we are, pretty lady. How about taking a walk in the woods with me?"

She arched her brow and whispered loudly, "Why, of course. I thought you would never ask."

Amid the laughter, Tolliver said, "Wait now. If anyone goes to the tobacco markets, it will be Darlene and me." This fun talk continued until the group reached the tree line. Then each segment moved in different directions without saying anything. There were some nervous smiles directed at spouses, but no noise or demonstrations.

The trek through the forest was a fast paced movement with all senses alive. Jake led Samantha to the deserted school building and they hunkered down to observe the location. They quietly watched and waited but nothing moved—and they agreed that the site was deserted. Samantha whispered, "I don't believe that anyone is in there. I will go to right and circle to the back of the building." Without further words, she moved cautiously to the edge of the woods and turned toward her target. Jake watched her for a few minutes and started his approach. Their observations proved correct. The building was vacant. They paused at the back of the house.

Jake asked, "When we hit them, you want this side or the front?"

Her answer was, "You know some of these people and they may see you, so I will take this side where they will enter." The two plotters explored for a position for Samantha to take during the attack. Jake said that he would take the position in front of the building.

"We don't want to shoot each other," he said with a grin. She chuckled and they started for the house.

The old house had a deep crawl space that was a pleasant surprise because explosives could be placed in positions where no one or anything could survive the blast. They spent about two hours exploring and planning for the coming mission. When Jake was satisfied with the work, he suggested making their way back to the camp. He anticipated that the other teams would soon be returning. Samantha took the lead and set a fast pace—and after about fifteen minutes, she abruptly stopped. Jake froze and waited for her to explain. She moved slowly behind the trunk of a tree and whispered, "I saw some movement off to the right and I think it's a person." They stood frozen for a few minutes and both searched the surrounding area until they were satisfied that they were alone at this location. Samantha moved out slowly and in a few minutes made the same move and stood behind a tree. After the thorough investigation there were no further sightings of concern.

When they approached the camp, it was obvious by the campfire that others had returned. Carpenter was sitting on a log and Jacobs was lying on a table. George was making coffee with a very satisfied smirk on her face. Carpenter drawled, "Wheah did ya pick up this gal? She jest about run us ragged both there and back."

The other teams came in together and a thorough debriefing from all teams was made with questions, comments and suggestions. George said that they had found a location where the aircraft landing area could be controlled. Carpenter noted that he could disable the plane from the position. Silvers and Lydia described their plans to control the transportation vehicles. Tolliver and Darlene explained how they would handle the unloading crew. All agreed that more observations of the area and planning should be carried out.

During the conversation, Jake had seen an attractive young woman who appeared to be interested in the camp. She had hiked all around the site and at different times she would take a seat from which she could see movements and probably hear a few words of the conversation. He didn't think that she could have heard enough to be a threat. Someone offered a cup of coffee and he didn't pay any more attention to the observer. "Probably a camper checking out the neighborhood," he mused.

Carpenter and Silvers came to where he was seated and Carpenter said in a low voice. "Navy, they is a young woman thet seems mighty interested in us." Silvers said that Samantha had noticed her and told him of the return trip to camp.

After telling all of the campers to act as if they were not paying special attention, Silvers warned them about the young woman and suggested that she should be kept under casual observation while near the campsite, and said, "Sarg, she probably will think that you are asleep. Watch her and see if you can spot her destination when she leaves here."

Chapter 5

The campers spent the remainder of the day discussing the different plans being formulated by the different teams. Jake asked Samantha to start it off by discussing the attack and controlling the headquarters of the Nazi/Klan organizations. She told about the trail that leads to the old school and said, " I believe the girl over there was observing us on the way back this morning." Samantha took a deep breath and described what she and Jake had found. The story was continued with the information that told of the locations where the two observers would station themselves early in the morning of the exercise.

With a chuckle she said, "Don't anyone shoot us if you see movement." The entire group was interested when she spoke of the building that had at least four separate rooms and the high crawl space.

"You have any dynamite to put under that house?" asked Tolliver. He was answered with a negative and a shrug of the shoulders.

Jake didn't say anything but mused, "I didn't think of that sort of material. Better watch it guy, you are getting old."

Jacobs stood up from the table and said quietly, "Our little friend went into the fourth tent up the trail." The others casually spotted the indicated campsite and continued talking of the coming exercise. Samantha continued with her description of the Klan building. The other teams would be expected, if practical, to bring as many of the enemy they could to the building. Jake had already said, "We don't need to leave bodies all along the lake front." Here again there was a reminder not to take chances. The idea was to shoot first if there was any problem and if possible, transport the body to the building.

Samantha stated that she was sure the Klan/Nazi people could be held in the building. She said, “Jake will take the left side of the building and I will take the other. We should be able to keep their heads down until we want them out.” Someone asked what would happen if anyone escaped the building. She said with a wan smile, “Then I guess we will have to throw them back through the windows.” She turned and asked, “Have I missed anything, Navy?” She had used the name given to Jake during the Korean War.

“You covered that very well, but I think we should obtain some explosives for that building,”

Green replied and said, “Who’s next?”

George spoke up, “The Sarg and I will take care of the aircraft crew, and Carpenter has found a location to take out the airplane.” She and Jacobs went into detail about taking the crew by calling from the hidden location. If that concept worked, the people could be captured, but if capture became a problem, the crew would be taken out by gunfire. Everyone turned their attention to Carpenter and he told them that from his location he would be able to fracture the propellers of the aircraft.

Jake said, “Sounds great, old buddy, but what if they keep the propellers turning?” Carpenter answered with one of his long discourses of what would happen.

He drawled, “Then she comes apart when the gas tank goes.” That appeared to be one of the longest sentence the sniper had ever used.

Silvers asked with a grin, “Where did you learn all those words? I bet Lydia has been holding school call on you.”

The sniper broke up his audience as he put his arm around his wife, “Maybe so. She learns me a lot of things, and I lak school.”

Tolliver took over and started discussing his and Darlene’s plan for the load transfer from the plane to the transport vehicles. He said, “Now, every body, if possible don’t shoot until the dope is loaded into the transports.” Darlene told how they would capture the local characters by confronting them after the other personnel were in hand.

She said, “There is a three-sided cabin where we will leave them tied together and then tied to the structure. If we have time, we will gag them, also.” Then their plan was to join Silvers and Lydia at the transport site, and if needed, they would help to bring the other prisoners to the loading area for movement to the Klan headquarters.

John Silvers said that he and Lydia would remain out of sight until the contraband was loaded. At that time they would attempt to capture the group from the airplane. He said, "Both of us will keep track of the leaders to make sure they don't escape. We will or should have the seller and the buyer under the same restraints until we get the transport back to the headquarters. Lydia will drive the load back and the others of us should clean up any traces of our participation." Everyone seemed to be satisfied with the different operations and all agreed that the time remaining would be utilized in planning and scouting the entire location of the mission. It was planned for all units to be familiar with the different locations of other sites. This would make it easier to respond to any unexpected actions from the enemy. Tolliver spoke up and said, "That is enough for today. I would like some of those fish we bought at the market. Of course, we can still say we caught them in case someone asks where we found them."

It wasn't long before the odor of fresh coffee was wafting through the air. The fire was crackling and the cooks were waiting for the bed of coals for cooking the fresh trout. Jake turned to Tolliver and asked, "Hey, Jarhead. You think you can handle some explosives? If you can, you and I will wire that old building." Tolliver indicated that he would be glad to show any swab how to use things that go boom.

Jake retorted, "Well then come with me, General. I think I know where we can get at least a supply of dynamite. You may have noticed the large construction area out on the highway. It must have an explosive shed." He continued, "We will be back in a short time. At least save us some bones to chew on." The others chuckled and watched the marine and sailor took off on a dangerous mission. The campers noticed that the vehicle movement caused some stir at the camp area where the young girl had entered. She and a man came out and started to follow Jake and Tolliver until Jake waved to them. The girl returned the greeting with grin and a three-fingered scout salute and turned back toward the camping site.

The marine was driving and Jake kept track of their rear. After a few miles he said, "I guess they aren't following us."

"Where is the construction site?" asked Tolliver.

Jake answered, "Turn right on the highway. It is about four miles with two entrances. We take the second road. That should take us up to the east side of the property." They discussed any problems that had to be faced and agreed the most likely hindrance would be a guard. Jake said, "You know more about explosives, so you take that job and I will take care of any watchman."

About twenty minutes after leaving the camping area, the van turned off the highway and started a slow movement toward the target. There was a break for them because the equipment shed was beside a drift fence that was at ground level near the explosive shack. Tolliver stopped just as the building site could be seen from the vehicles. They commenced the approach at a stealthy pace until they had a clear view of their target. After a few minutes of observation they agreed that there was only one watchman, and he appeared to be dozing in the warm sun. Jake walked up behind the sleepy guard and slammed his full arm across the victim's shoulders. As soon as the man went down, Tolliver turned toward his target. The guard started a struggle to get up until he received a slap alongside the head with the handgun. He halted his struggles when the weapon was lowered to his eye level. He was tied up and gagged without seeing his tormenter.

Tolliver had found a simple clasp lock and opened it by striking it with a nearby piece of I-bar steel. When Jake turned to the shed, he could see a box of dynamite and fuse coils. He spoke in a low voice, "I have the fire cracker box and will take it to the van." There was a muttered acknowledged from his partner. Jake stuck an arm through the fuse cord and lifted the box to his shoulder. After a careful scan of the site, he ran toward the van and could hear Tolliver a few steps behind. They secured the material that included C-4 plastic explosives and a carton of detonators. This was a plus because with the detonators, it would make it a simple operation to cause the planned explosion. They were back in camp in less than hour and a half. The young woman came out and waved as vehicle went by. Tolliver muttered, "Wonder who she is and why is she so interested in us. You know, she could be a lookout for the bad guys." Jake didn't answer, but he was considering the same idea.

The cooks had delayed cooking until everyone was in camp. Tolliver told them what had occurred at the construction site. He and Jake would wait until Saturday night to wire the Klan headquarters. Darlene broke into the conversation and said that the girl had left her camp and walking leisurely toward them. She said, "I think I will go talk to her and invite her to dinner." The idea was good but as soon as the young woman noticed that she would be intercepted, she turned away and walked out of the campgrounds and was not seen again. The campers discussed the mission while eating a great dinner that had been cooked by the Carpenters. Some tried to rag the sniper, but he ignored all hands. They decided to take Thursday off and go fishing on their own. Friday and Saturday, though, would be full days of exploring the entire operation site. They wanted to see where their comrades would be located and rehash the plans for completing the mission.

Chapter 6

The day off on Thursday lasted until the early afternoon. Jake left the camp and started scouting different possible approaches to the lake. He was only alone for a half hour before he met Tolliver and Jacobs. They teamed up and started toward the Klan head quarters and were hailed by Carpenter. The Klan building was in a cleared meadow, and the four men took up positions and looked for ways to get to the building and to see if anyone was in residence. After observing the area for 30 minutes, they decided that they were alone and approached the old school house. Jacobs and Carpenter entered through a broken window. Tolliver and Jake scouted the crawl space and discussed where to plant the charges on Saturday Night. Tolliver summed it up, "We can place the C-4 on each bearing beam, and divide the dynamite into four bundles and throw that under each room. The C-4 fuses should be tied together and forked off to each bundle of dynamite. When the C-4 goes, the building should begin to collapse and the other explosives should completely demolish the entire structure and anything in the building.

Friday and Saturday were scouting and familiarization days. The time was spent exploring the entire area of operations. Tolliver and George went for a walk on the shoreline and explored the three-sided shed and a boat dock. Carpenter ambled down to the aircraft landing facility and sat on the dock watching kids as they fished from the pier. On Friday, Jake was certain that he had seen movement in the trees along the path to the old school house. He discussed it with Samantha and they agreed to a possible ambush on the stalker. Saturday morning, Jake slipped out of camp before daybreak after telling the others of the plan. He found a place near the trail where he wouldn't be seen unless he moved or someone stepped on him. Jake smiled at that thought because if that occurred it would probably be a struggle for him to capture anyone while lying on his back. The plans were for everyone to leave the camp in a group and split up at the edge of the woods with Samantha the first to disappear. She would double-time to catch her partner or make it seem that way.

Jake heard Samantha's cautious footsteps before she came into sight. He gave a low whistle and she bent over to tie her boot. Jake whispered for her to go around the next bend and listen for the ambush. She had disappeared around the bend in the trail when he saw a branch move without any wind. Then the stalker cautiously stepped into the trail and followed the path. When an old growth cedar tree separated them, Jake came to his feet and with one step was in the path. The hunter had paused at the tree and appeared to be listening to the different sounds. Samantha played it smart with a noise, and the person moved away from the tree, but before a step was taken Jake slammed a full arm across the shoulders and then stepped into the middle of the exposed back. He had pinned the stalker with hardly a sound, and said, "O.K., now I am going to let you up. If you struggle or make a racket, I will hurt you. Understood?" The head nodded and Jake moved away and recognized the girl from the camping area. She obeyed him by dropping her gun and knife and kicking them away.

On his bidding, she sat down with arms and legs around a small tree. There was no resistance when he tied her hands around the tree. Samantha rejoined him and asked, "Well, whom do we have here?"

The young woman looked at her and a faint smile was shown. She wouldn't talk to either one, and Jake stood up and said, "Samantha, tie her feet. We have work to do." The girl almost said something before the jaws clamped tightly. She struggled momentarily when a gag was tied, but then relaxed as Samantha checked the snugness of the material covering the mouth. Jake looked back, as he approached the bend in the trail, and saw her lean against the tree. She apparently had accepted the present situation.

The rest of the day was filled with casual walks over the region and staying out of reach of tourists who were out walking. At 1500, Jake and Samantha had returned to the old school building, and Jake showed her the plans for detonating the structure. They then moved out without seeing or being seen by anyone and started for the campsite. Their friends were waiting where the prisoner had been left tied up. She had been released and was still stretching her muscles from the day of captivity. Sarg Jacobs said, "You two are mean for leaving this poor little old girl tied up."

The “poor little old girl” evidently didn’t appreciate that descriptive phrase. Sarg had to dodge her attack. George and Darlene stopped her, and Darlene said, “Whoa, honey. He ain’t worth much, but he is mine. You can’t have him.”

The girl joined in the chuckles. She relaxed and for the first time spoke, “O.K., I will be good if you will let me go pee. I have been holding it for hours.” No one made a move to hinder her as she stepped around the big cedar.

They returned to the camp and the girl accepted their invitation to have a cup of coffee. She was sitting at one of the tables and Jake took a seat across the table from her. He asked quietly, “Now, what about your story? Why have we become so interesting to you and what is your name?”

She smiled, as he continued, “We are tired of calling you all the nasty names.” The young woman took a deep breath and said, “My name is Waseka Standing Fawn Stone, and I have been watching you scout the KKK headquarters—and for personal reasons, that’s what I was doing, too.”

Lydia reached over and took a trembling hand and gently asked, “Honey, why are you scouting the Klan?”

Without a pause the answer came with blazing eyes, “The Klan killed my father and raped my sister. I am going to kill the Grand Dragon. He is the one who tied the noose and gave my sister to his friends.” She continued with some heat, “If you are after drugs, you will have to kill me because I don’t like drugs.”

Tolliver laughed and retorted, “Lighten up. Lighten up, Waseka. We are after the drugs and we think the Klan is a dreg, so you might get what you want. The drugs will be left for the police, but not many of the people handling them. Now you know what we are about and if you try to leave us before the raid is over, someone will kill you.”

The silence lasted for a couple of minutes before she answered, “I will stay with you if I can help at the school house. If I can’t help you, shoot me now.” That statement caused the silence to last for a number of minutes. Each member of the group studied her and then their comrades. She accepted the moment and didn’t let her eyes drop while she was being studied.

Carpenter broke the silence, “Shoot, I cain’t hurt something that pretty.” There was general laughter around the table when Jake offered his hand. She grabbed it with both hands and tears started to flow.

Samantha ordered, "You men get a fire going and lets have some coffee." While the fire was being built, the women gathered around Waseka and soon had her talking and laughing freely.

As daylight weakened Jake and Tolliver began preparing for the night mission. The explosives were fused and the detonators were set to activate with heat. When they were ready, the backpacks were carefully fitted and lifted to the shoulders, and as darkness deepened Jake moved out first, soon followed by Tolliver. The separate movements were made a part of the mission to prevent possible sighting of a large shadow. Just inside tree line, the partners shook hands and without words started the silent trip to the target. When the building came in view, all that could be seen was its outline in the evening light. They went to ground to explore the scene for possible movements. After a half hour Jake whispered, "O.K., Jarhead let's go."

Light chuckles were heard when Tolliver responded, "Lead on, oh, master. Lead on." They moved out with about ten steps apart. When the structure came into full view they stopped for another period of observation. There were no acts or sights that disturbed them, but the final approach was made on their bellies.

With the use of hooded lights, Tolliver took the lead because he would be placing the C-4 charges on selected load bearing beams. Jake followed with the dynamite and placed bundles under the four rooms. They left the remaining explosives under the major meeting room. Tolliver left the crawl space but as he straightened, Jake watched him freeze and stand motionless. The cause of his alarm was a car rolling up into the front yard. Three Klansmen and two Nazis started noisily unloading the vehicle. They could be heard discussing plans for the following day. The partners picked up some good information. According to the workers the plane would be in at 0630. They also said that five members of the Klan would supervise the loading of a pickup truck. They would also escort the bosses to headquarters. There would be four Nazis sentries around the operating area. Tolliver had slowly regained a position in the crawl space and in whispers, suggested that a fuse be laid to the tree line. The fuse was prepared and attached to the nearest C-4 position. This would be a precaution against a possibility that the detonators did not work. With educated guesses, the timers were set for twelve hours. If need arose, they would ignite the fuse and hope no one spotted it.

After completing their chores, the visitors left. While waiting for the car to disappear, Tolliver spoke quietly, "Let's see what they have in there." Jake led the way to the broken window and stepped through the opening. The room appeared to be empty, and Tolliver eased into the mean meeting room. It was loaded with Klan and Nazi materials needed for the scheduled parade at noon on Sunday. The partners lifted a cover from a stack in the center of the room. They found weapons and ammunition, more explosives and 25 gallons of gasoline. Jake said, "We are just in time. These jerks are after someone."

Tolliver laughed and said, "Just think what is going to happen when this stuff combines with our stuff. There is going to be an explosion and fire that will go down in history. Better make sure Samantha is clear because the neighborhood will be leveled and she will be only a short distance away."

Jake and Tolliver returned to camp and shared the information gleaned from the work party. Waseka was assigned to work with Samantha in controlling the rear and sides of the building. Tolliver spoke up, "Samantha, when you see the dope truck arrive, head out as fast as possible. Jake and I really know how to light off fireworks, and the entire area is going to be leveled and probably burned."

Waseka said quietly, "I am going to shoot the Grand Dragon. Don't anyone get in my way."

No one responded for a few minutes until Jake answered, "O.K., you can have him, but not—I say again, not—before I tell you to get him." Then he turned to the others and continued, "According to our friends, the plane will be in at 0630. That means we should to be settled and hidden from view no later than 0500." There wasn't much conversation after that and soon everyone was in the tents. Waseka was invited to bunk with Sarg and Darlene Jacobs.

The next morning, the campers roused at or near 0400. When the Jacobs came out, they had disturbing information—Waseka had left sometime during the night. This started a conversation about the plans for the day. Carpenter spoke up. "If she gits in the way, ah'm goin to shoot her."

Jake spoke, "O.K. She has been warned, and..." he was interrupted by and amused giggle.

Waseka was standing by one of the tents with a full camp coffee pot. Pertly she asked, "Anyone want coffee?" A collective chuckle offered a relieved tension.

Jacobs retorted, "Just for giving us a bad time, you pour." And offered his canteen.

George spoke, "Sarg has a good idea. Use your canteens, because we should be getting out of here." The canteens were filled and a few drinks were taken before Tolliver and Darlene left the table. That was the signal for all. Without any talk, the group left and headed for their locations. All knew that they were going into harm's way, but none would turn back now.

Chapter 7

The ambushers were in place with cover by 0445. Each of them had their own thoughts concerning what was to occur in the quiet little fishing village of Porter Lake, Idaho. A successful mission would put the entire area under national or even international scrutiny. It would change the future of many people. Three natives of a South American country were expected on the aircraft loaded with contraband. A father and son operation out of Boise, Idaho, would be in the truck with three employees and would have the money needed to buy the contraband. The estimated strength of the Klan/Nazi contingent was 15 to 20 people. This group was made up from local citizens of the white supremacy chapters of the northwest area of the United States. A few Porter Lake people were anticipated as the labor force.

Jake had settled into his position when Samantha and Waseka had gone to ground. He attempted to review the entire mission and was confident that it could and would be carried out successfully. Jake's problem concerned the withdrawal of his people because when the explosion occurred the entire region would go on an alert. He and John Silvers had discussed this problem and agreed that in a very short time after the discoveries by the local officials roadblocks would automatically be set up. They had decided that the safest possible actions for them were to rapidly get back to the camp. John suggested that the best cover would be a camp break down and packing while waiting to eat breakfast. The biggest problem here would be to have a hot fire going when and if law enforcement discovered the paths between the attack location and the local campground.

Silvers and Lydia took cover under an oak tree that was near the anticipated loading site. A question always lurked, "What if they don't do what we think they will do." They briefly discussed this possible scenario but with shrugged shoulders, they agreed that that problem would take care of itself when it happened. As previously agreed, Lydia would walk through the mission as she could see it and John would criticize and make suggestions. The major problem facing them would be when to make a move, because at this signal the others would begin their movements. Everyone had agreed that this was the most important moment of the mission. If it went wrong, it would be a private fight to get away and probably most would be killed. Jake had required this discussion to be carried out a number of times.

Lydia said, "John, if we run into problems, go for yourself. I will be O.K."

Silvers smiled and said, "Same for you, lady, but I think we will be more successful if we stick together. Remember, you're the driver—don't leave me."

She chuckled, "Move fast, friend."

Darlene Jacobs asked, "Tolliver, how are we going to do this if the locals arrive at a different time than the airplane?

He replied, "I've been thinking along the same lines. We can't have separated groups. If we do, we have a problem. Why don't you take up a position in the shed and keep track of the locals, and I will try to handle the visitors."

"Good idea," she answered. She left for the shed and was hardly settled before some decisions had to be made. Darlene watched six people as they approached the landing site. One of them was talking loud and she heard that they were planning to help unload the plane. Except for one man, they appeared to be in their teens. She looked for Tolliver but he had already gone to ground. The group was allowed to approach the shed and as they did, Darlene stepped out and ordered them to halt.

She said, "Now, turn around and get your butts out of this area or I will shoot your butts out of this area." The adult of the workers tried to get a look at her and she said, "Don't be a fool."

He watched a hand with a gun come out of the shadows. He sputtered, "O.K., O.K. We will leave."

Tolliver stepped up and said, "Do it fast. I will give you a count of three to get to full speed. If not we will shoot six times."

"Good job," he whispered and turned back to his location. Darlene watched the runners and they were still a full speed when she lost sight of them. She heard Tolliver's low whistle—which was the signal that the plane was in sight.

Mrs. Tolliver was worried about her husband and had made up her mind to tell Jake not to call again. She smiled as the thought crossed her mind that Little Tolliver would appear in about six months—Pop did not know yet. Her mind started wandering over the time and circumstances she had known Jake Green.

She mused, "I don't know him as Jake Green; to me he is still the Leader."

The sound of the aircraft halted Mrs. Tolliver's thoughts, and George picked up and checked her weapon.

"What now?" Sarg Jacobs asked and both of them chuckled. Carpenter heard the engine noise a couple of minutes before the plane arrived over the area. It circled the area twice before started the landing run. As soon as the airplane came into view, the sniper started tracking the whirling propellers. The pilot coasted up to the pier and as lines were put out, he cut his engine. Carpenter smiled as he aimed at a propeller blade.

The three passengers stepped out on the pier and immediately became agitated. There was no one to greet them. Jacobs was near enough to hear their cursing and threats. Just as they started to cross the pier for the plane, a pickup truck came into view. Almost before it stopped, a man jumped out and tried to explain why they were late.

One of the South Americans snarled, "Senor, if you want this load, get it out of my plane." Their problems continued when they discovered that no laborers had appeared. After some argument, the driver of the truck told the five guards to start unloading the plane." Some grumbles could be heard, but they headed for the airplane. The father and son buyers were talking to the pilot and they all agreed to work. When the door slammed after the last bale had been put on the pier, Jacobs whispered to George, "Every thing has changed. Let's move over to the nearest oak tree to be able to assist John and Lydia." Silvers saw them making the move and turned to Lydia. She nodded and held up a thumb.

When the last package was loaded the South American said, "My money, senor."

The older man replied, "Here, look at your money while I look at my dope." The money bag was handed over, and when the seller was satisfied he started to hand it to one of his men to secure in the plane.

Before any one could move, John Silvers stood up and said, "Nope, you guys are confused. That's my money and my dope. Everyone freeze." Two of the Klansmen and one of the South Americans grabbed for their guns and were shot before they could get control of their weapons.

George spoke out from the shadows, "Who else wants to use their guns?" Before anyone could respond, the Sniper's rifle barked and a propeller blade fell from its mount. The three bodies were loaded on the truck and the others were put in restraints and also loaded with the dead men. Lydia and John went to the truck. Silvers said, "Lydia, take Darlene and Samantha and get that truck out of here, George. I hate to say this, but lead us out of here and do it fast."

Sarg Jacobs groaned and a satisfied expression came over a pretty face. In a very short time, George had them not far behind the truck.

When the truck wheeled into the old schoolyard, two Klan members were shot as they tried to get out of the house. In just moments, gunfire erupted at the back of the building and one Klansman and two Nazis sentries fell back with shots taken by Waseka and Samantha.

Jake called out, "In the house—we have your money and your dope out here, so back away from the doors and we will send you your bosses. Shut the doors until they get there." He turned toward the truck and said, "Look over here. We have all the bosses. The Grand Dragon is trying to hide, but Mr. Mayor, I see you. Get over there by your buddies."

The seller, buyer, and the protector were lashed together and ordered to their knees. The other four men were untied and told to take their dead comrades, including the sentry bodies, to the house. When they entered the door, Carpenter discouraged anyone from looking out with a shot to the doorframe.

Samantha and Waseka called out and joined the others by the truck. The seller, buyer, and the protector were ordered to their feet. The Grand Dragon said shakily, "Look, I am not one of them. I am the mayor of Porter Lake and I have been working under cover for the police. I am not a member of the Klan—no matter how it looks. You've got to let me go, please."

Waseka walked over and backhanded him across the face. She said angrily, "I know you and you are a Klan member—and have been for a long time. Do you know me?"

He whimpered, "No, little girl. I don't know you, but help me, please." His head shook again when the barrel of her rifle banged him alongside the head.

Then in a low husky voice the girl said, "I am Waseka Stone. Do you remember Waneta Stone?" He shook his head and she continued, "Waneta was my sister. Do you remember Wesley Stone?" She glanced at Jake and received an affirmative nod.

The Grand Dragon had wet his pants and whimpered, "That was a long time ago." He didn't finish begging, Waseka shot him in the groin. "That's for Waneta."

He crumbled over in pain she shot him in the neck, and said, "That one is for my father."

Tolliver said, "Jake, it is almost time. What do we do with these clowns?"

"Shoot 'em," he answered. Two guns spoke and a tremendous explosion from the building almost knocked them off their feet.

Jake yelled, "George, get us out of here."

They started the sprint back to camp, two other major explosions sounded, and then a crackle of ammunition. Tolliver called out, "Don't stop, that ammo was in the building." It didn't take them long to get back to camp. George slowed the pace to a walk at the tree line. There was a surprise waiting. A campfire was burning with a hot bed of coals and a full coffee pot was on the table. Samantha took over and said, "Quick now, let's get that bacon cooking. Throw a couple of slices on the fire. We want the smell over the area in case someone comes this way." The fire flared from the burning bacon and the smell of cooking permeated the area.

Jake turned to Waseka, but before he could say anything she said quietly, "Uncle Mike made the fire and coffee. Here he is. I have to go."

Before she turned, Jake said, "You did a great job for your family. Don't blame yourself. Now, do we have anything to worry about?" With a wan smile, she shook her head and ran for the truck. It was moving before she could close the door.

The men started breaking camp while the women cooked and helped pack the equipment. Lydia called out, "Here they are."

The law enforcement officers walked cautiously out of the tree line. They spread out over the campsite and started asking questions. Three of them came to where the ambush party was starting breakfast. One of them, with corporal stripes of the county sheriff office, asked, "How long you folks been here?"

Sarg Jacobs spoke up and answered, "We have been here all week. I believe we checked in last Monday. Why? What's happening?"

Another official spoke up without answering, "Have you heard and seen anything strange this morning? Tolliver responded, "We haven't seen any thing strange but about 40 minutes ago there were three heavy explosions over in the direction of Porter Lake. Is that why you are here?"

The Corporal retorted, "We would like to look in these vehicles."

Jake spoke up, "Look as long as you want, but don't tear up anything, as we are leaving after breakfast. We have plenty of fish in that red cooler. Have some if you will."

The deputy said, "No thanks for the fish and we won't mess up anything."

There wasn't any talking until the search parties started back toward the lake. When they disappeared into the trees, Samantha said, "I was afraid they would find all those weapons. What did you do with them?"

Carpenter made them laugh, "Navy, yuh has still got guts. Guns are in the red fish box."

Chapter 8

When the Porter Lake posse stepped back into the tree line there was a controlled rush to get all the equipment into the vans. After they had finished loading, Jake took all their room keys and suggested they leave the area as soon as possible after returning the vans to the rental lots. Tolliver spoke and said, "Jake, don't call on us anymore unless you are coming for dinner. I just heard I am going to be a papa."

There was deep throated laughter when his wife spoke, "If it is a boy, we will call him George" There were hugs and handshakes and the vans were loaded. They drove out of the area at controlled speeds. When they turned onto the freeway, the speeds went up and the caravan soon was at the Lake Side Motel in Coeur d'Alene.

After the vehicles were returned, the couples all left at short intervals. Jake was soon alone and was reflecting about their mission when a newsbreak appeared on television. The news out of Porter Lake was sensational. After the explosion was heard, Police Chief Coppage formed a posse to investigate. They found the old school house completed destroyed and burned. The chief of police also took possession of a pickup truck loaded with cocaine and marijuana and alongside the truck, she found a satchel filled will bundles of money. She also found three bodies, which included the mayor of Porter Lake and two unidentified men.

The county sheriff and some of his men joined the investigation. Deputies spread out through the area questioning campers and other people who were near the lakefront. Nothing out of hand was found with the searches, but an airplane was found with a broken propeller. After some investigation, the detectives reported that there was residue of plants and powder collected from the plane. This material would be sent to a laboratory for identification but the local sheriff predicted that the material came from the dope seized by Chief Coppage. While the reports were being made Jake decided to check out and return to Venture. The young woman didn't ask any questions when he returned the keys from all room occupied by his friends. Silvers and Jacobs had joined with Tolliver and asked not to be called for any future mission.

John Silvers laughed and said, "Navy, it's always exciting when you are around but no more for us. You are always invited for dinner."

Sarg Jacobs held out a hand for a shake and said, "Me, too—and don't be long before you come to dinner." Jake left and was soon on the freeway, heading west for home: Venture, Washington. As the mileposts ran past, Jake reviewed what had happened and was certain that none of the team could be identified. A thought came, "Hmm, everyone asked not to be called for another mission except Carpenter." The sniper had squeezed his shoulder and Lydia had stopped for a hug.

Late in the afternoon, after a long day, Jake crossed the Columbia River and breathed a sigh of relief as he stepped inside the "big house down by the river." The telephone, to his relief, didn't have any calls. As the lights came on, the telephone rang and he was welcomed home by the friend who looked after the house. Jake went to kitchen and fixed a sandwich and took it and a drink to his den. He picked up the television remote and turned it to a news station. Porter Lake had become the center of the universe. News media personnel outnumbered the citizen population by a wide margin. The locals were being interviewed so often most of them went home and drew the blinds. Jake laughed when Darlene Coppage came on camera. She looked worse than she did with the leeches hanging off her body. He thought with a smile, "Seaman, now you know what leeches really do. They feed off anything with blood and the news media is always looking for blood."

Tents were all over town because Porter Lake did not have enough rooms to house all the visitors. Some reported having lodgings 20 to 30 miles away. Jake could see three tents with law enforcement logos and names. The state police had assumed lead in the investigation under the auspices of the governor. The local agents were miffed, but the state police were the bosses. During an interview, Major Molenski, of the state agency, said that the FBI and DEA and other federal outfits were on the way into town. The local people were being asked why their mayor had been killed with the drug people.

Someone finally said, "Go out to the school house, the bodies will be identified as Ku Klux Klan and Nazi skinheads. Willingham was the Grand

Dragon of the Klan and most people know it." This led to another feeding frenzy by the news sharks.

Jake watched the Porter Lake situation as it appeared in the media. The television crews started packing up and heading out by the following weekend. The print media hung on for a few more days. The Porter Lake people came off looking well. Most of them stood their ground about not knowing that Mayor Willingham was a member of the KKK. Some were yelling for the criminals who did the killing to be brought to justice.

This came to an abrupt end when the local newspaper editorial stated:

"It appears to this paper that most of the criminals involved in this case have been brought to justice. A South American drug lord lost his life, and the dope he was carrying to be sold to our children is now in the hands of proper authorities. A major distributor from Boise lost his life, and the money he was using to buy the narcotics for our children is now in the hands of proper authorities. The local KKK has lost a Grand Dragon, and the Nazis lost their colonel, because the two organizations were offering protection to the drug rings. Others lost their lives because they were henchmen supporting the drug traffickers. Some of our community members have lost credibility and reputations because they have known that local people were members of these two organizations. In that stead, Porter Lake has lost a mayor because he was the Grand Dragon of the KKK."

The second Saturday after the news media had left, Jake returned to Porter Lake to check on Chief Coppage. He wanted to see how she had come through with the law enforcement organizations, and to see if her standing in the community had suffered. Jake arrived at the local restaurant and went in for breakfast. He requested the table that Darlene normally used, and was sipping his first coffee when she arrived. He was recognized with a wave and big grin.

The patrons of the restaurant received a surprise that turned into laughter when their chief ordered, "Stand up, pal, and assume the proper position. I never hug a man when he is sitting on his butt."

She sat across the table and in a quiet conversation Jake was assured that she had made out well with the local and other authorities. She chuckled and asked, "Would you believe I have been offered a position with the FBI and DEA—and some of the people of this town have asked me to run for mayor?" She leaned across the table and whispered, "Thank you, Jake, for helping with the leeches, but how in the world did you do it so fast and so complete?"

She laughed quietly, and continued "No, no. I don't want to know."

The waitress came by for orders and Darlene said, "If it's OK with you, Jake, I would rather wait for someone else." They were talking about going lake fishing during the day. He replied that waiting was not a problem but he didn't want to be late in catching the "big one." He glanced up as a man come to the table and pulled out a chair after being greeted by the Chief.

Jake looked up, and with a big grin said, "Well I do declare it's my old friend Walter T. Swackhammer."

The grin was returned when the FBI agent responded, "Jake Green, what the hell are you doing here?"

Darlene broke in, "Where did you two guys meet. I would have sworn that I was going to introduce two strangers."

Jake laughed and said, "Oh, Walter and I go back a long way—when I was working in D.C."

Swackhammer ruefully said, "Yeah, I chased this guy all over the D.C. area, which included Virginia and Maryland."

The breakfast was served and enjoyed by all three. Darlene said, "Jake, I can't go fishing with you. Some chores have to be completed, but you are welcome to use my boat."

Swackhammer spoke up, "I would like to go fishing, Jake. I will show you how to get the big ones." When breakfast was over, Chief Coppage drove the two fishermen to the pier and helped launch the boat. Jake headed for the location where he and Darlene had the success during the last fishing trip.

The boat drifted up close to the fishing hole, but before they could get rigs into the water the FBI agent asked, "Jake, what are you doing here? I know you and the chief of police are friends, and I don't doubt you are a fisherman. How are you involved with the actions that occurred in this area?"

The answer was with a laugh, "Now, Walter T., don't start that crap again. Why is it that you feds start seeing ghosts when I am around?"

The laugh was returned when Swackhammer responded, "Jake, when you are around, strange things happen, and old pal, I need someone who can make strange things happen. I have wondered often where you had disappeared to, and I almost crapped my pants when I saw you having breakfast with the local chief of police."

Jake was silent for a few minutes while the tackle was rigged and put into the water. Then, "Walter, are you talking as an FBI agent or is it Walter T. Swackhammer saying some strange things?"

The immediate answer was one word, "Both."

The trout started striking and the conversation ended as the other boats started closing in on the action. The two men released most of their catch, but kept some for Darlene, who was planning to make their dinner. When they got back to the pier, the boat was cleaned and secured.

Jake said, "Let's walk back to town."

They approached a bench and without speaking took a seat. After some time, Jake said, "OK, Walter you have my attention."

The federal agent didn't speak for a few moments and actually appeared to be hesitant to speak. Finally, he said quietly, "Jake, we didn't have this conversation. No one can figure out how you can take care of problems so efficiently." He paused and then continued, "We have a real problem in Oklahoma. You probably have heard the news of the federal prison riots and the take over outside Oklahoma City. The prison bosses have given us an ultimatum that if the gates are not open by next Saturday night, all of the hostages will be killed. If we storm the walls we can stop the uprising, but that would kill over a hundred civilians. There are four prisoners who are calling the shots. If we can take them out, the riots will subside with little or no more killing. We can't do that officially. Can you or will you take on that type of mission unofficially?"

With a long pause, Jake said, "I will need good pictures of the four bosses and someone I can trust with my life. If I cannot satisfy myself with the operation, the answer is a flat no, and also if I don't have complete control of the action, I won't participate."

"I can understand that," Swackhammer said quietly. "I will send you someone who looks a lot like me—the assistant warden, my brother Jason.

Chapter 9

Jake left Porter Lake after dinner with the FBI agent and the chief of police. He smiled with the thought about associating with law enforcement and considering an illegal act proposed by the federal agent. Walter Swackhammer had talked with almost a halting speech pattern. He probably was under heavy pressure to solve the federal problem in Oklahoma. The idea of shooting prisoners trapped behind locked walls offered Jake some strange fleeting thoughts. The troubling thoughts had been replaced with the information from Swackhammer. Innocent people were in danger of being murdered in exactly one week. The prison bosses had given the officials until Saturday to open the gates or the hostages would be killed. The authorities were in a hard situation. They couldn't open the prison gates and allow hardened criminals to get into the population; nor could they storm the walls, because the hostages would be killed along with scores of prisoners. Many of the prisoners would be innocent of any part of the uprising but had no way of stopping the revolt. According to the information from Swackhammer, the four bosses were hardcore murderers serving life sentences without parole.

The decision to go to Oklahoma wasn't a final decision to take on the proposed mission. Jake wanted to get a personal feel for the situation before making the decision to take on the job. He had no known contacts in the area except for the business card of Jason Swackhammer the Assistant Warden of the state federal facility. Those thoughts were still running through his mind Monday as he boarded the airplane for Enid, Oklahoma. The flight's ETA to Enid was 0730 before continuing to Oklahoma City, but Jake wanted to arrive and call the Assistant Warden before being observed by other people. During the flight he started to make plans to take out the four bosses. He couldn't bring up an idea that would make it possible for one person to do the job. The operating area would be too confining for one person to take four shots, and it wouldn't be feasible to have more than two operators. They would have to be good enough to shoot four targets and then walk out of a facility that would be as alive as a beehive. The only two people he could imagine doing the job were Carpenter and himself.

Before leaving Enid, he made a telephone call to the Ozark Mountains. Lydia Carpenter answered and Jake asked, "Is this the most beautiful woman in the world?

She answered, "If you say so, I won't dispute it." Her pleasant laugh caused a smile from her caller, she continued, "Do you want to talk to one of the skinniest people in the world?"

Carpenter came on the line, and stated, "Yeah, wheah do we meet and when?"

Jake asked, "Do you know Oklahoma City? If so, pick a place, and I'll find it."

"The Plains Motel," Carpenter replied.

Jake answered, "Tomorrow afternoon about 1630."

The conversation ended with those short comments. The ride into Oklahoma City did not take long and in that time he found the location of the Plains Motel. A man across the aisle tried to strike up a conversation and after a few words Jake stretched and complained about being tired and said that he still had to find a place to sleep. The man recommended the Plains Motel and how to find it. When the bus ride was over, Jake waited for his new friend to leave and walked across the street to a rental agency. He took the car and, instead of going to the motel, he headed to the freeway and watched for a sign giving directions to the federal prison. The idea was to get a feeling for the local area and to find a place for observations that wouldn't cause any undue attention.

The parking lot at the prison was almost full and many people were walking or running to and from the prison. At first, this situation appeared perfect for his purposes. Then, as he continued to observe the area he realized that there was no way to complete the mission without notice from many people. The automobiles in the lot were mainly law enforcement and news media, and many of them had observers in the vehicles. Jake noticed that the media would swarm to anyone who started for the prison gate. He surmised that those running were law enforcement, hoping to stay out of reach of the reporters with microphones or cameras. Jake started the engine and slowly moved out of the parking area, but instead of turning for the traffic exit, he turned on the road that paralleled the prison wall. He knew that there was a liability being taken in case someone became interested in the vehicle following the wall. To lessen the chance of curiosity he drove at almost an idle speed. His interest was directed toward the guard towers. To his surprise, most of them appeared to be empty, and those occupied weren't showing a watchman capability. The people appeared to be maintenance workers, but there was a good chance that many of them were armed. When he rounded the western corner of the prison, he found what he was looking for—a place to scale the wall at a minimum chance of being discovered. This side of the wall was hidden from the surrounding community by a large growth of trees. Jake smiled when he thought that the civilians probably had raised a ruckus because of the view from the countryside. The road traversed the wooded park and he regained the traffic corridor out of sight of the prison. He was satisfied that he and Carpenter could solve the problems that would affect the start of the mission.

Jake walked into the Plains Motel to register, but the Carpenters were waiting. They had booked two adjoining rooms with a kitchenette. After getting unpacked and a shower, Jake knocked on the common door and was greeted by Carpenter and a smell of bacon being cooked. He said to the Sniper, "Your wife must have picked out these rooms, because you wouldn't have the brains to do so—come to think of it I wouldn't, either."

Lydia called out, "Take a seat at the table. I am serving breakfast for dinner." She brought in dishes of bacon and eggs. As always with friends, the meal was enjoyable and pleasant. When the dishes had been washed and dried they again took seats around the table. Jake said, "Lydia, I expected that ugly husband of yours, but I didn't expect you."

She laughed and replied, "Where he goes I go, and you probably didn't consider transportation and a driver."

He laughed and told her that she was right. He hadn't thought of transportation to and from the target, but he didn't want to put her in danger. She took Carpenter's hand before saying, "Where he goes, I go—and by the way, he is not ugly, he's my little Pookie."

Jake almost fell out of his chair with laughter, he said through tears, "Pookie, I have wondered about your first name. Now I know it is Pookie." Carpenter sat there smiling and still holding his wife's hand.

They sat talking about their friends and Jake asked, "How about Josephs and Linda? Where are they? I haven't heard anything about them."

Lydia spoke up, "They are right here in Oklahoma City. Josephs has been governor of Oklahoma for a couple of years, but we have almost broken contact with them. I think they are nervous about the past association we have with them."

Jake said, "That's too bad. I always liked them because both of them would take care of anything." He chuckled and continued, "Especially Linda. She was or could've been a terror. I am pleased that he was elected governor. Glad you warned me that they appear nervous about us, because I don't want to bring them any grief." The three of them spent some time talking about old times.

Carpenter pushed his chair back and asked, "Whut ya got, Jake?" Jake leaned back also and replied, "I went back to Porter Lake to check out things and was approached by an FBI agent. You may have heard me speak of Walter T. Swackhammer—he was one of the people trying to tail us around D.C. He suggested that I might be able to cure a problem here in Oklahoma. I'm sure you have heard about the riots over at the federal prison. It seems that the prisoners have put the officials on notice and gave them until Saturday evening to open the gates—or they will kill the hostages being held. Swackhammer said that there are at least a hundred hostages. This puts the government between a rock and a hard place. If the gates aren't opened, over a hundred citizens will die and if the gates are opened it would send hardened criminals out into the neighborhood. So this isn't an acceptable solution. On the other hand, if the prison is stormed, that would lead to the murder of the hostages, along with many casualties among the prison population. There are four lifers running things and the authorities seem to think if they can be taken out in some manner, the takeover would end with relatively few causalities."

Lydia spoke up and asked, "Jake, how are we supposed to take on a mission like this? It will have to be done inside the prison. So how do we get in, take at least four shots, and then get out safely? If you get out, you still have to get away from the area before someone picks you up."

"You are a very smart lady," Jake replied. "I have been mulling over all those points. The only way that I will ask for your help is that we have complete control of the mission and are satisfied that there would be a acceptable route out of town."

Carpenter broke in, "Kin we git in the prison?"

Jake answered, "I don't know, but I have been asked to call the Assistant Warden. I don't know him, and the only thing I do know is his name—Jason Swackhammer, Walter's brother. Before we call him we should scout the prison and its surroundings."

They decided to take a run out to the target area. Lydia was driving so she would become familiar with the roads, streets and highways that they might take during the next few days. Jake suggested that his earlier route be explored. A local radio station was broadcasting, according to them, non-stop until the problems were solved. It was tuned in so the scouts could pay attention to their travel and hear what was happening in sight of the radio reporter. Lydia turned off the freeway and followed Jake's instruction into the prison parking lot. It was busy with people running or walking fast to and from the vehicles.

After about fifteen minutes, Carpenter said from the back seat, "We cain't do hit from dis place."

Jake answered, "I agree."

The car was put back into action and Lydia drove slowly out of the lot and took the road that paralleled walls of the prison. She drove at an idle speed and no one seemed to take note of the automobile. One nervous moment passed as they came to the curve around the corner of the building, as an official vehicle with five passengers was meeting the scout car.

The driver gave a salute that was returned by a wave from Lydia. She glanced at the mirror and said that official car hadn't stopped. As they continued on toward the highway, Jake turned in his seat and looked at Carpenter who said, "This is the place we could git outten if we kin git in."

Jake nodded in agreement. Nothing more was said as the car turned back toward the city. Lydia regained the freeway about 1700, and Jake had seen this route twice and completely agreed with Carpenter that plans for getting inside the facility would have to be made before the mission could be attempted.

When they got back to their rooms, a couple of hours were spent just talking about the possibility of taking on the mission. It was decided that Jason Swackhammer wouldn't be contacted until Thursday or Friday. They didn't want to be seen with the Assistant Warden until his information would be needed for the final decision and, as Carpenter pointed out, that official might back out of the deal and start talking.

Jake agreed and said, "It would be a catastrophe if we would be forced to take him out. That would bring Walter T. and the entire federal establishment down on us." After some discussion, it was decided to make a night run to the prison. They took the same route as before. The parking lot was quieter, but not much. It would still be dangerous to use it as a site for leaving after the exercise was over. There was another problem, also. When they started down the road alongside the prison, it caused an immediate reaction from the authorities. Jake and Carpenter stayed as much in the background as possible as Lydia explained she was looking for the highway. The young cops didn't question her, but told her that no one was allowed on this road during the evening. That answered one more question—it would be safer to take a chance during day light hours.

The next two days, Tuesday and Wednesday, were spent in the library, planning offices, and the prison museum. They were looking for any information to be found about the prison. Each took a building and worked alone, striving not to bring undue attention to their work. Lydia took the planning offices that posed more problems than the other areas. She had to work closely, at times, with the county officials. She was looking for any information that would show the prison as it was being built and possible changes made over the years. Carpenter spent his time at the museum, and was looking for any information about prison history. The subject he was most interested in was the construction and the changes of the facilities over the years. Jake spent his time in the library researching past prison breaks and riots. He was looking for information concerning the movements of the local authorities and how they operated with the federal people. In the evenings, the researchers discussed what information had been gleaned. Lydia found that the initial building plans were filed in the 1930s, yet Carpenter found that the complex was built before Oklahoma entered the union, and the back wall was over three feet thick. Jake's major input offered a newspaper story about a break in the 1920s in which over 20 escapees gave up their lives before getting out of the state. He also found a story that matched the present situation. The prisoners had rioted and captured some of the guards and service personnel. Their demands weren't met and two people were killed and others threatened if the warden didn't authorize other actions. The authorities issued a warning that if the hostages weren't freed, the prison walls would be stormed. State, local, and federal officers marched along the top of the wall, and the prisoners responded by marching the hostages out of the cellblocks. When the column turned toward the gate they were mowed down with a barrage from the men in the building. The situation was finally resolved when the lawmen stormed the cellblocks. According to the reports, 77 people had lost their lives.

Friday morning, Jake called Jason Swackhammer. The telephone was answered, and Jake said, "Mr. Swackhammer, your brother suggested I give you a call concerning a problem you might be facing."

After a moment of silence Swackhammer answered, "I'm not sure of what you are talking about. I don't have any problems. Who is this?"

Jake answered, "My name doesn't make a difference, and if you change your mind about my help, I will call you again in 15 minutes."

Before hanging up, he heard a question that wasn't acknowledged, "Where are you located?"

They waited for almost 25 minutes and Carpenter made the call, "Mistah Warden, we are waiting fo yo answer."

He listened for a moment and broke in, "Hit makes no difference to me, but if you need help we believe we can do hit."

He handed the phone to Jake, and the warden was surprised when Jake stated, "Mr. Swackhammer, I could care less about your questions. This is the last chance for us to get together. If you want to meet with us, come immediately to the Plains Motel, room 206."

He broke the connection and said, "Let's get to the automobile and watch him before identifying ourselves."

Jason Swackhammer was in a quandary. He had told Walter about the problems at the prison and had said something to the effect, "We need someone to shoot those four bastards."

There were no expectations on his part that Walter would react in this manner, and it was a sure thing that he wouldn't recognize these people. One of them sounded as if he was educated but the other appeared to have a limited vocabulary. He told his wife to make an emergency call to Walter in Washington, D.C. If she could connect with his brother on the radio, she was to transfer the call to the vehicle that he would be driving. He drove slowly to the Plains Motel, hoping that he would be able to speak to his brother before meeting these people. The call didn't come through and his frustrations and worries almost ran over when he didn't get an answer at the motel room. There was a surprise when he turned away from the door and came face to face with a young woman. She said, "Mr. Swackhammer, drive over to the gray Chevy and park alongside. Drive into the parking space, don't try to back into it."

When the prison vehicle pulled into the parking space, Jake lowered the window and told the assistant warden to come around the automobile and get into the back seat. Swackhammer was taken aback because as best as he could see the occupants, two men wore black masks and the woman had raised her scarf to cover her face.

Swackhammer thought, "What am I getting into, all of them are wearing masks? I can't even remember what the woman looked like." He hesitated but with a shrug did as he was ordered. When he approached, the back door of the automobile was opened for him. The man in the back seat was the one who had called his home. When the prison official settled into the seat, the person alongside said quietly, "Take it easy Jason. We are disguised for your benefit as well as ours because if you decide against us, our masks will save your life."

He was silent momentarily, then continued, "O.K., what can we do for you? Walter said that you might need help over at the prison. We believe we can give you a hand if there is a way to get two of us on the south wall just as the shift changes this evening. Understand now, we will have to spend the night on the wall, so there better be a way to keep patrols from our position."

The silence deepened and Jason tried to relax by shrugging his shoulders. Finally he responded, "We have a real problem in the prison proper but we still control the walls and watch towers. I can get you to the wall with a cover story for your being there. Two of our tower floodlights have been knocked out. I will go out now and convince people that the repair crew should be under the cover of darkness. Meet me this evening at 1930 and I will have coveralls and tool boxes for you." He chuckled and continued, "Of course you can't wear masks, and the next time you see Walter, tell him to keep me out of his conversations. My big brother always tries to make things easy, but if he trusts you enough to recommend you for this type of job, that is good enough for me."

Jake replied, "O.K. We will meet you at the service station at the intersection before the road turns toward the prison."

Lydia pulled into the gasoline station that had been chosen for the meeting with the assistant warden to receive their working clothes. Swackhammer was planning to take a good look at the team who would attempt to settle the prison's problem by shooting four men. He smiled weakly to himself when they pulled up alongside his vehicle. They had white breathing masks over their features. They told him to remain in the car and they would take care of the equipment. The two men took the packages with the worker uniforms and headed for the station bathroom, and the woman took care of the toolboxes.

She said, "You best leave now. We will be at the service gate at 2015. If you aren't there, we leave."

He was creating the biggest stake in his professional life with these people and didn't know who they were. His only contact was with his brother and he doubted that Walter would ever discuss it with him. He mused, "I wonder who these people are and where they came from." Walter had always said that the FBI did operate wet covert operations. If successful, this would be wetter than wet because the blood would be flowing when the guns were silenced. Jason was at the service gate and the team arrived at the precise time that had been planned. The two servicemen were unrecognizable because of helmets with face shields and facial hair. He introduced them to the watch commander, who had just come on shift. He led them up to the wall walkway and, upon their suggestion, agreed that no patrols would interfere with the work of repairing the floodlights.

The repairmen started down toward the first damaged tower and waved at the guards as they passed. The watch commander was instructing the patrols not to interfere in case the prisoner lookouts would see what was happening. Jake and Carpenter did as they were instructed and ducked their heads to be below the wall line. They made a point to enter the first tower for those who may be watching. They remained in the tower for almost an hour before easing out on their bellies. The crawl was slow and steady, and it took them about 30 minutes to make the next tower. Carpenter went on to find a likely route for escape and Jake prepared the shooting positions. He took some black plastic out of the bags and fashioned a screen on the broken windows, then at the side of each he formed a gun port that wouldn't be observed from the yard below. Carpenter returned and approved of the ambush platform, but he had some disturbing news. Their escape plan called for rapelling down the outside wall and retrieving the grapple hook by pulling the rope through with a knot catching the shank of the hook. Carpenter related that there was no way the hook could be anchored in such a manner allowing its retrieval. It took all night for them to bore and scrape a position for the hook to be anchored. When they were finished, Jake chuckled and said, "I hope that holds until both of us are on the ground."

Dawn was breaking when they got back to their shooting ports. Their rifles were assembled and they took care as the weapons were put through the port with flaps of plastic covering the barrels. The plan had been made to cover their presence from the prison yard. Shouts and taunting curses were heard as the prisoners started milling around below but the shooters didn't attempt to see any of the action. They had spotted the four leaders with aid from the pictures that had been furnished by the assistant warden. At 1000 each morning, the prisoner demands had been discussed.

This morning was no different. The four leaders moved in front and started jawing with the guards. Carpenter pointed as the assistant warden made an appearance and began talking by demanding that the prisoners drop their weapons, release the hostages, and form a column across the exercise area. The four leaders stepped out of the crowd and started their own demands. Carpenter whispered, "I got the two on our left, you take the right." Jake answered, "O.K. You count us down for the first shot and we will take the next as we can."

Carpenter said, "We shoot on three, not before I say it."

The weapons spoke as one voice saying two words, and four men had been executed with perfect head shots. Under the confused noise, the shooters made it to the back wall and the escape line. Carpenter went first and held the line taut for Jake. He released his hold about ten feet from the ground and as he fell, the grapple hook landed beside him. The shouting and orders could be heard, but they were in the escape vehicle before it completely stopped. Lydia had the car moving at full speed before the shooters could get up from the floor. Carpenter climbed over the front seat, and he and Jake took off the coveralls and stuffed them into the bags.

Lydia said calmly, "Jake, our car is at the service station where we met the warden."

"O.K.," Jake replied. "I will take this one. It is always a pleasure to play with you guys. I will see you some other time."

There was no more talking as Lydia pulled into the service station parking lot. The Carpenters hastily changed automobiles and Jake followed them out of the lot. He stayed with them until a rural road was noted. He made an immediate turn onto it and increased speed. In a few miles he was reading signs for the freeway, on which he turned west. The westward run was stopped after about 60 miles when a notice of an airport came into view. He carefully parked the rental automobile and paid for two days parking fees, and after putting on dark glasses and a moustache went into the waiting room door. He didn't spot anyone who might be a policeman. The clerk didn't pay any attention as he issued a ticket to Denver, Colorado.

In Denver, Jake went to the ticketing desk of a small airline that offered flights in many directions. The first flight out fitted perfectly into his plans, it was scheduled for Spokane, Washington, and that was where his personal automobile was parked. He made his way to the departure gate, attempting to stay in the middle of a group. At the gate, he sat down with a newspaper and he was sure that no one had paid any attention, at least not enough to describe him. The loading ramp was opened and Jake was one of the first passengers to board the airplane. His seat was at a window and he made sure that his interest in the operations outside remained constant. When the aircraft started to taxi, he asked for a pillow that he used throughout the flight. During the flight, Jake mulled over the past few days and felt comfortable except for one instance. During dinner on Thursday night Governor Josephs and his entourage entered the restaurant. Josephs came directly to the table with a big grin and an out stretched hand. He was effusive in his greeting and moments of small talk. As he left, Jake noticed an appraising look from the governor.

Carpenter drawled, "Jake, whuts wrong with Josephs? He seemed to me lak he was upset there at the last."

Jake replied, "I had the same feeling, but it was good seeing him. He's been a good friend over the years."

Nothing more was said about the situation, but when the waitress came with the bill, Jake noted that one of the governor's staff was coming their way. The staff person gave a sealed envelope to Lydia. She held it until they were on the way to the motel. Jake opened the seal and read the message to the Carpenters.

"It is good to see you people, but if you are not here to see me or other state attractions, be careful. I would hate to think that you have other situations to attend. If so leave my state!" The note was unsigned, and the group didn't discuss it. The airplane landed, Jake retrieved his automobile and headed for the big house down by the river.

Chapter 10

There were no further thoughts about Oklahoma, except listening and reading about the raid on the federal prison. Many people were giving their opinions, and some even charged that the shooting of the convicts was an act by the prison officials. This caused some politicians to start calling for congressional hearings. The warden of the facility called a news conference and tried to assure the news people that his employees had nothing to do with the incident. No one paid any attention to him, and the speculations continued. Jake noticed that Jason Swackhammer was keeping himself in the background, but a television crew caught him in the parking lot and asked him who he thought may have carried out the murder plot. He firmly told the television audience that the warden had everything in hand and the media should back away and allow the well-planned investigation to be carried out. This sort of relieved the federal people, and the attention was turned to the governor. Governor Josephs appeared agitated when he was asked about the incident. Josephs looked at the camera and spoke to the audience, "Whoever did the shooting broke Oklahoma laws, and this state will not allow this type of incident to go unpunished." One of the reporters asked the governor if the state agents had any idea who would or could do such a deed. Again, he looked directly into the camera and said, "I have some ideas which will be investigated to the fullest. My people are already investigating some leads and should soon have people of interest in for interviews."

Jake thought of calling the Carpenters because he felt that Josephs had been talking directly to all of them. Before he could do anything further, his private telephone rang. It was Lydia Carpenter and she asked if he had watched Josephs during the news conference. She said, "Jake, we felt that he was talking directly to us." Jake responded that he had the same feeling. Then she said, "We are going to cover here in the hills—not trying to hide just to stay out of circulation."

"Good idea," Jake replied. "I am going to wait for the governor to make the first move. Josephs may think I will protect his good name, but I am not going to let him get away with that idea; or at least I'll make him think he can't get away with that crap." After the conversation was over, Jake started thinking about what could happen if he challenged Josephs. The very least would be a confrontation between the two of them. The most and worst which could happen would be that the Silvers and the Jacobs be drawn into the picture.

Thursday morning following the governor's interview on Tuesday, Jake took some visitors fishing on the Columbia River. They remained out all day fishing, exploring, and eating part of their catch for lunch. All of the party was tired upon reaching the pier at Venture. Jake told them that he was going home and to bed without even taking a shower. Some of them accused him for being so old that he couldn't keep up with the younger folks.

He laughed and said, "You whippersnappers come back during deer season and I will demonstrate how old I am." He left the pier and was surprised to find an automobile parked in the driveway. Two men were out of the car before Jake pulled into his parking space. They told him to pack a bag because they were taking him on a vacation. He was surprised but tried not to show it, he asked, "Just who are you guys?"

One of them retorted, "It doesn't make any difference who we are—either you go inside and get ready to leave we will take you from here." Both of the men had flashed their holstered weapons, and Jake decided he needed more room and cover before responding to the implied threats.

He turned to the door and visitors were crowding him from both sides. After they took seats, Jake said, "O.K., you have my attention. What's this all about? And where do you think you will take me?"

The older man said with a grin, "The governor of Oklahoma wants to see you, and what the governor wants, the governor gets. We are taking you to Oklahoma City. You can make it easy by cooperating or you can make it hard on yourself."

Jake said, "One question. What is your authority to make such statements?"

The Oklahoman said, "We are from the state police barracks near the city, and you are going with us, so get busy with whatever you have to do and do it within 30 minutes." Jake raised both hands and said, "O.K., O.K. I have to call a friend to have my furnace fixed. It was out this morning."

The policemen relaxed with a smile between them. Jake dialed the telephone and after a moment said, "George, I have a problem, my furnace is out and I have to leave town in the next few minutes. Will you take care of it tomorrow?"

Jake listened as Constable Lou Prysylbilski asked, "Do you really have a problem?"

Jake chuckled, "I sure do have a problem. That thing went off this morning like Roy Rogers and his two six guns—scared me out of at least a year's growth."

The constable had caught on, he asked, "Do you have two visitors who are armed."

The answer was, "You bet, George. Run down here and I will give you a key." Jake turned to his visitors and said, "Let me clean up a little and when George gets here, I will be ready."

The agent who had been speaking said, "O.K." Then with a grin he asked, "Can we watch you wash up?"

Jake answered with a laugh and said, "Why, shucks yes. I would be honored." His levity caused them to relax more and he completed his plan by inviting them to have coffee. When he returned to the room, the Oklahomans were sitting comfortably in easy chairs drinking coffee. Jake mused, "Mistake, guys. Never get too comfortable in a situation like we have here."

Jake attempted to keep his visitors relaxed by just holding a quiet conversation. He heard the constable as he entered the house from the garage. Neither of the Oklahomans heard any thing because Jake told a funny story about going fishing. Lou stepped into the room and surprised the two visitors when he spoke, "Jake, what problems do you have here?"

Jake responded, "Lou these two guys want to meet you because they carry badges also, and they are trying to kidnap me." The two visitors were so surprised that it took them a few moments to react to the situation. They were too late because Constable Prysylbilski had his gun on them.

He said softly, "O.K. gents, pick up your coffee and with the free hand take out your guns and drop them to the floor." When the guns fell to the floor, Jake reached for both of them. The agent who had been talking attempted to tell the constable that they were state policemen who had come from Oklahoma to take Mr. Green back for questioning in a criminal investigation.

"Why didn't you say so?" the lawman asked, "Where are your arrest warrants?"

They were not covered by warrants and Prysylbilski asked to see their weapons permit. The two men started talking at once both trying to say they did not need permits to carry arms because they were law enforcement agents.

"Not in this state," answered the constable, then he even surprised Jake. "You two are under arrest until we can straightened this mess out." They were still sputtering indignantly as the handcuffs locked them together.

Lou Pryslybilski had moved to Venture ten years before the arrests occurred at Jake's home. He had become friends with The Fisherman after a trip up the river for salmon fishing. Lou decided that if a man could find the big fish at any time, he would be an invaluable partner. This had been the first time Jake had called on him since suggesting his name when the town began thinking of local law enforcement. Constable Pryslybilski soon realized that there was not much call for law enforcement in their town. He had served in the position almost five years before he made his first arrest. This occurred when three fishermen had paid more attention to their beer cooler than they did the fishing tackle. One of them had hooked another after failing on a cast. When they got back to the pier a visiting doctor removed the hook, and the victim decided he was going to pay back his friend with a sucker punch alongside the head. The fight had hardly gotten started before Lou had them spread eagled against their vehicle. The third one decided to come to the aid of his buddies and made a mistake by throwing a punch at the constable. This unlucky fisherman was the first to sober up after he found himself gasping in the water. Lou had fended off the blow and swung a backhand that had landed flush on the man's nose causing him to fall off the pier. The other two decided to come to the aid of their friend and found them selves gasping for air after Lou put them in the water. The constable arrested all three and kept them in custody until they were sober—twelve hours later. They left Venture with no fish, damp clothes, and sore noses and black eyes.

Chapter 11

The Oklahoma State Policemen were taken to the county jail after Jake had told them, "When you get back to Oklahoma, tell your governor that I declined his invitation, but I will visit him sometime in the next few days—on my terms. Also tell him that I would have come had he called and invited me." Jake called the county sheriff and told him what to expect, and asked him not to release the visiting policemen until authorities from Oklahoma called.

The sheriff said with a chuckle, "You are a mean man, Jake. Do you want to press charges?"

He laughed again when Jake answered, "Nah, they are two guys under orders. No need to give them any more bad times." He smiled when he started imagining what was in store for the two police officers when they returned to their state. Governor Josephs had disappointed him because either he or his wife Linda could have arranged a visit just by calling. They had been friends for a long time and had taken some unexpected steps in that time.

Jake mused, "Have they forgotten that they were involved in some mighty tough situations in the Ozark Mountains and Washington, D.C.? Did they consider what could happen to them if the word got out about their past?" Jake also wondered to himself if he would expose them if the Governor gave him a bad time about the Federal Prison. The prison operation had to be the cause of the governor's actions. A decision was made to take a trip to Oklahoma City to visit an old friend in about two weeks. It would be interesting to see how Josephs would react to the plans.

Jake landed in Oklahoma City at 1830 on a Friday night. It had been over two weeks since the visit from the policemen. He checked into a motel across the street from the airport, and after settling into the room—called the governor's mansion. He was surprised when Linda Josephs answered the telephone.

He said, "Hi Linda, this is Jake Green. It has been a while but I thought I would check in—I'll be here a couple of days. Is the governor in?"

There had been a gasp on the line when he identified himself and there was some hesitation before she answered, " Jake, this is a surprise. No, the governor is not at home yet, but he should be here at any time." She paused before continuing, "Are you here on a friendly visit?"

Jake replied, "It will be a friendly visit if I can control the situation." They visited a few more minutes and the governor's wife did not mention or ask the real reason for the visit. Jake told her where he was staying and the telephone number for his room.

Governor Josephs did not call—he arrived at the room door in about 20 minutes from the time Jake and Linda ended their conversation. The two old friends shook hand with guarded looks and mumbled greetings. Jake brought coffee to the table and poured two cups. His visitor took a few moments to prepare his coffee. Jake had decided to wait for Josephs to open the conversation.

The governor's first words were, "Navy, why were you and the Carpenters here a few weeks ago? Don't give me a dog and pony story I want and demand the truth."

Jake replied, "I was here by invitation and the Carpenters were here on my invitation. With your attitude, governor, why we were here is none of your damned business. So, what are you going to do—arrest me? I was not impressed with the two toadies that you sent to my home."

Josephs had turned red and was sputtering, "Watch yourself, Mr. Jake Green! I just might send you to one of our secret boarding houses. We have them in Oklahoma, just for people like you."

They sat staring at each other for almost five minutes with neither speaking. Finally, Jake broke the silence, "Buddy boy, I could take your ass in Korea and I can still do it, and you had best call others than the two you sent after me. I have already out smarted them and I can take both of them. So governor, you had better bring in your best people."

For a few moments, Jake thought he was going to have to fight the Governor of Oklahoma. Gradually the tension eased, Jake sat back in his chair and Josephs flexed his shoulders and sat back, and said, "O.K., Navy. You guys put me into a bad position by taking on the prison and killing those four men."

Jake responded, "Now listen, old friend, you don't know a thing. You are imagining something that you can't prove."

Josephs grinned and replied, "You are right that I can't prove anything, but you and Carpenter are the only people I know that could have done a job like that because Captain Silvers and Sergeant Jacobs wouldn't get involved with you."

There was another pause, and a larger smile spread across the governor's face, "Now, don't tell me that all of you were in Utah a few weeks ago."

Jake chuckled and responded, "O.K., I won't tell you anything."

Josephs said, "All right, I won't ask what happened in the prison or in Utah, but how in the world did you get in and out of the prison?"

They both laughed when Jake replied, "I just promised that I would not tell you anything."

A light conversation was held between the old friends until Josephs said, "I better get along, Linda is probably worried, and Navy, don't push your luck in my state"

They shook hands and Jake opened the door to see four very large Oklahoma State Policemen. He waved his hand at them and said to their boss, "Governor, you come well prepared."

There were chuckles all around as the door closed. Jake walked back and picked up his coffee cup and muttered, "Now what, old friend, now what?"

Later that evening the telephone rang, and it was Linda Josephs. On his answer, she said, "Navy, the governor is upset with you because you have put him into a bad position. As a matter of fact, I am mad as hell at you. You evidently think you can go anywhere you want and do anything you want. That's not going to happen while we are governor. If he won't do it, I will get your ass thrown into jail, and we will see who will be believed."

Jake waited patiently until she had vented her anger enough to listen to what he had to say. Then he replied quietly, "I hear you talking, pretty lady, but just how the hell can you get me thrown into jail? You folks are just imagining things. Who would believe you or the governor if you charge me with anything concerning the federal prison?"

She sputtered, "We might not charge you with anything. But the federal officials are looking for the cowardly murderers who ambushed those prisoners. We know that you are good at ambushing people. The feds will want to talk to you if we say anything."

Jake calmly spoke, "I heard that the four people who were shot were murderers threatening to kill over a hundred hostages, so tell me Mrs. Governor, who were the cowards in this story? I would like to hear your story if you try to link me to any ambushes."

She almost screamed, "Don't call me Mrs. Governor. We can prove you have run ambushes in the past."

"Listen to me, Mrs. Governor," Jake retorted. "Where are your witnesses? I remember a couple of times you and Mr. Governor came along."

"You bastard," she screamed. "Our friends will back us up."

"Lady," Jake said quietly with menace. "You may be able to trust the Marines, but you will have problems with the Navy—in more ways than you want to think about." With that he broke the connection.

The Oklahoma governor's mansion was hot with threats that evening and into the night. When the governor arrived, he found his wife in a very upset stage. She told him about the conversation with Jake and demanded that he be arrested. Josephs was also upset with his confrontation with his old friend. They discussed whether or not the other former Marines would back up their story about the ambushes Jake Green had led. Neither of them seemed to remember any part they had played in the other missions. They became more upset when their other friends refused to back their charges. When John and Samantha Silvers were called, the Oklahomans were betting their charges would be supported. That didn't happen because John was adamant that he couldn't support such an outrageous idea. He tried to point out to Josephs that all of them were as guilty as Jake. The phone was slammed with a broken circuit, without a goodbye. The governor and his wife were livid when Sarg and Darlene Jacobs supported John and Samantha, and their telephone call to the Carpenters wasn't answered. They spent hours suggesting ways to get Jake without becoming involved. Each plan had to be put aside because they would have no support from their friends. Linda even suggested that the governor use his powers to send Jake to prison and keep him hidden from the public.

Josephs appeared to approve of this suggestion until it was discussed further. He ended the night's conversation by saying, "Babe, it doesn't appear to me that we can do anything about all of this. Sometimes being governor is not much fun. Navy was a good friend. I hope we will be able to get together again somewhere in the future."

Chapter 12

Jake didn't wait, after he hung up the telephone on Linda Josephs, he grabbed his unopened bag and left the room. It only took a short time for him to check out and get a taxi to the airport. He had decided not to stay around to see what Josephs would do, and muttered to himself in the taxi, "Better not push it." The governor would have the advantage in Oklahoma, and Jake knew that he would never give up his friends. He shrugged his shoulder when he considered whether are not he would give up Josephs. When he left the cab, he went directly to the Northwest Airline counter and checked in with the return ticket he had purchased for the trip to Oklahoma. Jake spotted two of the very large state policemen he had seen with Josephs. He avoided them and surprised a young man by giving him the ticket to Ellensburg, Washington, by the way of Denver and Spokane. The youngster was heading for Denver. Jake had heard him enquire about the schedule and price of the ticket. Before the young traveler could thank his benefactor, no one was alongside. There was no need to try and find anyone, because the young man was reaching for the ticket rather than looking at the man who passed it along.

There was no hesitation on Jake's part when he gave the ticket a way. He turned immediately to the gates with the private airplanes. It only took him a short time to charter a jet to Ellensburg. He was the only passenger on the business jet, and no one appeared interested when the plane landed. There was a rental agency open and he rented a car and in less than an hour was back in Venture. He called a neighbor's sons and hired them to take the automobile back to Ellensburg early the next morning. Jake had enjoyed his actions, not because of any thoughts of danger, but because he had left a pretty tough trail for anyone from Oklahoma to follow.

Life in Venture was what he needed to return to a normal thought pattern.

Since Darlene Coppage had called, Jake had been living on the edge for almost two months. His first day back was spent at home, and he kept busy working on his hunting equipment and stocking supplies. The hunting season for horned game was scheduled to open on 15 October and the licenses and tags had to be picked up at the same time. Jake had applied for hunting licenses in Washington and Idaho. Some of his friends had invited him to hunt on the first day in the potholes area of Eastern Washington. He was looking forward to that because this would be his first trip to the inland desert of the state. For the past couple of years he had been guiding hunting parties in the high mountains of the two states. He did not let the upcoming hunting frenzy keep him off the river. The second week back he packed and took off for a five-day trip to the upper reaches of the Columbia River. His fishing had included forays into Canada, and this trip was suggested by one of his friends from the border patrol. The Canadians were betting that they could outfish the Washingtonians. Two of the Washington patrolmen were from Yakima, Washington, and had made a number of hunting trips with Jake.

The visits to Canada were relaxing and fun, the Canadians were great hosts and won the fishing tourney. Of course the Washingtonians never accepted that and wouldn't admit the facts. One night, after a feast on trout and fried potatoes the party of six were starting their nightly poker game, the Canadians' radio blared a warning about a possible attempt to cross the border with a load of dope and possible human contraband. Sergeant Freeland of the Mounted Police recognized the position coordinates of the possible crossing.

He said that the crossing attempt would pass their position by about two miles. The three Mounties started preparation for intercepting the smugglers and suggested that Jake and his party throw another log on the fire and settle in for the night. Jake retorted, "No way. I am going with you because I want to see if the Mounties are half as good as the public relations people say."

The Washington patrolmen argued that the border also came under their purview and started their preparation. Sergeant Freeland shrugged his shoulder and said the Mounties would protect them from harm. Lieutenant Sanderson of the Washington Border Patrol asked what the plan of action would be. The Mounties did not hesitate and it was clear that the smugglers wouldn't be arrested if dangers were perceived. Jake asked, "Who is going to clean up the strike zone if the attack is a success?"

Freeland laughed and replied, "We put them down and leave, then someone will find them and wonder what occurred."

As it happened, there was no attack because when the smuggler's camp was found, no one was alive. The victims were Asians and had been executed while chained together. The incident was reported and the Washington people packed to leave. Sergeant Freeland took Jake aside and said, "Jake, you appeared to be relaxed during our move to this site. As matter of fact, you took over when you signaled each of groups to fan out on your left and right. If there is an unusual border problem, can I call on you?"

Jake handed the policeman a card and said, "My telephone number. If you call it, no one will hear any secrets."

The trip up river was a success. The fishermen had great time fishing and telling stories. The Canadian Mounties were outstanding hosts, and the smuggling attempt was exciting. It was a mystery how and why the smugglers had killed their cargo. Jake surmised that it was possible that the smugglers had intercepted the report that had come over the Canadian Police radio net. He was also intrigued by Freeland's comments about possible future operations with the neighbors to the north. With a shrug, he turned his thoughts to big game hunting. The weather appeared to be cooperating because the high mountains of Idaho and Washington had been receiving steady snowfall and the season would not open for two weeks.

The weekend after deer season opened, six hunters from Venture headed for the Pot Holes. The weather was miserable. It was raining and cold, but not cold enough for snow. Lou Pryslybilski was acting as guide and he was trying to make the hunters feel better when he said, "O.K., go out that way and that way and that way and that way and someone will find something to shoot. Don't worry, I have had good luck in all four direction, so I will stay in camp and keep the fire going."

One of the hunters retorted, "I know I will find something to shoot because when you step back into that tent, I am going to shoot it down."

Pryslybilski laughed and scolded, "Oh, come on now—this is the weather we have learned to love in eastern Washington." When they settled down after the good-natured kidding, it was decided to go hunting in only two directions. Jake led a group to the southeast and Lou took the others to the southwest. They had hardly cleared the camp area when the first deer sprang up and one of shooters in Jake's party took it with only one shot. They gathered around it to tag and gut it before going back to camp. While they were working, another shot was heard to the southwest. The two parties entered camp within minutes of each other with two four-prong bucks.

Jake said, "Lou, you are the expert hunter so you have to teach us how to cook—and we are starving. I want a roast now and innard stew for the evening meal." There was some good-natured razzing for the proposed cook, and all the while, a fire was built and the animals were butchered. Each man cut a selection to be roasted on the fire and helped cut the liver, heart and other innards for the evening stew. The rain and wind almost doused the fire before a cover could be rigged. All of the hunters were experienced and soon a three-sided tarpaulin structure was protecting the cook fire. A large pot was used for the stew and the meat, potatoes, and other vegetables were soon at a slow simmer. The smell was so tantalizing that they could hardly wait for the roasts to cook. Jake started another good-natured argument when he said, "Stew pots, potatoes and carrots? You people don't know how to rough it. Maybe sometime this winter when the sun is shining I'll take you into the high mountains for some real hunting. There will be no vehicles to take your gear so you will have to pack the stew pot. And I insist on innard stew with all my parties."

As the hunting season went forward, Jake was guide to hunting parties almost every weekend and a few times during weekdays. Most of the hunters were sportsmen and gladly gave the meat to the food banks and public kitchens. Some of them would take a hindquarter for the meat and all of them wanted the hides and antlers. The innard stews soon become the watchwords for hunting parties in Idaho and Washington. Some of the hunters would struggle to take the stew pot into the mountains. On one trip into Idaho, Jake made a stop at Porter Lake to visit with the chief of police. Darlene told him that the town had become boring since the raid against the drug runners and the supremacists and that she was thinking about resigning as the town's police chief. Jake said, "You are a pretty good hand, seaman, but take some time making that type of decision. If you do leave, come see me. I might have an interesting story to tell."

She laughed and replied, "Jake with comments like that I think I will resign now, but I will have to take some time with such a decision. Porter Lake may be boring, but it is my town."

On one Saturday that there was no hunting party, Jake was in the local restaurant at "the table" with some of his friends. They were telling new stories which were really old stories that were changed each time a different person told it as the "truth."

He had not noticed any of the customers until the restaurant owner came over and quietly said, "Jake, those two guys at the back table have been asking about a man called The Fisherman. Jake casually moved until he could see the two men. They were both big and looked very capable of taking care of problems.

He turned back to the restaurant owner and said quietly, "O.K., Walt. I don't know them. Let me know if it sounds like any trouble may be brewing. If they ask for me again, try to find why they are looking for me. I'm sure it is nothing. They probably have heard of The Fisherman and are curious about the name." When the two men finished their meal, they left the restaurant and Jake watched them turn west on the freeway toward Seattle.

In the intervening weeks, the hunters slacked off on their activity and Jake had more time to spend with his neighbors. He helped a boat builder construct three riverboats. Then turned his attention to a pier for his own use. He had been planning such a venture for months, but it took about two years before all of the permitting process had been answered. Jake had all of the provisions for the job delivered to his back yard. When the pile-driving started, his friends visited to watch the progress. The piles were finished late one afternoon. The next morning, Jake was awakened by voices and hammering down by the river. He stepped out on the back patio and watched as a carpenter crew began building the pier. When he came out, there were razzing hoots about a city boy trying to do country boy work. With all the help, the pier was studded and braced by 1800. Lou Pryslybilski came over about 1700 and he and Jake started a pot of innard stew. The carpenters were told to call their families and extend an invitation to help eat the stew. Lou had out done himself by baking two pans of corn meal fritters. The dinner party lasted until 2000 and then everyone helped clean up before going home. Some of the women stopped by and asked for the recipe because they had heard the raves about the innard stew but had never tried cooking it.

Lou responded, "Shucks, ladies, all you have to do is fill the pot and let it stew. The longer it is cooked, the better the taste. The fritters are nothing but cornbread which is cooked by frying or on a grill like hot cakes."

One evening in March, Lou Prysylbilski called Jake and told him that there were two strangers at the restaurant asking for The Fisherman.

Jake said, "I'll be there in a few minutes. Let me see them before introduction." The restaurant was empty except for the local storytellers and the two strangers at a back-wall table. Jake recognized them as the two men who had been asking for him late in the hunting season. He hadn't approached them on that occasion, but this time he approached their table and said, "I am the guy you must be tracking. What can I do for you?"

They introduced themselves as Harvey and Marvin. There were no last names and it was obvious that they were close family and probably twins.

One of them said with a smile, "You can do us a favor by calling us Harv and Marv."

Jake responded with further mirth, "I'll be glad to if you will tell me who is Harv and who is Marv." The small talk went on for some time and Jake found that he was beginning to be at ease, and it was apparent that they were responding in like manner.

One of them finally asked, "Is there someplace we can talk?" Jake replied, "Sure, let's go down and sit by the river."

As the three were leaving, Jake gave Lou a sign to follow. The Constable wouldn't be interfering but Jake knew that he would keep the party under a watchful eye. The two strangers followed him down to the river landing that he had constructed earlier in the year. There were a number of seats and a table at the head of the pier and the three men took seats at the table. Jake maneuvered until he could watch both while they would be unable to gain eye contact without some effort.

After they had settled down, one of them said, "O.K., I'm Harv. We understand that you are the best guide in the area, not only for the river, but for the mountains, too."

Jake did not respond and his visitor continued, "We are from southern California and we have a serious situation. My boss's daughter was lost last fall on Mt. Shuksan. Do you know that area?"

Jake replied, "Sure. Mt. Shuksan is over near Mt. Baker. The mountain is 8 to 9 thousand feet and the terrain is very tough. I doubt if anyone could survive the winter unless proper plans had been made. You have to be in good condition before you tackle that hill."

Marv spoke up for the first time and answered, "I think we can hack it if you can." He grinned and continued, "The real problem is that the girl was probably abducted rather than just getting lost. We promised to find her or at least some sign of her. Will you take us up that hill?"

There was a period of silence before Jake responded. After some time with an appraising look he said quietly, "This sounds serious. If she is dead, there is not much we can do. My question is what do we do if she is living in a mountain man's shack?"

He was answered by one of the brothers, "Just get us to the area and we will take care of every thing needed to be done. You won't be involved."

Jake grunted, "I am already involved. When do you want to go on the trip?"

The men said that they could be ready on Monday of the following week.

As they had planned, there would be four days to prepare for the trip. Jake went to Lou and asked him to research a disappearance of a young woman in the Mt. Shuksan area. On Saturday, the lawman called and said that he had some interesting information. The report showed that Merrylynn Rogerson, 18 years old, had disappeared from a camp in the rugged mountains of the Northern Cascades in the state of Washington. Ms. Rogerson was from Riverside, California. She was on a trip to the northern mountains with the senior class of Riverside High School. The reports from her friends were vague, without any hard news of her actions. She had left camp for a morning hike and wasn't missed until lunchtime. Some of her classmates initiated a search. The others remained in camp to await reports or for her possible return. They also called the nearest ranger station and reported Merrylynn missing. There was a formal search for the missing young woman that lasted four days and the only trace of her was a kerchief one of her friends found on the trail heading up the mountain. Two days later, one of the searchers found tracks on a small creek bed. The footprints suggested two people, one large and one much smaller and they disappeared at a rock ledge about a quarter of a mile from the hiking trail.

Lou also had found the information that the girl's father was a Colonel Rogerson stationed at the Pendleton Marine Base in southern California. The colonel was deployed at the time of his daughter's disappearance, and the search had been called off before he could get to the area. Some of the Marine scouts from Pendleton came north and they searched for another week before the high mountains were filled with snow. This search didn't turn any more information about the young woman and Colonel Rogerson and the Marine scouts returned to southern California. Lou asked Jake what was going on and was told that another search would be made but for him not to speculate on any stories that might be told about this search.

The twins, Marv and Harv, arrived at Jake's place on Sunday evening. The three hunters packed a four wheel drive vehicle, and later that evening Jake said, "O.K., tell me who you are. I am betting that you are Marine scouts from Pendleton.

After a moment of silence one of them said, "You are half right. I am a Marine, but my brother is Navy."

Jake waited, but when no other information was forthcoming he growled, "You aren't telling me anything, and I am not about to take a Jarhead and a Swabbie up Shuksan." He continued by pointing at one of them and asked, "Harv or Marv?"

The visitors chuckled and the one pointed out said, "I am Marv."

Jake said, "O.K., you are the Marine. I can tell by the high-sided haircut. A sailor like your brother does not have that kind of crap. Of course, he doesn't have much more hair than you. But if you are just enlisted men, we can call this off now because I am not equipped to babysit anyone."

Harv answered, "O.K., Jake. I am a SEAL and he is a Marine scout. I think we can carry our load."

They all laughed when Jake retorted, "A SEAL and a scout. Why shucks, I have two baby-sitters and I shouldn't have to carry any thing up that mountain." He then stood up and said, "We should leave early tomorrow. Let's get some sleep." He pointed to three doors and continued, "That's a bedroom, that's a bedroom, and that's a bathroom. Good night."

Jake was up the next morning at 0400 and found his visitors busy packing their equipment. He handed them the keys to the four-wheel drive and made coffee. The twins came in and reported they were ready to leave. The coffee was divided into travel containers and they left for the mountains. They turned west on I-90 until reaching the exit for Wenatchee, Washington, and when they reached the town stopped for breakfast. There had been little conversation because the three of them were thinking and planning for the coming operation. Marv brought papers into the restaurant, which included a hand drawn sketch of the past search actions. Jake compared three maps and noticed that two of them marked the spot where the footprints were found in the small creek. He suggested and his companions agreed that this would be a logical place to start their quest for the teenager from southern California. They compared the sketches to a detailed map of the area. Jake said, "I can get us to that site without going through the trail-head camping area used in previous searches."

They were in the mountains a few hours after leaving Wenatchee. They discussed their best way to start their search and the twins suggested that Jake take the lead. He said, "O.K., we only have a couple more hours of daylight. Let's go to where we will start tomorrow and make camp." The automobile was left in a clearing near the road down the mountain, and the hikers started the climb. They arrived and prepared a campsite at about 1800. After setting up the tent, they moved out to the next trail and located the small stream where the footprints had been found. There was nothing suspicious or noticeable until they located a faint animal trail that led up the hill. Before they retired for the night, a decision was made to make their first search by exploring the animal trail and starting at first light. The next morning they had a breakfast of jerky and a handful of trail mix. Marv said lightly, "Jeez, the Marines won't allow me to eat this good stuff for breakfast."

Harv retorted, "Yeah, we know you jarheads start the day with ham and eggs and we swabs are required to have fresh fruit."

Jake responded, "That is why you guys have to call on a poor old boy like me for help. When we get back, you jerks can cook breakfast for all of us."

"Huh," said one of the twins. "Your poor old stomach couldn't take good food, so we will soak some of this jerky in hot water. That's what you're probably used to."

The next morning they quietly repacked the tent and other equipment so as to be ready to move to another location as the search dictated. At first light they approached the hiking trail and slipped carefully into the path heading into the deep forest. Sometime was spent orienting themselves to the area map. When they were reasonably satisfied that they were in the proposed area to start the search, Jake said, "O.K., Marine, you are the recon expert—lead us out. Harv follow at about 15 yards and I will bring up the rear to protect you guys."

There was a chuckle but no further talk as they quietly and stealthily started the upward climb. The first half hour the climb was easy but gradually became steeper. Marv signaled a break and they gathered off the trail because they did not want to be surprised by a man or animal. The searchers only spoke as necessary and just as they started to regain the trail they heard a noise that had not been present during the hike. Without words they went back to ground, with all them facing the trail. A few minutes passed and a gruff voice could be heard which was profanely directed at another person. The hunters also heard a weak mewling cry and then another curse. They burrowed closer toward the ground when a large bearded man appeared with a rope trailing behind. The weak cry was coming from a young woman who was at the end of the rope. It was tied around her waist and outstretched arms. The man was huge and filthy and was bragging to his captive about what she could expect at camp.

The man and his captive continued up the track and the searchers waited until they couldn't hear any noise on the trail. Jake whispered, "Let's follow, but Marv, keep out of sight. Don't get caught, there may be other people involved."

There were nods of agreement when he continued, "I have a bad feeling about the Rogerson girl. She may have been out here all winter with that son-of-a-bitch." They returned to the trail but with very slow movement and in a short time, could hear the progress up the trail. The girl had stopped crying and had begun to use words that her captor probably had never heard before. This bravado did not last long because a resounding sound of a slap was heard. The climb lasted most of the morning, but about 1100, the Marine gave a signal to halt and then asked the others to close up. When they closed up, Marv said, "I smell smoke and it is not far away."

His brother nodded and said, "I smell it and also camp odors. We are very close."

Jake said, "One of you go left and the other right. I will take the trail and let's not lose sight of each other." The movement was agonizingly slow but steady. The smells were becoming stronger and camp noise could be heard. Jake signaled a halt and then moved slowly up the trail and in a few yards the camp came into view. He motioned for his comrades to move up.

When all were ready, they stood up and could see into the camp. The man was untying his captive and slapped her when she complained. The blow had knocked her a yard or two and he followed and held her down with his rifle buried in her stomach and growled, "If you weren't mine I would fill you full of bullets, but I have plans for you, honey, and I'm going fill you up but not with bullets."

The observers were surprised when another man appeared in the door of the shack and giggled, "Don't shoot her until I get some. We need a fresh doe and she looks good." Another young woman came from the shack, and Jake could see that she was almost mentally blank. She did not respond when the new captive said, "Merrylynn. It's me, Annie Corbett."

The two men laughed as the big one said, "Look what I got, someone who knows the whore. This way they can learn together."

The second one said, "Nah, let's gut the whore and then we can share the new stuff." He pointed at Merrylynn and laughed, "I'm tired of her anyway—she has quit making noises. Won't even talk or bawl."

His last move was to unsheathe a knife and turned toward the girl. Two shots rang out and the men fell squalling to the ground. Jake watch and listened until he decided they may survive, he added two headshots to finish the job. The twins approached the two young women and it took some time before the new captive would accept the fact that friends had arrived. The other girl looked vacantly around as if she didn't hear or see anything. Jake settled the argument when he grabbed the girl by the arm and pulled her up close and said quietly, "Listen, girly, we have been following you all morning, waiting for a chance to take your friend. We started out looking for one and found two. If you don't shut your mouth, I'll gag you again. Get your friend up so we can get the hell out of here. The gunfire probably carried for some distance and we are not interested in any other person."

He continued, "Marv, you take Annie here and if she complains anymore, spank her ass." There was actually a giggle from the girl. Jake said further, "Harv, you take Merrylynn. We may have to carry her. If so, I will give you some relief. But for now, follow me down this hill. We don't have time to squirrel around."

Jake led off with a fast pace and it was not long before both women were being carried. The three men traded places about every 15 minutes. Whoever was in the lead did not slow the pace. A break was called at the intersection of the trails and Annie was questioned about her party. She told them that they were at the trailhead campgrounds waiting for the rangers. She grinned weakly and said, "I wouldn't wait for them and got caught by that ape about a mile from the camp."

They took twenty minutes and before departing, Merrylynn appeared to revive and fell into Annie's arms. Jake called for continuation of the trip and the girls started walking. Merrylynn needed help at times. Marv picked her up and said, "Let's go."

They hiked for another half hour before hearing the camp. There was a great combined shouts and cries when the girls came into view. The rescuers allowed the search party to take control of the victims. Jake signaled for a slow retreat to the tree line. When they reached the woods he said, "Let's choose up sides and get the hell out of here." They made the move to their equipment and within a half hour were back on the road heading toward Wenatchee. There were no stops and they arrived in Venture at about 1815.

The news media was enthralled with the story of rescue for the two young women. All of the people in the search party were interviewed at least once; Annie Corbett was questioned over and over by the media and law enforcement. Merrylynn Rogerson was taken to Harbor View Hospital in Seattle and was isolated because of her condition. One question was asked many times, "Who rescued and returned the young women to the search party?" Some of the observers only noticed one man; other swore that two men brought the captives into camp. Only one person held out to three rescuers, but she was only 11 years old so no one paid any attention to her claims. Annie also was questioned about her capture and why she left camp. She told that she was too impatient to wait for the search to commence. Her capture had happened when she spoke to a man on the trail. According to her he was a mountain man who denied any knowledge of the disappearance of Merrylynn. Then when she passed him, she suddenly saw him turn and strike out. She did not remember any more until she regained consciousness and was being tied up and gagged. When the rangers returned and told about finding the mountain camp with two men dead, the media went into another frenzy and Annie Corbett was taken from camp when it was hinted that she might have been a part of the kidnapping. There was some speculation that the entire story had been faked.

Later in the evening, Colonel Rogerson, Merrylynn's father, stated that he would very much like to meet his daughter's rescuers so they could be properly thanked and he chided the news media and authorities for suggesting some sort of collusion in the return of his daughter. One of the doctors attending the young woman made an appearance and made the statement that there was no way that Ms. Rogerson could have been a part of a false story. He said, "She is a very lucky person to be rescued, when she was, because it was likely she would not have been able to survive very much longer with the treatment she had been receiving."

Chapter 13

The remainder of the year in Venture was uneventful, and Jake only left home for two meetings that lasted two days each. He finished the work on the new pier, and returned to his quiet existence as The Fisherman. There was one week that he stayed on the River and an island that was just north of Grand Coulee. He had found that there were many types of fish in this part of the region and on this trip he was looking for river trout. Five nights were spent on the island that was not much more than sand spit. The other nights were spent on the boat as it floated down the river. During the trip he explored the possibility of taking the boat past Coulee Dam and then into Canada to the far headwaters of the great river. One night in Grand Coulee, he located a river man who promised to get the boat around the dam. They made a date for September if the trip could be arranged. A call to Sergeant Mike Freeland of the Northwest Mounties extended the plan for such river trip.

Sergeant Freeland said, "Jake, on another subject—if you can, meet me in Trail about 1500 on Thursday. I certainly would appreciate it. I will be at the first service station on the left as you approach." Trail, British Columbia, was a small town just across the international border, and the Mountie would not discuss the reason for the invitation.

Jake pulled into the service station at 1430 and, while the car was being serviced, the attendant took a telephone call. He approached Jake and asked, "Are you Mr. Green?" Jake nodded and took the telephone.

It was Mike Freeland, who said, "Jake, meet me in Penticton at the 5000 Motel. You will find it near the intersection of Industrial Avenue and Main Street. I am checked in at room 129. You'll find a key over the door. When you arrive, don't stop at the desk just go to the room and wait for me. I should be there no later than 1700." He hung up before Jake could ask any questions.

The trip into Penticton was taken at a slow pace and it was only 1600 when he arrived. Jake went directly to the room as instructed. He waited until 1715, when the door opened and his Canadian friend entered and they shook hands. There were a few minutes of small talk and Mike indicated the dining table as the place to take a seat. He turned the television on and selected a noisy program and said quietly, "No loud talking, and no screams when I tell you what I am thinking."

Jake nodded his head and said, "O.K., What is going on?"

The Mountie sat quietly for a few minutes with some appraising looks at his friend from the States. He lowered his voice and related to Jake that there would be a conference later in the evening with organized crime figures from both their countries. The meeting had evidently been called after the Canadian authorities had busted a number of illegal operations that ranged from a 30-pound pot bust to a 12-ton shipload off the shore of Vancouver Island. Sergeant Freeland leaned close and said, "Jake, don't hesitate to stop me from what I am going to say if you can't go along with my ideas. I have told myself not to involve anyone, but I can't handle this operation alone. Jake, I am proposing that you and I go to the meeting and wipe out over thirty people."

He quit talking and leaned back in his chair.

Jake leaned forward and said softly, "For an operation such as you are discussing, I would suggest automatic weapons and I don't happen to have one with me."

Moments passed before Mike Freeland said, "I thought you go for something like this—I have two specially made 12 gauge automatic shotguns with twelve round clips. They can't be traced, because they will be in the evidence room at the headquarters in Vancouver. When we finish tonight, I will clean them and return them to my friend in the evidence room." He reached into a bag and took out the two weapons. Jake took one and examined it in detail and said with a smile, "Partner, this is the ugliest gun I have ever seen. We could take on an army at close range."

When the television program was over they turned the sound down. As the sound was muted, they were talking about Canadian football while making coffee and sandwiches. At 2000, Freeland stood up and said, "My friend, I am going to leave. Got a busy day tomorrow."

Jake answered, " O.K., pal," while putting on his coat. They left the room and got into the Canadian's vehicle. It had a common, nondescript appearance. As they started moving, Mike Freeland described the building they would be entering. He stated that the only possible problem would be a switchback passageway. He was still talking when Jake recognized the target. The car started slowing but then the driver suddenly accelerated and passed the target without looking out the window. When they turned a corner, Jake questioned, "O.K., partner, what's up?"

Freeland shook his head and said, "That place is surrounded by every Canadian cop except for me." Jake knew of course that his friend was exaggerating but waited for him to continue.

Mike shook his shoulders and chuckled when he said, "Jake, let's go to dinner in case someone saw me. If they did, I may need an excuse for being in Penticton. I hadn't heard there was going to be a raid."

Jake laughed and retorted, "O.K., if I must have dinner, I want shrimp and you have to pay for them. Seriously friend, I am glad you spotted the stakeouts. Just think what a surprise all of us would have had if we were in there spraying when the Mounties tried to bust the place."

Chapter 14

On October first, Jake came in from the river and found a message light flashing on his telephone-answering unit. He was surprised to hear a familiar voice, "Jake, this is John Tolliver. The general wants to see you. Be in New Bern on the tenth of the month. I will pick you up at the airport."

The message ended abruptly and Jake sat at his desk with a faint smile. John Tolliver was an old friend from Detachment X-Ray days and had become a brigadier general of the U.S. Marine Corps. The general that the brigadier was referring to was Lt. General Sheffield, who was the officer in charge of Detachment X-Ray. When Sheffield was advanced to brigadier general, he was transferred to the White House for highly classified duties. He warned the Detachment X-Ray members, "Once in Detachment X-Ray always in Detachment X-Ray."

Jake reflected on the past and memories came flooding back about the past. Their duties included two raids on islands in the Caribbean. The first raid was to take out communist cells and the other an island dictator was eliminated. Detachment X-Ray operated out of the South Atlantic from Africa to South America. During that time Colonel Sheffield was the officer in charge, and after Jake had been separated for a number of years, he was ordered to report to New Bern, North Carolina, for a special operation for the general. And here again were orders, not a request, for him to return to New Bern. New Bern, North Carolina, is a small historical town on the eastern seaboard and was situated near Camp Lejuene Marine Base and the Marine Air Station at Cherry Point, North Carolina.

Jake did not question the fact that he would obey the orders and report to New Bern. He drove to Ellensburg and chartered a Cessna for the trip to the east coast. He told the pilot when he needed to be in New Bern, and they made plans to leave at 2200 on October 9. The next few days, Jake made arrangements to be away from Venture for a short time. He returned to the Ellensburg airport on the ninth, and at 2200 he was on the way east. A few stops were required during the night for fuel for the airplane and the passengers. The pilot was instructed to stay until Jake was ready to return home and was to find lodgings and that he would be reimbursed for all expenses. They joked about the pilot being loose in town. Jake said, "Do what you want and go where you want, but if you are not ready to return, I will contact your wife and ask her where you are."

Tolliver was waiting, as promised, at the airport in New Bern. The two old friends stood at the service counter and reminisced about days gone by. The general grinned and said, "The tobacco markets are open. Should we take a trip?"

Jake laughed and retorted, "Not me. If you remember, I was visiting the county sheriff's home. We could stop by Lake Waccamaw though. You think they might be still looking for us?"

Tolliver laughed and said, "Maybe we should go see the general. It might be safer than those places."

They had been referring to adventures experienced during their Detachment X-Ray days. The trip to General Sheffield's home was short and Jake recognized the house where the earlier meetings with the general were held. A young woman answered the door and was introduced as Gunnery Sergeant Whitestone. She led them into a library and told them that the general would soon be with them. Jake said quietly, "No one knows General Sheffield. Have you ever noticed that he is "the general" in all references to him?"

Tolliver laughed and answered, "That's because he is the general. Even the president refers to him in that fashion."

Gunnery Sergeant Whitestone returned with a coffee service and offered to pour the refreshment.

She laughed and blushed when Jake exclaimed, "No way. I have always been afraid of Marine Gunnery Sergeants."

Tolliver asked, "Gunny, where is the house staff? I am like Jake. I still get stomach cramps around a sergeant."

The marine smiled and responded, "The staff was given the day off for this meeting. The marines are here to protect you and the general. I am going to squeal to the other sergeants about the cramps. Sergeant Fernandez said that he was nervous just by being in the same house with one general, much less two."

After laughing loudly, Tolliver said, "Jake, wait till you see Fernandez. He is a puny little rascal—about 6'4" and 250 pounds. He wouldn't be nervous if there were two presidents around the area." They continued with the small talk for over an hour before an automobile came into the driveway.

The general spoke from the door. "Well, it is time to go to work. It sounded like you were having fun. None of that—we can't have any fun." He was smiling and continued as he shook hands with Jake. "Navy, it is good to see you. The brigadier and I have been thinking about you for some time. Take your seats again and I will be back after one telephone call."

"He is checking in with the White House," Tolliver whispered. Thirty minutes had passed when the door opened and Jake knew it had to be Sergeant Fernandez. He growled, "The general will see you now in his office."

Jake felt small as he walked past the "nervous" marine. Fernandez knocked on the office door and opened it without a word and indicated two seats in front of the desk. the general ended the telephone conversation and turned toward Jake, still without saying any thing. The two men stared at each other without a twitch for at least five minutes. Finally, the general broke the silence with a smile and chuckle, "Navy, it is nice to see that you can still hold a man's eyes."

The tension was broken and Jake said, "I had a good teacher with the eye contact. You used to make us sweat with that stare." The three good friends remained in the library getting reacquainted and enjoying the visit with reminder stories of their common past. No one said anything about why the meeting had been called. Jake was tempted to ask a couple of times but decided wait for one of the marines to open the discussion. Fernandez interrupted the conversation when he made the announcement that food was waiting for hungry people. Tolliver stood and said, "We better go while there is food for us, because Sergeant Fernandez is famous for his appetite."

After everyone had pushed back from empty seafood platters, they went back to the general's office. He closed the door and took a seat with his visitors. He looked at Jake for a few moments and then began, "Navy, I need you to do something for me, and it may seem a little farfetched. You were one of the best from Detachment X-Ray, and we need people for that same type of work. This time, though, it has to be completely secret. If you do it for us, the three of us will be the only ones who know exactly what is happening." He hesitated for a couple of moments and when Jake did not say anything, he continued, "We want you to recruit a team such as you had in X-Ray. I think you called them the Wise Asses. The new team will be for the same type of actions and must be good enough to complete such tasks. Plainly, if they cannot execute people, we don't want them—we don't need them. If you do this, the people you will be going after will be much the same type targets as the X-Ray teams went after. This time the action will be by my orders only and no one else will know about you. Tolliver will be the advance man for me—I am the advance man for the president. That is all I can tell you. Basically, we need an assassination team to be on call at our convenience." He leaned back and waited.

Jake moved forward in his chair and responded, "General you are asking a lot. Detachment X-Ray is no more. I only know two from X-Ray besides Tolliver, and one of them, I heard, is going to have a little Tolliver. If I can recruit such a team, how would they be compensated? I don't need any money, but the ones I am thinking of are hard working people. Also, if we do this, I am the leader of the team. Neither of you are to try and dictate. If that happens, I will quit even if you have direct orders from the president. You furnish the information needed to select the targets and I will take it from there. There will be no plans discussed with anyone. And I have to have your word that I will be independent in all of the actions. I will not allow visitors on any mission, and I don't give a damn who wants to visit. If we agree and I can recruit, there will be six or eight people other than myself. That is if I can get the ones I want."

Tolliver spoke up and it lightened the tension that all could feel, he said, "There is a little Tolliver, you know."

The general spoke up with a smile and said, "You have got it, Navy. No one will interfere and you can tell your people when they come on board that an account will be set up with one million tax-free dollars in their names. The one stipulation is that they will not be able to access the accounts for one year. After that, it is for their use and as they see fit. Also, each will be paid one hundred thousand a year with no regards given to the number of missions. Any more questions or comments?" After a few moments of silence he said, "O.K., you both are welcome to stay as long as you wish, but the sergeants and I will be leaving at 2300."

Without more talk he left the room, and Tolliver said, "Jake, we have a suite downtown if you want to see Mrs. Tolliver and little Tolliver."

They both laughed when Jake responded, "I don't know any Mrs. Tolliver, but I would sure like to see George, if it can be arranged."

It was arranged and George was still a delight, especially when she was showing off the little Tolliver. She was good as her word; the little boy had George as his middle name. The three friends stayed up late into the night just enjoying the company. There was no talk about the past and the future was mentioned casually when Tolliver told his wife that Navy would be working for the general, and she took a long look at both men and said, "Jake, you are my friend, so be careful--be very careful—I don't want to have to go looking for you."

After a few hours sleep and breakfast with the Tollivers, Jake returned to the airport and his friend with the Cessna was standing at the ticket counter flirting with the clerk. She giggled when Jake walked up and said, "Miss, if this guy is bothering you, call the cops, and I will testify to anything you want."

They all laughed when he continued, "No, wait, don't call the cops. I will get him out of here," then to the pilot, "Norman, go wind up your toy and let's go flying."

When the airplane leveled out and headed to the northwest, Jake leaned his seat back, intending to sleep but he began thinking about the people to recruit for the new adventures. He was satisfied all of them would at least listen and not discuss the subject with others. There was no way for him to know if any would join the effort because what was to be offered would take some hard long considerations for all of them. While he was talking to the general, he decided on the recruits he would be looking for: The twins, Harv, Marine Recon and Marv, the Navy SEAL (or was it the other way around?); Carpenter, the marine sniper and his wife Lydia; Marlene Coppage (Seaman) chief of police of Porter Lake, Idaho; Waseka Morning Fawn, the young woman who insisted on her right to kill the man who brutalized her family, also from Idaho; and Mike Freeland, Canadian Northwest Mounted Police.

Jake knew that he would have to contact the twins fast because they were trying to decide whether on not to stay in service the last time that he had seen them. They said their enlistments would be over in November. The problem facing the recruiter would be locating the two men. The only possible locations would be the SEAL Team School at North Island, San Diego, California, and Camp Pendleton Marine Base near Riverside, California. Jake smiled when he remembered he did not know their surnames. The Carpenters could be a problem because they were well known it their region, but the marine sniper would be invaluable in a time of crisis. Lydia Carpenter was a small, beautiful woman but could handle a gun or knife and would not allow her husband to go alone. She said in jest, "I let him go to Korea alone and see what happened—he got himself captured."

Darlene Coppage had offered a number of times to assist Jake any time he wanted. She would be a great ally because of her skills and determination. The leeches had affected her for a very short time—by the time she was dressed in the dry clothing she was laughing about the situation. Waseka Morning Fawn was an unknown and Jake had decided to take some time with her before asking her to join his team. He had decided that if she handled herself in the same fashion she did at Porter Lake, she would be a real asset for spying and tracking. Mike Freeland of the Canadian Mounted Police would have to be approached cautiously because of his position with the Mounties. He had asked for Jake's assistance on one occasion, but they took no actions because of police involvement of another sort.

During the night at one of the refueling stops, Jake asked the pilot if he would be willing to fly to San Diego. The answer was, "Sure, I haven't been down that for over ten years." He continued, "Jake, what kind of business are you in—first we fly to the southeast and now you want to go southwest. Whatever it is, keep me in mind for the flying jobs."

Jake laughed and retorted, "O.K. Let's go home and get a couple of nights rest, then on Monday, it will be off to the California desert. I will be there for a few days. Will that fit your plans without problems?"

The pilot assured him that a few days in San Diego would give him time for a few hours in Tijuana, Mexico.

Jake said, "Watch it in TJ. Those cops will put you in jail for your protection and keep you there until you are protected."

That caused the pilot to choke on his coffee because of a burst of laughter. "I know," he spouted, "They will protect someone until they squeeze all the money they can from family and government." Jake spent the weekend preparing for at least a week away from home. While he was working on the boat dock Lou Prysylbilski stopped by for a visit.

Jake mentioned that he was going on a trip for a few days and the constable offered an observation, "Jake, you have been taking quite a few trips in the last few months—and most of them, you haven't let anyone know where you are heading." Then he asked, "What are you into, my friend? Why all the traveling?"

Jake answered quietly, "Frankly, Lou, I do what I want and go where I want. I stopped answering to people a long time ago." The lawman looked at Jake for a few moments, shrugged his shoulders, and left without another word.

Monday morning, Jake stopped at the restaurant for breakfast. He spied the town constable and walked back to the table. Lou smiled and said, "Have a seat, my friend, but don't tell me where you are going."

Jake laughed and said, "O.K." They talked about mundane subjects until the lawman started to leave. He said, "Jake we are friends, but I am a policeman."

Jake replied, "I understand, pal. You won't be tested in Venture."

During the drive to Ellensburg, it started raining and the wind was getting strong. There were some concerns that the trip to San Diego would have to be delayed, but Jake shrugged his shoulders and said to himself, "Well if we are delayed, there is always tomorrow."

He was concerned about the possibility of not being able to fly the Cessna in this type of weather. The wind let up some but the rain continued in a steady downpour. Norman Olsen, the pilot, was waiting in the passenger terminal when Jake arrived. They started discussing the weather and Jake made a comment about flying the Cessna. His friend grinned and said, "If you don't want the Cessna, there is a Lear waiting to be lit off".

With a laugh, Jake retorted, "What are we waiting on? Are you afraid to fly in the rain?" He picked up his bag and continued, "Let's go flying."

Olsen took the bag and said, "Let's go. I hope you don't mind a fellow passenger."

The fellow passenger was a young woman that squealed with delight when the pilot said, "Go start those engines, girl." He turned to Jake, beaming, and said, "That's my co-pilot."

The weather cleared as the plane reached cruising altitude and three hours later, the tower at San Diego International airport gave permission for a landing. When the plane was secured, Jake said, "Before you two get too busy, let's go have a cup of coffee and discuss what you are going to be doing."

The co-pilot laughed and retorted, "You'll have to talk to me, because he would faint if he knew what's going to happen."

Norman pleaded, "Oh, please don't make me do those things."

They were still kidding when the coffee was served. Jake said, "O.K., guys. When do you have to have the plane back to Ellensburg? I plan to be here three or four days." He was assured that the plane could stay in southern California for the entire week. Jake told them to check at the information booth and as soon as he could, he would leave a telephone number to be used for coordination of the return trip. "When you get the number, you are free for three days. If you are able, call the number. I will leave a message or will take the call," he said with a leer.

The co-pilot retorted, "I will call, because he isn't going to be able, and he may have enough strength for the return trip when you are ready to go home."

Jake laughed and said, "Keep talking like that and I will trade jobs with him."

The pilot moaned, "Please, please protect me from her. She is an evil woman."

Jake walked out of the terminal and took the first waiting taxi on the street. The driver asked for directions and he was told to go to the best motel in the community—not too close to the airport. The cabbie did not reply. He let his movements do the talking. He turned away from the airport for the waterfront and Jake recognized the area when the taxi turned on Shelter Drive. After a short trip the cabbie dropped his rider at the Bay Club Hotel and Marina near the end of Shelter Island. After checking in and being shown to the room, Jake called the information booth at the airport and left a message for the pilot, with the name of the motel and the telephone number of the room. He had lunch at the Bay Club Bar and Grill. The name was simple but it was apparent that money was needed at all facilities. The service was great because in less than fifteen minutes he was unfolding his napkin while looking at the $4.00 cup of soup and the $7.00 ham and cheese sandwich. The waitress told him what bus route he should take for the San Diego waterfront. There were no intentions for a bus ride, but he was using the conversation with the waitress as cover. The habit of covering tracks came as second nature since the days of Detachment X-Ray.

After walking about six blocks, he flagged a taxi and told the driver to go to Fleet Landing. He was dropped off near the water taxi pier. The ride to North Island was a trip back in time. He had made the trip a number of times when the transportation was called the Nickel Snatcher. It was a short ride and Jake picked up a bus heading for the Naval Amphibious Base, Coronado. The bus let him off at the gate information center and he was directed to take a shuttle to the Combat Training Tank on Guadalcanal Road. The driver stopped in front of the SEAL Team training office and information booth. A young seaman offered him a visitor's log.

After signing in, Jake smiled at the young sailor and said, "This is going to be dumb but I am looking for one of your team members and the only thing I know is that he is a SEAL and his name is Marv." Jake listened as the information was relayed to someone, and he was invited to take a seat.

In a short time a lieutenant commander came in and said, "You must be looking for Chief Gunner Marvin Whiteside. What is your name, sir?"

They both laughed at the response, "My name is Green, but the chief will remember me as Jake." The officer said with a smile, "Well, since you are such good friends I will see if the chief remembers you."

Jake waited for about 30 minutes before the door opened and his friend entered with a guffaw, "Hello, Mr. Green. It's nice to see you."

Jake responded, "Hello, Chief Whiteside. It is my honor."

They went for a cup of coffee and Marv walked to the far side of the cafeteria and took a chair. He said, "Jake it is great to see you, but I would like for Mr. Green to explain why he came all the way to San Diego."

Jake leaned over the table and spoke just above a whisper; "I would like to talk to you and your brother about you future career plans."

The chief looked across the table for a few minutes before sliding his chair back and suggesting they go for a sightseeing tour. At the gate, Marv turned south toward Imperial Beach.

They rode for a couple of miles before Jake asked, "Can we get in touch with Harv? I would like to talk to both of you at the same time."

Marv replied, "Sure, he is coming down tomorrow. We have been planning to take a few days of leave to discuss our future plans. Maybe you will help us decide." They both chuckled when Jake said that there would be no maybe about it.

It was getting late in the afternoon and Jake invited the sailor to spend the night on Shelter Island. The offer was refused because he was expecting the marine recon twin to be in town early. Jake invited them to breakfast at the Bay Club Bar and Grill. The twins were not married, much to Jake's relief, nor did there seem to be anyone special in the background. When their visit ended, Jake took a taxi back to Shelter Island and settled in for the night.

Chapter 15

The next morning, Jake entered the restaurant at 0700 and found the brothers already seated. He joined the twins and said, "Marv, I see you located this jarhead. Did you have to look for him?"

Harv snorted, "No sailor can find me when I get lost. That's why I left Riverside last night. It only took me nine hours to find San Diego."

The waitress interrupted them and took the orders. In a short time the three were visiting and eating. The marine regaled them with stories about an exercise the recon teams had completed on the past Saturday. The exercise included a beach approach and landing. The inflatable boats had been previously loaded on a helicopter and everyone knew that someone else had checked the equipment before deployment. The boats were dropped and the troops followed. All of the boats were retrieved, but to all hands' amazement, the drain plugs were missing. The helicopters had departed as the last jumps were made. The marines were in the water with their equipment strapped on their back and their boats were sinking.

Harv laughed and said, "We had to destroy all of our packs and sink the boats, then swim about 15 miles for an ass chewing session that will last me all of my days to come."

Amid the laughter Marv sputtered, "Fifteen miles is nothing but a loosening up exercise." His brother responded by saying that he would be loose for the rest of his life.

When the meal was completed, Jake asked the waitress for coffee at one of the outside tables. The three settled in and the SEAL leaned across the table and said, "O.K., Jake you found us. Now, why did you go to all the trouble?"

There was no response immediately because Jake was studying his friends. They both held his eyes without a tremor. He leaned forward after taking a sip of the coffee, and said quietly, “Let me get something out of the way first. What I am going to talk about may upset you. I must have a promise from both of you that this conversation will never be disclosed. If you can’t keep a secret, tell me now because in the future it’s going to very dangerous for anyone who talks. No matter what you two decide, I will be talking to no more than ten people and those ten are the only ones with a possible need to know.”

There was only a moment of silence before Marv said, “O.K., Jake, you have our attention but don’t make threats because we are big boys who understand how to take care of ourselves.”

The brothers again come under close scrutiny before more was said. Jake leaned forward again and said, “Marv, I don’t make threats. I make promises. Now do we continue?”

The marine quietly said, “You sure have our attention, so tell us about it.”

After a few moments, Jake started, “I am going to organize a team of people to go against “bad guys.” If you come along, you have to leave the Navy and Marine Corps. The government will be paying you but will deny ever knowing you. You can expect protection from no one except us.”

The conversation livened as the two brothers became interested. They assured Jake that they would never divulge the plans for forming such a team. Jake told them about who would be approached and assured the twins that each of the prospects would be approached in like manner. There was some surprise when Jake mentioned that some members would be women but he gave assurance that all members would be well trained and motivated for the work ahead.

When the conversation lagged, Jake said, “I will be leaving San Diego Wednesday afternoon. I will need your answers before then. If you can’t meet that deadline, let’s be friends and you are invited up for salmon fishing.”

Before the twins prepared to leave, Harv responded, “Jake who are the bad guys?”

Jake gave a faint smile and said, “I don’t know. No one has told me, but I would guess that we may visit drug dealers, organized crime, and possibly some foreigners who someone higher doesn’t like.”

Harv broke in, “O.K., you have recruited me. I can’t speak for this swabbie. Of course he might be afraid to go along because he is nothing but an unorganized SEAL.”

His brother interrupted, saying, “Huh, a good SEAL could take a full squad of recon marines. Jake, our mother made me to promise to take care of this jarhead, so I'm in for the duration." They were invited to a Venture, Washington, for Thanksgiving dinner.

Jake called the airport and left a message for Norman Olsen to be ready to leave San Diego the following day. During the afternoon on Tuesday, he explored San Diego by taxi and mulled over the plans for the future. He had recruited two good members for the team, and was hoping that the Carpenters would join. Jake decided if that happened he would be able to field one team of five people, but he wanted at least ten people for two teams of five. He decided to call on the sniper before returning to Venture. The cab dropped him off two blocks from the motel and at the first telephone booth he called the Carpenters. The call was answered by Lydia and Jake asked if it was O.K. for an unannounced visit. She assured him that they would look for him. He said, "That's great, beautiful woman. I will leave San Diego early tomorrow morning and fly to Popular Bluff."

The answer, "Jake, we will be waiting for you at the airport." Nothing was said about transportation between Popular Bluff and the Carpenter's home.

Norman Olsen was standing at the information booth of the airport. He waved to Jake and pointed to the exit that would take them to the private parking area of San Diego International. As they approached it was obvious that the co-pilot was prepared. She had the engines running and was following the pre-flight check for the jet airplane. As they a turned around the front of the hanger Jake said, "Norman, I need to go to Arkansas. Would it be possible for you to fly me to Popular Bluff? That is up on the Ozark Plateau, and we can be back to Ellensburg sometime Sunday night."

The pilot quickly assured he could make the trip but would have to re-file the flight plan. He said that take-off time would be approximately fifteen minutes. The co-pilot took the documents back inside and was back with the new plans within 10 minutes. They rolled out to the apron pavement near the hangar and received immediate permission to head for the flight line. They were in the air at 0830 and the estimate time to Popular Bluff, Arkansas, would be approximately four hours.

The Popular Bluff airport was not busy and when the jet landed it was instructed to taxi to the hardstand at the hangar marked Ozark Rotary Wing Airways. Jake smiled with memories of rotary wing experiences in the hill of the Ozarks and wondered if it could be—yes it could be—because when he left the jet he was immediately tackled by a redheaded, freckle face buzz saw.

He had known her as Doreen O'Halloran, the best defensive driver in the D.C. area. There were tears, laughter, blushes and hugs and kisses.

She finally backed away and Jake said, "Don't tell me you followed that broken down helicopter pilot to these mountains."

There was the proof because Charlie Daniels came trotting over with a big grin and a hand out. Jake grabbed him and hugged both of them, and said, "Two of my favorite people, Doreen O'Halloran and Charlie Daniels."

Doreen giggled and responded, "You mean Doreen and Charlie Daniels." Jake turned to the jet crew and said, "I want to leave at 0800 tomorrow morning."

Almost an hour and a half later, the helicopter turned into the wind for a landing, and Jake remembered the beautiful home of the Carpenters. Lydia was waiting near the landing pad and welcomed him back to the mountains. He could see his friend, the sniper, standing on the front porch. Lydia was saying, "Come in, come in, come in," and Carpenter grumbled, "Yeah, come on, guess you wan sum of my likker."

Jake almost shuddered at the thought of the likker—pure mountain moonshine—you could use it as a level by turning the bottle on its side and watch the bubble respond to any movement. They took seats around the kitchen table with the shine and coffee. Jake looked around and remembered the prior visits to this, as Carpenter described, li'l ole mountain shack. The only part of his description that was correct was the word mountain. The li'l ole shack was big, beautiful and sprawled over almost a quarter acre. Jake had visited twice, once during the Gorman episode and the other for Thanksgiving week when the plans for the killing Long Ball Qwong were formulated.

After visiting for some time, Jake leaned back in the chair and said, "I have come recruiting. The other folks asked me not to call again, but you folks never did. Are you still listening or do you want me to sit and drink this poison, referring to his drink?"

Lydia said, "We will always listen, Jake. You are always in the middle of something exciting."

Carpenter grunted, "Yeah, count us in. We need a vacation from all these hillbillies."

Jake warned them not to be hasty and continued, "I am forming a team of, for the lack of a better word, assassins. We will be working for the government, but if we need help the government will not know us. I have no idea what they are looking for, but in the past I have helped against foreign governments and against rebels opposing such outfits. There have been times we were called on to oppose organized crime or smugglers. You saw some of it in Idaho and Oklahoma except that was not authorized by government. I did it to help a friend."

Lydia said, "O.K., Jake what are you concerned about? We said that we would go."

The sniper drawled, "Yeah, if the gov'mint is gonna pay, I want sum of that."

Jake said with a smile, "They are going to pay. When we start, an account will be set up for each of you with a million bucks. Your annual pay will be a hundred thousand, whether you work or not. I am looking for about 10 people and we will meet at my place for Thanksgiving."

Carpenter grumped, "Huh, bout time we git to eat yo grub."

The trip back to Ellensburg was smooth, and Jake used most of the time planning for the next interview. He decided to head for Porter Lake and approach Darlene Coppage. He realized that this could get sticky because after all, she was a chief of police. She accepted the favors from the operations in her area but never admitted taking the actions. He knew her well enough to close the conversation before any information would be offered about the future plans in her presence. Jake also wanted to speak with Waseka Morning Fawn Stone. She had proved handy in the earlier Porter Lake excursion. The problem to be faced was that he knew nothing about her and her family except what she had discussed about her father being killed and her twin terrorized by the Klan members. That girl evidently was still under constant care by the Stone family and doctors because she wouldn't leave the confines of the family home.

Upon arrival back in Venture, Jake stopped at the café for a sandwich before going to his house by the river. A number of his neighbors waved or called to him when he took a seat at the counter. A few minutes after his arrival, Lou Prysylbilski entered the café and took a seat alongside.

He said, "Welcome home, neighbor. We have missed you."

Jake grinned and retorted, "Missed me? I have only been out of town for three days."

"Yes, but when you leave, a big hole is left in our community," Lou drawled. "Where did you go?"

Jake responded, "Well, let's see, I went to San Diego, that's in southern California, you know," then with a grin continued. "After California, I moved over to the Ozark mountains and went to get a drink of the whitest corn whiskey you've ever seen or heard about. Then I come back to town and in a short time I going home to my bed. I have had a tough three or four days." Then, "Oh yes, Lou, I will be gone for the weekend, too. I am going over to Idaho for some trout fishing." The constable laughed and said, "O.K., O.K. I was just being neighborly. Bring me some trout just to prove you went fishing. I can tell if they have been frozen or not."

He called Porter Lake Police Department and left a message for Darlene to return the call and for her to call on the "leech line." She would know to call his private number from a public telephone. Jake had just returned to his office from the shower when the telephone rang. He picked it up and without identifying himself, asked if the weekend would be a good time to take some action for the "big one" down in the lake. She laughed and told him that any time would be a good time to hook the "big one" in front of him. They talked of the visit for a short time and Jake asked, "Darlene, do you know Waseka Stone?"

She responded, "Sure, the Stone family is well known around here. As a matter of fact, they live up at the head of the lake. Why are you asking?"

Jake answered, "I would like to talk to you and Waseka about some plans of mine. See if she will come down and go fishing with us."

"This is beginning to sound intriguing," Darlene retorted. "I will call her now. See you on Friday."

Jake left home before daylight on Friday morning. He had a nine-hour drive and did not want to get to Porter Lake late in the evening. Shortly after 1400, he checked in at the Porter Lake Inn, located at the head of the public pier. There were a number of people who recognized him from the previous visits. They waved and spoke, but none of them interrupted him at the table. The word passed fast because the chief of police came in before he had finished his coffee. After a cup of coffee, Darlene suggested a walk down the pier. They walked slowly toward the boat-launching ramp and bait shop but before getting to the ramp, Jake led her over to a bench. He said, "Darlene, what I am going to say may upset you, and if it does, tell me and I will end that part of our conversation. I am forming a team of operators who will be looking for the bad guys." He paused momentarily and when she didn't respond he continued, "Now, from this point, if you don't want to hear more just tell me. But if you do, I have to insist that you will never talk about this conversation. If you talk, you may never hold another conversation. Do you understand what I am saying?" She didn't respond except for a nod of her head.

He continued, “Darlene, this operation could lead to many confrontations as happened here with your leeches. We will be working for the government, but if we get into trouble, the government will never acknowledge our existence. There is no assurance that we will only work in this country. It is possible that we will be called offshore at times. In all cases we will be outnumbered and outgunned. I am looking to recruit no more than ten people for this team.”

She interrupted him by squeezing his arm. Two people approached and Jake recognized the editor/publisher of the local newspaper.

George Strong smiled and said, “I heard you were in town. Are you still looking for the “big one?”

Jake answered, “You bet I am—and he’s mine this time.”

The newspaperman laughed and then said in a serious bent, “The last time you came through you didn’t get the big one but a couple weeks later someone did get the BIG ONES.”

Jake chuckled, “I watched all the excitement on television. Porter Lake became world famous. Did anyone ever solve the puzzle or did anyone try? If I remember correctly, the community is better off now than they were before that weekend.”

Strong said, “No, no one solved the puzzle, but we are still looking.” He turned to the young man that was standing nearby and said, “This is one of my reporters who has promised to solve this mystery, and that is why I wanted him to meet you and the Chief.”

Jake responded slowly, “George, don’t put the young man in over his head. That was a big story.”

The person in question broke in, “Mr. Green, I am Lester Lewis. Is now a good time for the interview or would you rather do it later this afternoon?”

Jake grinned, “A good closing Lester, but I am not going to stand for an interview.”

The editor laughed and said, “Keep after him, Lester. I think he knows what we are talking about.”

The newspapermen waved and walked away and Darlene said, “Jake, I have heard enough. Count me in. I have been getting a little bored in Porter Lake anyway, but I am not rich.”

Jake laughed and said, “You will be rich now. When I give the word, a million dollars will be put into an account for you. You will not have access to that money for one year, but you will be paid $100,000 a year whether we work or not.”

She laughed and retorted, “Jake, sign me up twice. I like this job already.” They left their seats and walked further down the pier. As they approached the landing ramps a young woman stepped out and waved. Jake recognized Waseka Morning Fawn. After the greetings, Waseka was invited to take a boat ride.

Darlene steered out toward the middle of the lake and Waseka asked, “What’s going on, chief? If you want to fish you would have better luck in near the shore.”

Darlene responded, “We are not after fish.”

She laughed and continued, “This guy is after you. He has quite a story to tell. I have already joined him.”

To keep up appearances, three lines were rigged for trolling. Darlene steered in a direction that would not approach other boats. Jake started talking and used the same warnings about keeping the information a secret. Then he said, “Waseka, I really don’t know how to approach you. I’ve known the chief for a long time so an approach to her was easy. We were impressed with your actions when we went against the drug smugglers and the Klan. There will be about ten members of the team and we will be working for the government but will not be recognized by the government. Once we commit we will be on our own. Take your time, because this is a big step for all of us. Do you think you could join such an organization? If things go wrong at anytime we could all be killed or captured.”

Nothing more was said until Darlene turned the boat back for the shore and retrieved the fishing tackle. Waseka asked quietly, “Could I talk to Uncle Mike before I decide?”

Jake said, “Sure, just don’t talk about what I am asking you to do. Tell him it will be dangerous but you will be well paid for your service.”

There was no more talking and when the boat nosed up to the ramp, the young woman jumped out and left without speaking or waving her hand. The next morning at breakfast Jake and Darlene were talking about his invitation for Thanksgiving dinner. She volunteered to come to Venture early and do the cooking for the holiday. With a grin, he accepted her offer because he said that it would be embarrassing to have the dinner catered. Darlene placed her hand on his arm, and they watched Waseka coming toward their table.

She smiled shyly while taking a seat. She refused breakfast but said, “Mr. Green, I would like to join your team.”

Jake spoke up abruptly and retorted, “If you call me mister again, you can’t join me.”

She joined in the laughter and replied, "O.K., Jake. I want to join your team. Uncle Mike said that he would like to help, too."

"I need to talk to him," Jake replied. "You are invited to my place for Thanksgiving, and bring your uncle with you."

Mike Freeland accepted the invitation for Thanksgiving when Jake called him at the office. The conversation didn't last long and Mike promised to call after leaving work. Jake gave him the number for his secure telephone and told him to call after 1800. He said, "Mike, I can't tell you what I am looking for on a telephone. But I will tell you that if you have or had any reservations about the last mission we attended, maybe you shouldn't return this call.

The call came through about five minutes after the hour and Mike Laughed and said, "You said not to call before 1800 and not to call if I have reservations about some actions that may be taken. After that, I had to call, and I am calling from a public telephone booth."

Jake replied, "Mike, once I start talking, interrupt me if you need to. After you hear everything, it is almost too late to back out." Jake continued, "I am putting together a team to carry out such missions as we had in Penticton. The pay will be good, and you will be paid whether or not any work has been done. My government will pay your salary, but if there are problems, no one in Washington will know any of us."

The Mountie said, "O.K., I will see you when you get the turkey on the table." Neither player said another word; the two telephones broke the connection together.

Thanksgiving morning dawned with a cloudy sky. There was an intermittent rain with flakes of snow falling. Jake entered the kitchen at 0500 and found coffee made and the maker sitting with a cup. Darlene grinned and said, "It's about time someone started moving on this nice warm sunny morning."

Jake growled, "That must be some strong coffee or did you brew more than coffee?" She had arrived in the afternoon the day before and by 1800 the Thanksgiving turkey and ham was ready to be baked the next morning. There were great odors coming from the stove as she prepared bacon, eggs, and potatoes for breakfast. Jake brought his coffee to the table, but before sitting down he stood behind her and cupped her face, saying, "You keep this crap up and I am going to kidnap you."

She chuckled and looked up at him and said with a laugh. "My, my, would you like to have some ham, too?"

When in close proximity of each other, Jake had noticed that their hands came together often, or one would leave a hand on a shoulder or leg for long moments. In the evening at bedtime they parted at the guest room door after stopping and looking at one another for long moments. The spell was broken when she kissed him lightly and turned immediately to the door.

After breakfast, Jake started for the boat house to look after the moorings in case the wind came up. Sometimes it would be quiet on shore but with gale blowing down the river gorge. Darlene grabbed her coat and insisted to come and help. Jake asked her to board the boat, a 28-foot cruiser, and turn on the heaters so the cold moisture would not form. After checking all the lines and fenders, he joined her in the cabin of the cruiser. The heaters were warming the cabin and Jake said, "It's getting warm," and took off his coat.

She looked at him for a few moments, grinned and removed her coat. Then it became a game, his shoes, her shoes, his shirt, and her shirt. They were standing without speaking and she slowly lowered her trousers and let the bra slip off her shoulders. He dropped his trousers and reached for her. They came together for a lingering kiss that became more intense as they moved in unison together. He felt her hands shoving his shorts over the hips and as he stepped out of them he pushed her away and said, "Why did you take off your clothes? I don't see any leeches."

She smiled and said, "I see one, oh no, that's not a leech." They both chuckled huskily and reached for each other, and what happened then; happened then.

The Navy SEAL and Marine Recon, Harv and Marv Whiteside, were driving up to Washington from southern California and had been discussing Jake Green's offers or suggestions for them to join his new team. They had discussed leaving the military after 12 years of service and what that would mean to their future if Jake's plans did not pan out for them. They had admitted to each other that they were nervous about the choices. They stopped in Ellensburg for breakfast and while they were eating, Marv said, "You know, Jake made a threat about talking about this deal. I don't plan to talk, but he better lay off the threats because I won't accept them."

Marv answered, "Take it easy little brother. We have seen him in action and he's pretty good, but so are we. I think he was just warning us as to how restricted his plans are, rather than making threats."

The marine chuckled, "I suppose you are right, and if we go into any type of combat I will not mind having him on our side."

The SEAL continued it with a grin, "Yeah, I still remember two head shots before we could use our weapons." They continued their trip without much talking and arrive in Venture at 0830 Thanksgiving morning.

The other guests arrived at about the same time. Mike Freeland waited for Waseka Morning Fawn and her uncle Mike Stone before ringing the doorbell. They were making introduction when Jake opened the door and said, "Get off my porch, I don't want to buy anything and I am not going to invite the likes of you to my Thanksgiving dinner."

Mike Freeland grinned and said, "We don't need you to invite us. We have invitations from your boss. He warned us about a wise-ass stable hand." Waseka was giggling but her uncle moved back away from the door. She grabbed him by the arm and said, "Uncle Mike, this is him. This is Jake Green."

There was only a hint of a smile on the young man's face as they shook hands. Jake said laughing, "Don't mind me, crowds make me nervous."

When they started to enter, Jake took Mike Stone's arm and said, "We need to talk. Let's meet the others and get a cup of coffee and I will show you my boat and the moorage."

The next was a rap on the door. Jake laughed and said, opening the door, "Here are some real hillbillies. Well at least one of them is. The other is too gorgeous to be a hillbilly."

Lydia laughed and Carpenter snarled, "Wheahs yo likker. I need it cause ahm dry."

After the meeting and greetings were over and a general conversation was started, Jake signaled to Mike Stone to follow. On the way to the door, Carpenter was invited along.

The three didn't talk until they reached the boat shed. When the guests were finished with exploring, Jake motioned to seats. They settled in and Jake asked, "Mike, what do you know all about this meeting and more important, what kind of tracker are you?"

There was a long silence before Stone started talking, "I only know what Waseka told me about Porter Lake. She also has suggested that you may want to talk about some future plans. I can track anything you put in front of me. I learned to cut signs as a boy." There was no bragging noticed by either Jake or Carpenter. A thumbs up from the sniper was enough for Jake.

He said, "O.K., Mike. This can get dangerous and you can make it more so for you if you start talking about our plans. The plans will include damaging property and killing people. The targets selected will need killing. That's as far as I can go. If you don't want to join, say so now and have Thanksgiving dinner before you leave. But if you elect not to work with us, nothing can be said about us. If you talk, you're dead."

The young man sat quietly for a few minutes without raising his eyes. Still not talking, he walked to the end of the pier apparently deep in thought. Jake and Carpenter were visiting when Mike rejoined them.

He said quietly, " I'm in, Jake, if you want me to help."

Jake looked at him with a smile and said. "You have just become a rich young man if you stay with us for a year. Let's go eat some turkey."

After a look at Carpenter, who nodded an agreement, Jake continued, "And drink some likker, too."

"Yuh fin'ly said som'un worth hearing," Carpenter drawled.

Chapter 16

The day after Thanksgiving turned out to be the start of the new team's work. Jake called General Tolliver and said, "Old Buddy, I have myself a team. There will be eight of us, and we need some training together as a team. If push comes to shove, we can turn out in 24 hours."

Tolliver paused and then said, "Stay right where you are for at least an hour. I am going to make a call to the general. He will probably want to talk to you."

Jake only waited about 15 minutes when Tolliver called back and said, "Meet us in San Antonio Sunday morning. We will be at the Homewood Suites, 27 N. Saint Marys. You will have a reservation under the name Hank Burlingame. We will be in the adjoining suite and the general will find us. I never know where he'll be."

Jake didn't hesitate. He immediately called Norman Olsen at the Ellensburg airport. When the pilot came on line he said, "Sure I can go anytime after 2000 tonight. Where are we going?" Olsen laughed when Jake gruffly asked him what he was talking about and who did he think he was talking too.

The pilot said, "Shucks, I know your ring." Then he said, "I don't know why I knew it was you. What do you need?"

"I want to go to Texas, and I'll tell you where when I see you tomorrow morning. By the way, why do you have to wait until 2000?"

He received a chuckling answer, "My co-pilot will be flying in about 15 minutes and we have a lot of work to do before I go anywhere."

They both laughed when Jake responded, "Yeah, what are you going to be doing, off-loading cargo? I'll drive over about 1300 tomorrow afternoon."

The trip to San Antonio started out with a flight plan to Birmingham, Alabama, and during a period of rough weather the pilot was instructed to change his flight plan to Dallas-Fort Worth. Just before reaching the eastern Texas airspace, the flight changed to San Antonio. When the course had settled in for San Antonio, the pilot came back and took a seat across from Jake and said, "O.K., buddy. What's this all about? Are you getting me into trouble?"

Jake smiled and said, "No, no. No troubles for you. Everything has been legal. I change my mind often these days." He chuckled and continued, "Honestly, you won't have any trouble. I just don't want many people to know where I am going. How long can you stay in Texas?"

Norman wiped his brow with an exaggerated swipe and whispered loudly, "As long as you pay, I'll stay."

On a serious note, Jake said, "That's great, but you have to stay in touch with the airport. There could be chance that we will need to leave on a moment's notice." They made arrangements for the pilot to check in with a friend who worked in general aviation. This was accomplished by radio before calling the San Antonio approach control.

Jake took a taxi to the hotel and at the check-in desk the clerk was waiting for, and had a message for Mr. Burlingame. The only notice on the envelope was the address to Mr. Hank Burlingame, Homewood Suites, San Antonio, Texas. When the hotel bellboy left, Jake opened the envelope carefully to find one sheet of paper with a key card for a door. The message said, "Howdy, podner. We is nex' door and dis card will open the adjoining door. Knock before yuh come in or you might see somethin' that yuh'll never forget." Jake chuckled when he read the name George. He immediately knocked on the door and Tolliver was waiting. After exchanging greetings, the two men turned toward the guest area.

There were some hugging and kissing going on after Jake held out his arms and said, "My goodness, here's Ole George." Of course he was addressing and old comrade from Detachment X-Ray days who had become Mrs. Tolliver shortly after the general's mission off the North Carolina and Virginia barrier islands.

Tolliver said, "Quit mauling my wife and listen. The general wanted to see us two hours ago. He will meet us at some place called Joe's Crab Shack. I have looked it up. It is over on College Street just off the River Walk, so let's take a walk." The two old friends found that there was not much to talk about because neither could fathom why this meeting was called in South Texas.

On their previous occasions, the general called them to North Carolina.

Tolliver had smiled and said, “Can’t talk about that,” when Jake asked him what Generals Sheffield and Tolliver were doing. The name Joe’s Crab Shack didn’t support the restaurant. It was a nice clean upscale house. They were shown to a table reserved for Mr. Tolliver and Mr. Burlingame. They ordered coffee and told the waitress that they would wait to order when another party showed. They didn’t have to wait long before the general appeared at the table—neither of them had seen his approach. He shook hands with Jake and took a seat across the table so he could observe both men and all doors. He said, “Let’s order before we talk.” Jake tried to question him but he only said, “We will get to that.”

The seafood feast was just about ending when the general leaned on his elbows and quietly asked, “Jake, do you have your team ready?”

“I have eight people, including myself,” Jake answered and continued, “But they aren’t ready as a team. There are four of the men who could pass muster on a simple problem, but two of them are still on active duty.”

The general nodded and said, “Let me have their account identification and the accounts will be opened tonight, local time. Yours is already open under the name Leader. As I said before, the money won’t be available until after one year of service. We will advance them half of the annual salary as soon as you report them as being ready.” He glanced up and his demeanor immediately changed.

Jake and Tolliver caught it but did not look around. The general said, “I could have a problem. There are two guys that I don’t want to see standing at the door scanning the crowd.”

“What do they look like?” Jake whispered. “They are wearing blue jeans; white shirt and both have New Orleans Saints baseball caps. The one on the right as you look at them has his cap on backwards and he is the most dangerous. Why don’t you guys just get up and move out of the way?”

Jake said, “No way, General. When they spot you and start back, nod your head and both of you hit the floor when I jump up and start cussing you.”

Jake could feel the .38 automatic on his shoulder and knew it had a round in the chamber. He felt that would give him an edge on the intruders. The general nodded his head slightly and Jake reacted by jumping up and kicked chair out of the way. The air must have turned blue with his language as he stomped around until he had recognized both men. They were about ten feet away and had stopped and were reacting to his railing. Neither of them had weapons visible. Jake kicked the chair again and started toward the door. He noticed that both of his friends were on the floor. The two intruders didn't have a chance as Jake faced them he drew the weapon and hit one of the men in the right eye and the other in the left eye. He didn't stop or slow down. At the door he glanced back and the only ones watching him were his two friends, and they were moving toward the door. The restaurant was in an uproar and no one had noticed him as he stepped into a taxi.

He calmly said, "Take me to the airport." That was cover because at the airport he told Norman Olsen to be ready to leave early the next morning and then returned to the hotel.

Still unnoticed, he returned to his suite and tapped on the adjoining door. This time George let him in and motioned to the two Marine generals. General Sheffield offered his hand and said, "Thanks, Jake. You still react pretty well. No one noticed you through the commotion and I don't think anyone paid any attention to us as we sheepishly crawled up off the floor." Tolliver continued the story, telling how much of an uproar followed the gunfire. He said that both men had died instantly and the police were told many graphic and conflicting stories. Some said the shooter was a tall white guy while another said the he was tall but black. No one even mentioned that he had been sitting in the chair that had been kicked around.

George interrupted, "Shh. Here's the news." The television cameras had caused more excitement and soon the place was in a real uproar. It became so bad the police finally had to clear the restaurant. They kept two eyewitnesses and as before, they come up with confusing stories. The police finally gave up their questioning when the detectives arrived and took over the investigation. The lead detective called a news conference and said, "It's simple, and I don't know what the hell happened except two guys were killed in a roomful of people. No two witnesses can agree on anything except they heard many shots, but our investigation finds only two bullets. It appears they were hollow points and exploded in the heads of the victims. Both of those men were heavily armed. We surmised that they were after the shooter. There has been some discussion about another party causing a ruckus near the spot of the shooting. We want to talk to this person. He was already standing and might be able to offer some insight as to what went down."

After the news, the old friends sat down with coffee and discussed what had happened. The general said that the two shooters were from an operation that he participated in with the DEA. They had been arrested but were released because of lack of evidence. When they walked out of the courtroom, General Sheffield and DEA Field Supervisor Abrams had been threatened. He said, "We should get out of town as fast as we can. Jake, do you need transportation?"

Jake answered, "I have arranged to leave at 0600 tomorrow. But before we go, what in the world am I doing in this town?"

This drew a chuckle from his friends and Tolliver leaned forward and said, "We have some bad guys coming to upstate New York, but we don't know exactly where they will locate. We know that there will be four men from the Middle East looking to get into Israel from the United States. The prime minister is the target, and we want to stop them without telling anyone. With your new team, do you think this could be handled?"

Jake thought for a few moments and responded, "Yes. There will be four of us—one will be a driver, but when will we be moving?"

The general spoke quietly, "We know that they are on the way to Canada now and by the time you get home, we hope to have their final location—or at least where and when they will cross the border. Are you sure you can do this?"

Jake answered, "Let me know where we have to go as soon as you can. If I don't hear anything before Monday morning, we will head for Buffalo."

Norman Olsen met Jake as he left the taxi, and the pilot told his passenger to follow closely. He led Jake around the building and entered a gate directly to the airport. The plane's engines were turning as they boarded. It started moving as Olsen closed the door. Jake heard him tell the co-pilot to make the takeoff. When the plane cleared the airport, the pilot came back and sat across from Jake.

He said, "I just assumed that you didn't mind leaving without notice from those in the waiting room. In case you didn't know, there were four cops talking to everyone."

Jake grinned and said, "Thanks pal, but I wouldn't have minded talking to the Texas Rangers. I have always been a fan of that organization. Of course I don't mind leaving San Antonio."

The pilot asked, "Jake, are you putting me and my co-pilot into harm's way? If you are, I want to know."

"No danger, Norman. If it comes to that, I will leave you behind." Jake replied and then grinned and said, "By the way, buddy, I need to fly to upstate New York Monday morning, probably to the city of Buffalo. Are you available?"

Olsen returned the grin and answered, "You know, my co-pilot has never been to that Buffalo city in cold weather. Maybe we will get snowed in over there, but a trip like that might cost you more money."

Jake leaned back and closed his eyes and said, "Name your price, pal."

Jake called Tolliver before heading for Ellensburg for the New York flight. The brigadier told Jake that the visitors from the Middle East were heading for Oswego, New York, and the estimated day for their arrival was Wednesday morning aboard a Lake Erie freighter. The two friends discussed the advisability of getting to Oswego so soon. Jake laughed and told Tolliver that it was too late because his team was heading for Buffalo if they did not get the word for change of plans. Jake had called the Carpenters and Mike Freeland upon returning from Texas and they had agreed to go to New York with him.

When he ended the conversation with Tolliver, he immediately called the Carpenters before they left home and he found Mike Freeland by radio. The Mountie was on his way, but he said there wouldn't be any problem getting to Oswego. Jake obtained a radio frequency from his pilot for a conference after everyone was in flight. When they come on line, Jake told them to head for the Thomas Inn on Rte 104 West, near Oswego city center. He had reserved rooms for them under their code names because it was forbidden to use their given names during the exercise—and they wouldn't establish public contact with each other until the targets were identified. After some discussion, it was decided to attempt to get their targets out on Lake Ontario for the execution. The Carpenters were to rent a car and small boat, and Mike Freeland agreed to arrange for a lake fishing boat that could accommodate 8 or 10 fishermen. Jake told Lydia Carpenter to become familiar with the area, especially the route to Oswego County Airport in Volney, New York, and to find a landing for the small boat when they started the extraction part of their plan. Jake said, "That's it. There will be a plane at the county airport to get us out fast when we leave."

Chapter 17

The team met for the first time in Sabha, Libya, and was transported to a Chadian rebel's desert training camp. They were in for a tough time because the Chadians were known for their brutal training before a weapon would be introduced to the visitors. Marksmanship instructions on four different types of weapons was to be focus of the training, but it was explained to them that snipers had to be physically fit to be of any use to the Army of Allah. A person in four different countries recruited the four-man team to be trained for a cold-blooded assassination of the Israeli Prime Minister. An English tutor was assigned to each man. The plan called for a fluent understanding of English to facilitate movement through Canada and the United States; therefore easing transition to Israel from a friendly location. The team members knew each other by code name rather than a family name. They were to be only the first team because the creators of Allah's Army expected to become a real force in the world of the Infidels.

Abra lived most of his life in Palestinian camps throughout Israel. His parents had settled on the West Bank years before the Israelis had come to power. When the Jews had arrived and taken over Palestine with the dictates of the United Nations, led by the United States and Great Britain, Abra's father vowed that he would never live under the fist of the Jews. He also promised Allah that his sons would not be allowed to accept the weight of the Zionists backed by the upraised arm of the United States. The father helped train and support his sons to become martyrs in the name of Allah. Abra's oldest brother died a martyr's death during an ambush by a unit of the Israeli Army. He killed two high-ranking officers and three soldiers before being gunned down with an AK-47 machine pistol. The second brother died in a flaming crash and explosion in a bus terminal that took the lives of six people and wounded dozens more. Abra was looking for a target when he was approached by a Muslim cleric. This man stood on street corners during the day preaching peace and evenings he recruited and helped train a different breed of martyrs. This force would be hunter killers and escape artists rather than martyrs killed by their own weapons.

Aziz came from a village out side of Baghdad and had lost his family during the so-called Desert Storm. He would never forget the explosion that had killed his father, mother, three brothers, and a sister. It came without warning—no one heard an incoming scream of the bomb. The screams of the people were the only noise heard by Aziz. He swore then that he would never rest until the Zionists and the Americans had all perished by his actions. The army would not take him because of his young age, but there were many veterans of the wars who offered training to the young men. Aziz joined and by the time he was old enough for the army he had already made two trips into Kuwait and had killed ten people—one he was sure was an American. The recruiting agent for Allah's Army was a double amputee whom Aziz had known for two years. This would be a great chance to serve Allah because he would be trained to kill, evade and live to kill again.

Abdul's family had lived in refugee camps in Jordan since the Zionists had been given Palestine by the "Great Satans" of America and Great Britain. It was known throughout the Muslim world that these two nations of infidels had caused the United Nations to declare a Jewish homeland. When his mother and then his father died of broken hearts, Abdul swore that he would not rest until the Zionists were driven out of his father's homeland. He was fourteen years old when he declared total war against the enemies of the rightful owners of Palestine. One night he was able to slip out of Jordan and found shelter on the West Bank. There, the youth of the country served Allah by harassing and baiting the soldiers of Israel. It was common for the Muslim children to harass the soldiers by throwing rocks and other street trash. One night, martyrs of Hamas attacked and Abdul found a real weapon lying beside a dead Israeli. From that time when his comrades were using slings he was taking aim with real bullets. It was not long before the enemy began to lose men to the village children. This brought down heavy attacks by the Zionists but Abdul just shot faster and more deadly. A leader of Hamas brought him into Allah's Army and some of his early training was raiding Israeli villages.

Ahab had lived his life in Syria and watched the Soldiers of Islam as they would move soundlessly into the countryside and wait for the Zionist's motorcades to pass. On his fifteenth birthday, one of the commanders allowed him to accompany the field soldiers heading for an unsuspecting Israeli convoy that would be heading to a kibbutz near the Golan Heights. This part of Syria had been overrun during the so-called Seven Days War and had never been returned to its rightful country. One of the soldiers instructed Ahab in the handling and operation of an automatic weapon. When the enemy convoy moved toward the ambush, Ahab was scared and was ashamed of himself. When the first explosions occurred and his comrades rushed to make the kill, he realized he was not afraid and killed his first two people. At first he felt sickened but then he stood tall and was proud of himself. The young Muslim continued fighting with the Syrians for two years and had become one of the most feared fighters of the war against the Zionists and their Great Satan protectors. The Jews put a price on his head and he became a prime candidate for the Army of Allah and was presented by his Syrian commander.

The Chadian rebels watched the recruits as they stumbled from the truck. Some of them had been traveling for days with very little water and no food. The instructors let it be known that there would be no food or water until the day's work was completed. There were thirty men, thirty shovels, and thirty sandbags were given to each of the men. The day's work was for the sandbags to be filled and placed as berms around the tents used only by the instructors. They were told that no one could have food or water until the bags were in place. Most of the workers turned stolidly to the tasks at hand. One man protested and was shot. Ten others passed out and were dragged to one side of the work area. The extra sand bags were divided among the ones working. It was after midnight before the chores were complete and the men were given food and water. Each received a bowl of mutton and a few pieces of potatoes. They also were given a water skin and were told that the water had to last for three days. The men who had fallen out were required to dig their own graves and were shot when the holes were about two feet deep. No one was allowed to cover the bodies and the next morning the scavengers of the desert found a food supply.

The training with the shovels and sand bags went on for two weeks before the recruits saw a weapon. Finally, one morning after they had eaten goat meat for breakfast, they were taken to the large tent used by the instructors for rest and recreation, but there was no rest and recreation on this day. Each man was introduced to an AK 47 machine pistol, which had been manufactured in Israel, and a .45 caliber Colt automatic that had once belonged to a soldier of the Great Satan. They were told that it would be an honor to Allah when a Zionist was killed with the machine gun and an American with the .45 caliber handgun. Other weapons were introduced, but the AK-47 and the Colt automatic were their prime weapons. Each man was trained in hand-to-hand combat that included the use of a knife. They were issued the standard bayonet of the United States Marines. The weapons training included shooting and knifing people brought in by the Chadians. The first few victims haunted the killers, but after a short time the killing became a part of the job. The sniper instructions were different. The shooter would be sent into the desert and took cover and waited for the first people along the trail. Some drills would be all day in the blazing desert sun; others would be all night in the desert cold. When a target appeared, they were required to ambush or be shot by an observer in the area. Two bodies were brought in one morning and the heads were missing because the caravan of women and children was not ambushed.

Then, praise be to Allah, the training was over. The new fighters were made up into four or five man teams with a stated mission—kill the Zionists and members of the Great Satan. The last chore before leaving the camp was glorious—the sand bags were emptied and a dune was formed over the bodies of those killed during the training. All traces of the camp were obliterated and the men were allowed to celebrate and have fun with all the water they wanted. Early in the evening, the teams were led out by a Chadian guide and were told that the graduation ceremony would be to raid a Chad village that supported the standing government. The instructions were to shoot all of the men and kill the women and children with the knives. The bodies would be delivered to the town square and left in one stack; the houses would them be blown by grenades and torched. The last part of the instructions was ominous; if captured by the Chadian army, the remaining comrades would honor only martyrs.

Abra, Aziz, Abdul, and Ahab met for the first time as they were formed into a team. With eyes and a few words they knew that they could depend on their team members. The new force became known by two names—used interchangeably: Allah's Army or the Army of Allah. When it was noted that their names began with the letter A from the alphabet of the infidels. They became known as Allah's Fist. They were transported by truck to a small village outside the city of Faya-Largeau, Chad. The raiders waited until the village became quiet and asleep. Each member of Allah's Army walked confidently into the street and then separated at the first house. For the next half hour their ears were filled with the sounds of shots and screams of men, women and children. Allah's Army didn't heed the instruction to shoot the men and kill women and children with knives. They systematically went through the village and used the automatic assault weapons on any movement. Then they reversed the assault by going back through the village and beheading all the victims. Some were still alive when the blades sliced through the throat.

It was said later that the Chadian guide was so sick he could not drive the truck to the Sudanese border and then to Khartoum where teams were left to negotiate movement plans for the remainder of the trip to North America. They had no money and to find funds they robbed and killed two merchants. One evening as they were settling in for the night they were approached by a woman and a man who offered them United States currency if a certain group of people was to disappear. The visitors stressed the requirement that no signs of a struggle could be left and suggested that the targets should disappear into the desert. The Fist of Allah accepted the assignment and the targets were four Christian missionaries. Two nights later, the missionaries were sent to their maker after being forced to walk three hours into the desert. After taking all personal possessions, the Fist of Allah stood three women and one man on a dune and opened automatic fire. The people were dead before falling into the sand and were soon covered by more sand. After the bodies were hidden, the four young soldiers ate a meal of dried mutton while sitting on the new sand dune. Upon returning to Khartoum they met with their employers and after receiving the promised pay, the employers were killed and robbed of all their possessions.

The Fist of Allah took the loot from all of the killings into the back streets of the Sudanese capitol and sold every item. Early the next morning they joined a camel caravan that was heading to the north. They had discussed riding on motor transport, but decided the caravan would be the safest way out of Sudan. The caravan took over a week before entering Wadi Halfa at the Egyptian border. The leader of the caravan told them that he would be heading back into Sudan rather than making the long trek into Egypt. Wadi Halfa was full by many different caravans, and the camel driver introduced Aziz to the leader of a motor caravan heading for Cairo. The Fist of Allah convinced the motorman that he should take them to Cairo. This was done when Aziz flashed a roll of American dollars. When the trucks left Wadi Halfa, the Fist of Allah were separated and rode in different vehicles. The afternoon before entering Cairo Abra told his comrades that he was sure that the truckers were planning to kill for the American money. That night the four men crowded under one truck and settled down with all four directions under surveillance. None of them slept and at about four in the morning Abra and Ahab warned that three men were approaching them. Without talking Abdul and Aziz rolled clear of the truck and started crawling to outflank the two stalkers. When they neared the trucks knives were flashed and they didn't have a chance. Four other knives were flashed and three men were dead. The leader of the caravan came running and when he saw that the Fist of Allah were the survivors, he fell to his knees begging for mercy. His body was torn apart when four machine pistols ran out of ammunition. The four bodies were buried and when the trucks left, the gravesite was indistinguishable. The caravan headed for Cairo with the new owners driving. All the goods and trucks were sold in just a few hours. The Fist of Allah was on a mission for Allah and the mission required money.

They stayed in Cairo and listened for news about the other caravan drivers and heard nothing. Three days later, they boarded a riverboat to Port Said. Here they came under the care of Hamas and were placed in a small hotel that was being used as a safe house. Their new comrades invited them to go into Israel and participate in Hamas raids against the hated Zionists. The four demonstrated skills that were above and beyond the Hamas soldiers. The commander took notice and allowed them to make their own raids. Soon the Israelis were reporting attacks more vicious that any experienced in the past. The victims were shot and beheaded with the attackers disappearing and leaving no tracks. Warnings went out for the people not to travel at night unless they were in company with army units. The epitome of the Fist of Allah work came when they escorted a 'martyr hopeful' into one of the desert towns. Many citizens were in the town market place when a truck came racing in and before anyone could take action it exploded. The news from this attack was different. When the aid units and police come on the scene, the marketplace come under siege by at least four sharpshooters. More people died from the automatic weapons than were killed by the explosion. By the time the Israeli troops could respond, there were no snipers in the area.

The Port Said Hamas Commander was laughing when he told the Fist of Allah that they should move out because they were making things too hot for the local soldiers. He arranged passage on a small coastal steamer bound for

Beirut, Lebanon, and a person to contact. They were told that the contact was not a member of an organized group but he was someone on whose head the Zionists had placed a price because he was so brutal. The story was that this person had not killed anyone, but the people he captured were tortured for hours on end. Some of the victims didn't live after the ordeals. Many of them committed suicide and others attacked the police and were killed. Abdul said, after boarding the ship, "This is the type of soldier everyone should honor."

Abra replied quietly, "Yes, we will honor him," he paused and then continued, "but he has a price on his head." No one said anything for long moments and then Abdul spoke again, "And we need money. Others can take his place."

When the ship arrived in Lebanon, the Fist of Allah went to a safe house that had been arrange by Port Said. They were told to stay inside and not to respond to any outside noises, and that someone would contact them in a short time. The four young soldiers obeyed the orders, even when a riot was joined outside the door. It was good for the rioters that none broke in the door. All entrances were cover by guards who did not mind shooting. The four young Muslims were disappointed that they couldn't join the fray and were hoping someone would attack the safe house. The only actions taken came from Abra's window. He shot a policeman who was bravely trying to break up the confrontation with young Muslims. When he fell, it appeared that the rioters were taken by surprise and the melee started breaking up. It was soon quiet throughout the neighborhood.

Later, when Aziz and Abdul were preparing the evening meal, a young street urchin came begging for food. He was brought in and shared the goat cheese and mutton with the Fist of Allah. The boy appeared to be 13 or 14 years of age, and later in the evening when Hamas came visiting, he was introduced as The Muslim Shadow. This was the name offered by the Zionists when the price was placed on his head. There was some general good-natured laughing at the surprise and embarrassment among the Fist of Allah. When the visitors left, the four soldiers began planning the next move. Aziz was the most upset from the laughing by the visitors and his friends and mused, "Laugh all of you. We will laugh when the money is collected from the Zionists for his head."

After that comment, the Fist of Allah started preparations for claiming the Shadow money. Ahab disobeyed their orders and slipped out into the street. He returned after the middle of the night and his comrades were waiting. When the four were gathered around the table, Ahab said quietly, "The price is fifty thousand American dollars. It will be paid in cash when the body of the Muslim Shadow is delivered to a motor caravan out side the city." A lengthy discussion kept them up for the rest of the night. A plan would be offered and discarded. A suggestion would be made and turned down. The sun was rising to the east and after morning prayers, the Fist of Allah agreed on a plan to gather money that would be needed to carry out Allah's mission. One life wouldn't stand in their way—no matter fame and heroism—the money would be needed to travel to Canada and the United States and then to Israel. They had been warned and were sure many bribes would be made before the Zionist Prime Minister fell at their feet. No one had mentioned, nor would they mention, the possibility of immediate death or worse—being captured.

The next day, Fist of Allah moved in four directions and spread the word that they would like to go on a mission with the Muslim Shadow. Just before evening prayers a representative of Hamas arrived at the room where they lived. He told them that the Shadow would invite them to go with him later in the night. Just before midnight, the young teenager arrived and told them that he was planning to cast a shadow over a motor caravan outside the city just before dawn. Fist of Allah was told where to meet and would be expected to take an active part in the ambush. According to the visitor, the caravan was the transport for Zionist sympathizers. Ahab said that he was certain that the caravan to be attacked was the one with the prize money for the Muslim Shadow. The plan called for the killing of all the men and burning the material. The women and children were not mentioned. When the four soldiers were alone, Ahab told them that the target was the caravan with the prize for delivering a dead Shadow. Abra held up his hand and quietly said, "Why don't we collect the money tonight. During the ambush I will shoot him, and Abdul, you cut his head off and we will throw it at the feet of the caravan leader. If there is any argument we will shoot one of them. And keep it up until they pay."

There was a hush when Ahab whispered, "After we get the money, let's finish the job that the Shadow started. That way the ambush information won't get back until the women move back to the city." Abdul continued the planning by suggesting that the women be killed, too. Three other heads nodded in agreement, and all knew that they would have to get out of Beirut within a very short time or Hamas and Hezballah would be tracking them.

Fist of Allah left the room one at a time and moved cautiously to the meeting site south of Beirut city center. They were sure that they were not trailed, but the Shadow materialized through the darkness and laughed because of the discomfort shown by the four soldiers of Allah's Army. They found a truck full of vegetables that Hezballah had prepared to ease their way into the camp. The camp was rousing when they moved into the campsite. The Shadow took charge and explained to the caravan leader that vegetables were available for their trek. The men of the caravan commenced to unload the truck and the five young killers separated and took positions so a friend entered no field of fire. When the truck was unloaded, Abra asked who had the money for the Muslim Shadow. The caravan leader stepped forward and was surprised and frightened when Fist of Allah turned their weapons on the Shadow and commenced fire.

Abra said, "There's the Muslim Shadow. Where's our money?"

All of the caravan members were in shock and when the money was delivered, the young soldiers killed the men. The women came running and the children were screaming but after more gunfire the camp was silent with dead bodies sprawled all around the area. Aziz said, "Let's go, comrades." They jumped into the truck and headed toward the Beirut waterfront. Hamas had chartered a small ship and they had passage to Tunis. They boarded the ship and asked the captain to get underway. Only a few orders were needed before the ship headed for the open sea. Later that day, the captain told Abdul that he had received a message that the Hezballah commander wanted his passengers. The ship's officer smiled and continued, "I told them that my passengers hadn't come on board before we left the harbor."

When the ship arrived in Tunis the young soldiers shook hands with the captain and Ahab left an envelope in his hand. They had paid well for his friendship. When he saw the $5,000 dollars he laughed and said, "Goodbye, my friends. I wonder what happened to my other passengers. I hope your travels will be blessed by Allah."

During a six-hour stay in Tunis, the Fist of Allah offered passports to be stamped and boarded a ship bound for Morocco. During the afternoon the young soldiers were visited by the first mate of the ship. This officer introduced himself as an officer of Al Qaeda, the leader of the anti-Zionist organizations. Fist of Allah was informed that Hamas and Hezballah were offering rewards for their capture, because their path from the Chad training camp to the assassination of the Muslim Shadow in Beirut had been followed. The officer commented that they had been very lucky to get out of Beirut, because the trackers and other investigators came to the conclusion that they were guilty of all the beheadings and the brutal assassination of the Shadow. Al Qaeda had arranged for the Moroccan bound ship rather than a motor caravan across the dessert that had been arranged by Hamas of Palestine. The four men were escorted to the bridge and the captain warned them that any allegiance from them would go to Al Qaeda or they would be killed and would disappear without notice. Such acts would keep them from being honored as a part of Allah's Army. They were also told that in the future they would be tracked and controlled by Al Qaeda.

The Fist of Allah was secretly transferred to another ship before arriving in Morocco. Their new destination was Brunswick, Maine, in the Great Satan's homeland. This ship was with Panamanian registry and the purser stamped their passports enough times to hide the recent movements and give notice of travel for most of the past year. The ship's officers suggested that they should remain in the cabins during the day, only come out at night. All meals would be delivered to the staterooms. During the night before arrival in Brunswick, Maine, the soldiers of Allah's Army was called at 0400 and by boat were transferred to a Canadian fishing boat headed for the St. Lawrence River. The Al Qaeda itinerary called for them to go ashore on a deserted stretch of the river and make their way into Canada before heading for their first United States destination, Oswego, New York. From this small Lake Ontario town, Fist of Allah would be in control of travel plans to Boston, Massachusetts, and go underground until further orders were given. They were to be prepared at all times to visit other cities on the northeastern coast of the United States to carry out Al Qaeda missions. Aziz questioned this order and enquired about the Zionist Prime Minister. They were told that that mission would be sometime in the future.

Chapter 18

Jake was taken aback at the small New York airfield. The airport manager met the plane and as Jake came down the ladder the official said, "Another stranger. We only have strangers during the summer. You are the fourth one through here today. I have been to the Thomas Inn twice. Is that where you want to go?" Jake had to make a fast decision. He figured that once someone had taken notice of the teams arrival others would hear about the strangers.

With a friendly grin he responded, "Yeah, take me to the Inn. It has taken me six months to get them up here for winter lake fishing. Has the freeze started yet? If not we will need a lake boat."

As they settled into the car, the airport manager said, "Your friends have rented a boat. I got a call a few minutes ago from Wright's Landing. They are shaking their heads because no one goes out in a boat unless they know what they are doing, and you people better watch it because the winter lake is dangerous to people with no experience."

Jake laughed and replied. "I expect you are right, but you may be surprised at the level of experience we can muster. Oh, by the way, have any other strangers come this way lately?" The airport manager said that he had not heard of any one else. Mike Freeman was at the check-in counter asking about messages. Jake walked up and said, "I got more messages than we need. The guy out at the airport has spotted the sudden influx of strangers."

Freeman chuckled, "Yeah, we were afraid of that. The Carpenters' plane came in right behind mine. We paid those pilots to beat it out of the region and they took our money and ran." Freeman said before leaving, "I'll see you at Carpenters' suite."

After taking his baggage to his room, Jake stepped across the hall and tapped on a door. It was immediately opened and a beautiful woman was offering a welcoming smile. Jake said, "Lydia, you get more beautiful every time I see you. Give me a hug before I see that ugly hillbilly you are married to."

"Hunh," was the answer from the marine sniper, then. "One Swabbie can give off more crap than a platoon of marines."

Jake answered, "Yeah, but look at the mess jarheads make where ever they go."

All the while they were shaking hands and Carpenter slapped Jake on the shoulder in a welcoming gesture. After the greetings were completed, the four-member team sat around the table and talked quietly about the situation. They had been noted by the local people and knew that within a few hours, many people of Oswego, New York would be aware of the presence of strangers. Mike Freeland suggested that since they were spotted, each one should go about talking and visiting with the New Yorkers. Mike continued with suggestions that a winter fishing trip should be discussed freely.

Lydia Carpenter agreed, "If the natives know what we are planning, that is what they will want to discuss—then to give advice to a bunch of stupid out-of-town visitors who don't seem understand how dangerous the lake could in the winter." They left the room and went to the house restaurant for dinner and to talk publicly about the planned fishing trip. They gained a lot of attention, advice, and warnings about the dangers on the lake. The heavy wind conditions that could strike at any time were the subject of most of the warnings, with advice to stay off the lake.

Upon returning to his room for the night, Jake called Tolliver. The telephone conversation was scrambled from both ends. He told his friend about being noted as strangers as they entered the airport. General Tolliver said, "Jake we have some disturbing information. A new terrorist group has been formed in the Middle East. It is called the Army of Allah, aka Allah's Army." He stressed that the new group was much more advanced than what had become the norm of many terrorists from that region. He said, "Jake, these people have been trained for search and destroy exercises. The thought of killing themselves does not enter in their minds. They have been taught to kill almost anyone who gets in their way. According to intelligence they have wiped out a village—men, women, and children—in Chad."

Jake did not interrupt and the information kept flowing. "The Army of Allah is a relatively small force that has split into four- or five-member teams. We believe that the team you will be looking for is called the Fist of Allah. These are young men from a mid-east terrorist organization, and Hamas and

Hezballah have put out a contract on them—dead or alive. According to our information, Fist of Allah has already killed so-called friends for money. One of them you may have heard of is the Muslim Shadow—the Israelis had a contract out on his head and Fist of Allah collected the reward and had to run from Hezballah and Hamas. They also wiped out a pro-Israeli caravan from whom they had received the money."

Jake was still mulling over the information from Tolliver when he entered the restaurant for breakfast. His three friends were already seated and talking to four men. Jake studied them as he moved back to the table, and asked himself, "Is this the Fist of Allah?"

The nearer he got to the table the four men appeared younger and younger, and there was a definite suggestion that they were from the Middle East by the physical appearance. When Jake took a seat, Lydia said, "Jake, these four Israeli students would like to go fishing with us."

He looked at them appraisingly, and responded, "Well if they are as crazy as we are, tell them to be at Wright's Landing tomorrow morning."

There were general chuckles around the two tables as Lydia explained what the phrase about being crazy actually meant. Mike Freeland spoke up, "We asked them why they wanted to go on a dangerous trip that the fishing expedition promises to be," he laughed and continued, "Their reason is very simple. They have never been on such a trip."

One of the young Arabs broke in and said, "We desire to have a great experience to tell our brothers at the University of Haifa." The conversations started lagging when the food was served.

The four young men left their table and as he watched them leave, Jake said, "It's nice out, let's go for a walk. I brought my coat, so meet me at Franklin Square by the Vet Bench."

Franklin Square was a small park in the city and the Vet Bench was the town's monument to the men from Oswego that had been killed in wars. The Carpenters and Freeman arrived together and they took seats on and around the monument.

Carpenter said, "What's the problem?"

They sat quietly as he related the information from Tolliver the night before and he finished by saying, "And folks, I think we had breakfast this morning with Fist of Allah. They look and sound like school kids, but I bet their sympathies don't apply to any Israeli or United States citizen."

Freeland asked what the plans called for as they related to the Fist of Allah. "Simple," Jake replied. "We kill them. Tolliver said last night that we couldn't afford to hesitate during a confrontation, because Allah's Army had been trained to kill and not care about questions and answers."

Fist of Allah also was meeting. A professor from Syracuse, New York, had arrived with new instructions. They were to ignore al Qaeda and go their own way on the mission for Allah's Army. The major part of the instructions caused a shiver of excitement to Fist of Allah. They still were slated to kill the Zionist Prime Minister but first there would be a target in the United States. Great Satan's president was the new target and the desired date of the mission would be the Christian day for celebrating the birth of Jesus Christ. That day was selected because it was such a day of celebration that some of the security precautions would be lax. There was also a warning that the enemy had targeted Allah's Army. They were warned not to mix too closely with the local citizens. When the proposed fishing trip was discussed.

The professor said emphatically, "Don't do something foolish. These fishermen may be looking for you or someone like you. We make fun of the Great Satan, but there are teams such as you that are looking for us. I advise you to leave this area immediately without prior notice and don't all move together." The four young soldiers went directly to the hotel and checked out. Ahab and Abdul elected to travel together but Abra and Aziz would move independently. Three automobiles were rented and left Oswego in three different directions. From a road atlas, they had decided to meet in Lewes, Delaware, a small Eastern Shore community. The Professor made reservations for Fist of Allah at the Sleep Inn, in Lewes, for the fifteenth of December.

When the meeting at the Veterans Bench ended, the four friends walked back toward the motel. Mike Freeland said, "I saw a sign to the New York Deli. Let's stop there and I'll buy you an early lunch but only if they have pickled tomatoes and a corned beef sandwich."

Jake responded, "Start looking for your money, pal. Any establishment called NY Deli will have the tomatoes and the sandwich, but I want a Rueben and some of those pickled tomatoes, pickled onions and a pickled egg."

Everyone broke into laughter when Carpenter broke in, "He's gonna sit by the door, or I don' come in."

During lunch they decided to track down the four men who had expressed a wish to go lake fishing, because the wind was at a reasonable rate and the sky was clear. The temperature was hovering at the freezing mark and Lydia mentioned that the weather should be watched. She said, "A sudden squall or high wind could break into lake-effect snow and whiteout conditions would not be an ideal situation," especially in the small recovery boat she had obtained and secured at a public landing site. The four partners spread out over town and met back at the motel after searching for their invited guest. As each arrived, they expressed that it appeared that Fist of Allah had left town. Jake came in last and confirmed the fears. He had stopped at the car rental agency and found that four men had rented three cars. The clerk in the motel advised that the unexpected checkout occurred at 1115 and the departing guests left in three automobiles.

Jake said, "Well, we missed them and I am sure they were the ones we are trying to find. There is a plane at the airport that will take you back home. I am going to attempt to do some tracking." With that he called directions to have the plane ready for three passengers for the flight back to Washington state. Jake took Carpenter aside and told him to get in touch with the others of the team and give the twins the responsibility of training. Carpenter said that he would take the team to his home in the Ozarks for field training.

Jake drove his friends to the Oswego airport and instructed Norman Olsen to fly them to Ellensburg and be on call for a further flight to the Ozarks. When the flight took off, Jake took the automobile to the rental agency and after finishing the paperwork, he turned to leave and then said, "I need to buy a car. Where can I find a sales agency?"

The rental agent laughed and said, "You just found one. Would you like to have the one you just turned in? It is full of your gasoline."

Before leaving, Jake asked, "The three autos you rented this morning, do you know where they are going?"

The man hesitated and said, "I couldn't hear where they were going, but I did hear them say that one would leave for the east, one to the west, and the other would head southwest." He hesitated and then asked, "Do you think I have lost three cars?"

Jake shrugged and answered, "Probably." He then left the airport and mused, "And we have probably lost a chance at Fist of Allah. Wonder what plans they are executing." While checking out, he looked at a New York road map and decided that he would search to the southwest because there were no major highways for some distance after leaving New York.

Jake drove back and forth between the small towns of southwest New York and found his first possible track in Wellsville, New York. There an operator of a mini-mart talked to a young Israeli student while another young man serviced the automobile. According to the operator, the students wouldn't discuss the destination except to say they had to be ready for classes on the fifteenth of the month and that they had taken Route 19 heading in a southerly direction. Jake learned that he was about seven hours behind his targets. He decided to drive until about 2200 before stopping for the night. He rounded a bend in the highway and saw a sign for the McCarty Motel, fifteen miles ahead in Fillmore, New York.

The motel had no vacancies but the clerk called and found a room at the Fillmore Hotel, and said, "They will hold the room for you, just continue on your way and you will find the hotel at the corner of Main and Emerald streets in beautiful downtown Fillmore."

He laughed and continued, "Be quiet you may wake them up down there. We close down the sidewalks at sundown."

The next morning Jake checked out early and the desk clerk recommended Ned's Diner for a fast breakfast. He said that the diner could be found further on Main Street. Jake chuckled when he looked around his surroundings and saw The Wide Awake Club Library across Main Street. After ordering the food, he looked at the neighboring diners and decided that he had found 'the place' in Fillmore, New York. He smiled and mused, "This place can be found in any town. The same people would be at the tables talking about and cussing the politicians, and there would be stories that had been told so many times they had become true. Many of them would start, 'This ain't no lie, or did I tell you. My friends in Venture will soon be at 'the table.'"

When the waitress brought his check, he looked at her nametag, and said, "Thanks for the good breakfast, Sally. Have you noticed any young Israeli students in your fair city?"

She responded, "You just missed them or maybe two of them. They stopped in and asked for food to go." Jake left without waiting for change and walked briskly out and trotted the last few steps to his vehicle. He spent most of the morning but couldn't find any further trace. It appeared that Southwest New York had swallowed them without a trace. He stopped at noon and headed for the Interstate highways heading west.

Chapter 19

When Jake regained the interstate highway system, he turned west on I-90 and set the cruise control on 75 miles per hour. He stopped for dinner at 1830 and tried to call General Tolliver, with no luck. After another three hours of driving Jake checked in at a Best Western Motel. This time Tolliver answered and Jake told him what had happened without an apology—none was expected. They discussed future plans and spoke about the training going on at Carpenters' place. Jake was to call in at four-hour intervals because the two men agreed that they would soon hear from Fist of Allah. They also agreed that the general probably could get a line on the terrorists faster than anyone else, and that it would be a waste of time for Jake to look for them without some idea where they could be found. It did not take long for Fist of Allah to take a swing. In a two-day period, six businesses were hit and 24 witnesses had been killed. Each of the victims had received a headshot and one woman was decapitated—all of the women were young. The attacks came from three different directions with information tying the crimes together. At each location the police had found a note: "All infidels, take this is a warning—you have now seen the results of Allah's Army attack on the Great Satan, as carried out by Fist of Allah. Fist of Allah is one small part of Allah's Army."

The first few attacks hadn't raise much speculation until the reports came in that a woman had been beheaded at each location. The news media and law enforcement went on alert. The media was in a frenzy trying to turn information and scoop the competitors, and law enforcement was busy with the investigations and trying to elude the news reporters. The attacks were in the same general area of the country but far enough apart to be seen as separate operations. One of the television reporters came on and said, "These murders are occurring at different locations, but our reporters are beginning to say a dreaded word. Terrorists—we believe that the United States is under an attack by terrorists from the Middle East, because in each incident young men described as possible Arabs have been observed on or near each scene. It only took a few hours for this word to spread worldwide. All headlines and broadcasts labeled their stories, "The United States is under widespread terrorist attack. There have been multiple attacks on businesses and in each case a young woman has been decapitated. So far the law enforcement agencies of the most powerful country in the world have been unsuccessful in capturing or even identifying the attackers."

Jake arrived in Venture at 0400 and there were two calls on his private and secure line. The first one was from Carpenter stating that the entire team was at his place and the twins were working them to death. He asked, "Navy, wheah you git these people. Firs' thet little old girl in Idaho run us almos' to the graveyard. Now these two young'uns is tryin' to finish the job. I lak this team and you will, too."

The second message was from General Tolliver. He asked, "Jake, when can you get that team in the field? The general said that Fist of Allah will likely join up somewhere on the eastern seaboard. Call when you arrive—anytime—day or night."

Jake smiled as he dialed the telephone. Carpenter had called him "Navy," the name that the marines had used during the Korean War. Tolliver answered the telephone on the first ring. Without waiting for Jake to speak, Tolliver said, "Jake, take a nap and then get your people to Kansas City, Kansas. Fist of Allah had talked too many times. The general said they would meet on the 15th somewhere near Kansas City before heading for the East Coast. According to the boss, Fist of Allah's target is the Prime Minister of Israel. They want to fly out of the United States, after having come through Canada, because it will be easier for them to get on a flight to Tel Aviv."

Jake replied, "Ask the general if he can furnish us locations of these cats in between the terrorist acts. If that can be done, we may be able to pick up a trail. I'll call you from the Ozarks about 1600 this afternoon. I can take the nap on the airplane. And we will be on the way to Kansas City tonight. How are they traveling, by the way? They left New York in rental cars." Tolliver would ask the general if he had any idea of Fist of Allah's location or direction of travel.

Norman Olsen had the engines turning on the executive jet when Jake reached the Ellensburg airport. As they boarded, Jake said, "Take me to the

Ozarks. I am going to sleep." He buckled the seat belt and was asleep before the small 12-passenger jet left the ground. Norman grinned at his co-pilot and said, "I wish I could do that. When it's time to go to sleep, he goes to sleep. If he can do that he will most likely awake with any noise,so walk quietly when you go back. I don't want to have to screw your head back in place."

She grinned and slapped him on the shoulder, "Shoot—I don't think you know what my head looks like." The pilot chuckled and leered as he pulled back on the stick and the plane rotated smoothly and took a heading to the southeast. Norman had not asked any questions, he told his co-pilot to file a flight plan for Popular Bluff, Arkansas. The flight was smooth and the pilot realized that Jake was standing in the cockpit when permission was received to land.

He said, "Let's talk before we open the doors."

When the engines were cut, the two pilots came back and took a seat. Jake said, "I may be getting you into some trouble—probably won't happen, but could. With that, if you can't go any further, I'll see you back at home. If you can go further, how much is it going to cost me?"

Norman chuckled, "With that, let's see you get rid of us. The cost—well let me see—pay as well as you have in the past, then we are yours."

Jake nodded his head and retorted, "I figured you would be dumb enough to go along with me." He reached over and patted the woman pilot on the knee and continued, "He has just made you a rich woman—share with him only if you want to."

They left the plane and Jake casually asked, "Is that plane for sale? If it is, have the ownership papers ready when I return. I will arrange the money. Buy it in your name as an agent for Mister X. Start with an offer for cash, but accept the seller's wishes for any payment plan. When you are ready, take off for home and I'll be in touch."

He waved to them and headed for a helicopter with its rotors turning. One of the crew was a beautiful redhead who was waving, laughing, and blushing. Doreen O'Halloran had not changed over the years except for her name. She and Charlie Daniels were married shortly after the Washington, D.C., operation against the future Prime Minister of China. He had been killed at a busy airport with at least a hundred security and law enforcement agents waiting for him to depart. Jake and his friends had been questioned for hours even though FBI and CIA operatives surrounded them before and after the shooting incident.

The flight to Carpenter's home was uneventful. Jake had Doreen laughing and Charlie smirking as Jake spoke of the first trip in the helicopter in a snowstorm. Doreen said, "Well, the pilot is quiet when I am at the controls. He is teaching me to fly, and I'm teaching him not to be a backseat driver."

Charlie spoke, "Jake, if you think you were scared that day, wait till you ride with this wild woman."

They all laughed when Jake responded, "I don't even want to think about such a ride. Charlie, your pretty little red-haired wife scared the crap out of me on a daily basis when she was driving for me." They were still enjoying being together when Charlie turned for an approach to their destination.

Lydia led the greeters and all of them gathered around, and Jake asked, "Where's Carpenter?"

Before an answer a mumble came from behind the house, "Ah'm hidin' mah whiskey. Ever time you come ya eat an' drink us dry." Lydia moved everyone toward the house and Jake's mouth started watering as he entered the door. The smells emanating from the kitchen was worth the long ride. Lydia would not allow shoptalk until after dinner.

She said with a laugh, "Whoever talks shop at my table will become the dish washer."

After dinner Jake checked in with Tolliver. The brigadier said, "Hold everything. Forget Kansas City. Fist of Allah has outsmarted us, and the general is steaming. Hold at your present location until we can update and clean up our information." He continued, "They are stealing cars every day. Almost all of the owners have been killed."

Jake responded, "That could be our trail—the stolen cars and murders. See if you can send us locations of the murders."

Tolliver said, "I have it. Where can it be faxed?"

The Carpenters indicated they had fax facilities and the general took the number and in a few minutes the information started flowing. The Whiteside twins took over the task of separating the locations of the crimes and they soon pointed out three possible routes. After the stores had been struck, the first two days with 23 people killed, the information pointed to movement toward Kansas or somewhere in the mid-west.

Marv Whiteside said, "Now take a look. I think you will notice that each party has changed directions of travel." Mike Stone was watching the situation and in a few minutes said, "They are heading to North Carolina."

Everyone laughed when Harv Whiteside said, "My goodness, you do talk, but how can you say they are going to North Carolina?"

Stone replied without a smile, "Extend their tracks."

Lydia took a ruler and extended the latest trail and the three intersected near Winston-Salem, North Carolina. Jake remarked that if they held to the track, all three units could meet in two to three days. He told everyone to pack because they may be taking an east coast vacation. Everyone had expressed light-hearted consternation about the training period at the mercy of a Navy SEAL and recon marine, and agreed they had rather be on the road than continuing the schedule as set by Harv and Marv Whiteside. The twins grinned and one said, "You ain't seen nothing yet."

"Carpenter, where can we rent a couple of vans?" Jake asked.

The sniper muttered, "Don' need rentals."

With that he dialed a number and said, "Bring me two vans." The two vehicles were delivered in less than an hour.

Jake smirked and said, "Jest a pore ole country boy."

"Jest friends helping a pore old neighbor," was the response from an unsmiling mountain man. They discussed travel plans and decided to send one van toward Winston-Salem to arrive as early as possible. Marv Whiteside, along with Lydia, Seaman, Waseka, and Mike Freeland would be the team to try and get in front of Fist of Allah and attempt to locate the three cars. Harv Whiteside would lead Mike Stone, Carpenter, and Jake in an attempt to nail down the traffic pattern and get behind the targets.

Jake said, "If we can get them between us, and figure out where they are going, we control the situation." When they were prepared to leave General Tolliver was advised of the plans and was introduced to Mike Stone who would take charge of the tracking information. The first van took off immediately and the second one waited until the next site was reported from Tolliver. In less than hour information came that it was likely that Fist of Allah would rejoin at the Mississippi River and cross into Tennessee on interstate route I-40.

Harv said, "Let's get out of here. If we drive straight through we may be able to catch up before they get to North Carolina."

Near midnight Stone said that the tracks were moving more to the north which would lead them into Virginia. General Tolliver called and reported another murder and again Stone spoke up and said, "They have crossed into Virginia, and we're catching up. When we left Mr. Carpenter's place we were almost five hours behind and now we are less than three hours behind."

Jake said, "Mike, you are some tracker. How do you make statements which turn out to be true?"

Stone's answer, "My grandfather told me how to track animals."

Carpenter was driving and called back, “Watch fo’ the law because we are going to get real close before daybreak.”

Harv laughed and said, “Now it’s my turn. I predict they will stop for the night around midnight.”

Stone replied, “If they do. We will catch up in Christiansburg or maybe Roanoke.”

“Roanoke is the largest but we have seen them running through the small towns,” Jake answered. A call was made to the leading van with the information about the likely stop during the night.

Lydia answered the call and said, “We have passed through Roanoke. Should we stop?” She was told to hold the line and after a brief conversation word was passed for them to continue until the next highway rest stop. One showed on the map about 25 miles east of Roanoke. The conversation continued and it was decided that Christiansburg would be surveyed with the best information available and if that came up empty they would continue to Roanoke.

The lead van was instructed to watch for three vehicles that appeared to be traveling together. Christiansburg was cruised, checked and rechecked, and a few questions were asked. It was decided to continue on toward Roanoke. A call from Tolliver led them to believe that the track was a good one. He told them that the last reported car theft and murder had been in Gatlinburg, Tennessee. According to the count Fist of Allah was in three recent thefts and murder vehicles, and an educated guess led them to believe that cars would not be changed until the Atlantic shore was reached. Everyone became silent, especially after Harv said that a total of 49 murders could be laid at the feet of Fist of Allah—and the young terrorists had only been in the country for nine days. Teeth were gritted, fists were clenched, and silent promises were made to Allah’s Army, this reign of terror would not control this country. As a matter of fact, it would soon be over. Each one of the hunters believed that Fist of Allah would soon be in front of Allah. None of them would be named, therefore a martyr couldn’t be identified.

The search in Christiansburg ended at 0630 when Seaman Coppage called on the radio and very softly said, “Jake, we believe the terrorists has just pulled into the rest stop. We are 25 miles east of Roanoke. There are other vehicles here, so be careful. Fist of Allah has moved to a table, and their autos are parked together near the men’s restroom. What should we do?”

Jake answered, “Move into position which will surround them and wait for us. That is, unless they start to leave. Don’t let them leave that rest stop.

We will be there in 20 minutes or less.

Carpenter was driving and he muttered, “Hit’ll be less.” He was good as his work, the van slowed for the rest stop entrance 14 minutes after the conversation with Seaman. The van was driven up to the three cars in question. Stone pointed out the other van parked near the exit lane.

Jake said, “When you get out, do a lot of stretching and locate the other team.” Fist of Allah was located at the table—two sitting on one side—two on the other side.

Jake spoke quietly, “Carpenter, walk past them and mark the one facing us. Harv, mark the one on the left side with his back toward us. Mike, you take the other one with his back toward us, and I will take the one this end of the table facing us. When we get into position watch for a nod. Take head shots. We don’t want them identified.” The men started a casual stroll while stretching and bending, and Jake waved to Marv for the others to close the area. Fist of Allah soon became aware of being crowded and started to stand up.

Jake quietly said, “You, at the table. Take your seats and keep your hands where we can see them.” The four young men slowly sat down and kept their hands on the table.

One of them asked, “What is going on? We are just resting before finishing our trip to D.C.”

Mike Stone responded, “You can forget D.C. tonight, because you have business with us.”

Jake spoke, “Do you recognize Allah’s Army? How about the Fist of Allah.”

The young men froze and Harv said, “We got ‘em before they got to the capitol.”

Fist of Allah started to move and Jake nodded and four weapons spoke as one and Fist of Allah unclenched in a lifeless heap. The teams moved to the vans and left at a leisurely pace. The other visitors to the park converged on the table and some screams could be heard as the people saw the last results of a terrorist group. None of the witnesses seem to notice the movement of the vans. When they returned to the freeway, Jake broadcast, “Easy now we don’t want to be stopped, so drive at or near the speed limit. If we get separated, head for the airport in Baltimore.”

He then dialed the Virginia State Police frequency and when he was answered in a few words he told the talker that they should head for the rest stop and on their way to call the FBI because the people shot were a terrorist group called the Fist of Allah, a team from the Army of Allah.

The next call went to Norman Olsen and Jake told him to get to the Baltimore/Washington airport a soon as possible. The pilot estimated the time of seven hours. He was told to land near to the general aviation gate. Tolliver was not in when a call went out to him. A message was left, "The mission is complete."

During the ride to Baltimore Jake asked, "Carpenter, what do we do with the vans?" Carpenter answered, "They ain't mine, so we have to take them back home.

Before anyone could respond, Harv broke in, "Marv and I will help drive. We want to look over your neighborhood."

Jake chuckled and quipped, "Sounds like the hill people might have some new neighbors. Watch them, Carpenter. They might steal your whiskey still."

The sniper said, "Huh. Ain't my still."

When they arrived at the airport Jake told everyone to spread out but stay in sight of each other but not close enough to have any association noticed. Carpenter's team was told to go directly home and get off the road as soon as possible—but not to get caught by the law for speeding or some other infraction. The vans took off and Jake walked casually into the airport and soon could see all of his team. After waiting for a couple of hours, Norman Olsen stepped through the door. On a signal, all hands moved slowly to the door. The airplane was near the door and was being refueled. Olsen said for everyone to enter casually and fasten the seat belts. "We will be moving in about ten minutes," he said. It took 12 minutes to get permission to take off.

After the aircraft leveled off and cut to flying speed, Jake walked to the cabin and gave the co-pilot a note and asked her to dial in a frequency. He looked at her with a grin, "We are the only ones who knows that frequency, don't tell anyone—not even this cat in the pilot's seat."

She handed him the speakerphone and before he keyed the mike said with a chuckle, "Just what is your name anyway? I can't call you 'co-pilot' any longer because we share a secret."

Olsen snorted and she answered, "I am Martha Hawkins and you are Jake Green. What do I call you? Bossman? Mr. Jake or what?"

He said with a laugh, "Just call me Jake." Then his attention turned to the radio and keyed the mike. When Tolliver answered, the speaker was switched off and Olsen handed back a pair of earphones. He listened for a couple of minutes without speaking. He didn't want to involve the aircrew even though they were curious.

His old friend relayed from the general, "well done." He told Jake not to call back and for the team to go to ground as well as they could in their neighborhoods. The Brigadier related that the news media was going wild and the FBI and the Virginia State Police were having a bad time because there was no explanation for the 'slaughter' until someone wised up and told the media that the people killed were terrorists that had marked the president for an assassination during the Christmas celebrations. This caused a frenzy of speculations as to what terrorist group was bold enough to target the president.

Jake took a seat beside Seaman. She looked at him with a wan smile and said. "You know how to give a girl some excitement. Is this what we are going to be doing?"

He chuckled and answered, "I'm afraid so. The people we are working for are working for the president so our orders will be coming from high places. Anytime we want to say no, we can say no, and that decision will be honored."

She nodded her head with understanding and leaned back against the seat, and Jake could tell she had relaxed and went to sleep. Jake looked at her a smile and, thought to himself, "You are quiet a lady, Seaman, and a real team member. I doubt if anyone else on this flight will sleep. It takes a while for most people to come down to the surface after doing what we have been doing for the past 10 or 12 days." He leaned back and in his mind started retracing the movements of the team and was satisfied with the way they reacted to the situation. He mused, "Wonder what the future holds? The Army of Allah is a real danger unless someone can take it apart."

With eyes closed, Jake smiled as a thought came to him. "I'll lay odds that the general will be on the line moments after we land." Seaman moved and brought him back to the plane.

She said, "Jake, I don't want to hurt you. What we had was great, and maybe sometime in the future we can play strip poker. What I am trying to say is that I am not ready for a complicated relationship."

She laughed huskily at his response, "Whew, I was going to suggest the same things. What we are doing is too dangerous for complicated relationships, but I cheat at strip poker."

She yawned, leaned back against his shoulder and said, "Goody."

Chapter 20

The Army of Allah was ordered to meet, by the leaders of the movement, in Cairo, Egypt. Some of the operating teams attempted to have their teams exempt from the meeting, but all of them were ordered to the Egyptian capitol. They gathered at a local mosque that had offered a meeting room for the gathering. The mosque clerics stood guard and would not allow strangers to enter that area of the building. One of the leaders had demanded that sort of protection because Hezballah and other Muslim units still had a reward for the heads of Fist of Allah. The guest speaker for the meeting was an American college professor, George Salaame of the University of Syracuse in New York State. Professor Salaame had been the controlling agent for Fist of Allah when the team landed in Oswego, New York. He was a third generation Muslim of the United States. He became active with the anti-Israeli movements after the Six Day War and had served as a control agent for Hezballah, Hamas, and now the Army of Allah. Much of his work in the United States was observing and spying on the infidels. He was able to do that kind of work because a university professor was allowed easy passage throughout the country. Professor Salaame was aware of an underground movement in the United States, throughout academia, that did not support the government's aid to Israel. He made many contacts through the university community and in turn he gained access to military and government meetings and seminars. As the years went past he had become known as an expert in Middle East affairs.

The meeting opened in a normal fashion with morning prayers, and then the leaders spoke about the work being done against Israel and the United States. The aim of the Army of Allah was the destruction of all Zionists and their recognized centers. The plans also called upon all Muslims to take up the fight against the infidel supporters of Israel especially the Great Satan—the United States. They told the audience that the first move would be by Fist of Allah whose initial target was the Zionist Prime Minister. Access to the United States was so simple that the target had been changed to the President of the United States. During a lull in the applause, a leader promised that the president would be sent to the hell of the infidels on the celebration of Jesus Christ's birthday. The hall came alive with all of the soldiers of Allah's Army begging to join the assassination team. "No one can join because Fist of Allah is in place and completing the plans," the leaders answered.

But a shocked silence soon reigned when Professor Salaame took the speakers podium. He said slowly and solemnly, "My brothers, pray to Allah that I might be wrong. I met with Fist of Allah when they first arrived in the Great Satan's country and someone had given them bad information 'to join the community and participate with the natives.' When I arrived for our first meeting, Fist of Allah had agreed to go on a fishing excursion on one of the Great Lakes. I told them that they were on the way to their death and for them to split up and leave immediately without speaking to anyone. At that time the target was the prime minister and I suggested they go to one of the mid-western states and go undercover until plans could be made for them to leave the United States for Israel. They were heading for Kansas City, Kansas." After a long pause the professor continued, "Fist of Allah started making some terrible mistakes. They would invade a business and take the money, a different vehicle, and kill the Americans." Some applause and talking interrupted the speaker and he waited for quiet before saying, "In two days, six robberies occurred and all witnesses were killed but the largest mistake happened each time when one of those killed would be decapitated—a woman. The people in that country are very protective of the women." He took a drink and then continued, "The target was changed to the President of the United States, and I sent them word to turn back toward Washington, D.C. After they turned back, the killings continued when they went after expense money. Some said that they assassinated over 50 people in less than a month. They were in three automobiles and disappeared somewhere in Virginia. After they disappeared, a story broke that four young men had been assassinated in a roadside park. It is likely that the four men were Fist of Allah, but no identification could be made because each was killed by at least two shots to the head and there were no fingerprints on file for any of the victims. I do not believe that the local police, the FBI, or the CIA carried out the killings. My Brothers, I believe that there is a new force in the United

States that has been charged to track down and liquidate Allah's Army or any other brothers wanting to kill the Zionist pigs. The stunned silence continued for many minutes.

It was evident that the leaders were distressed, or as others said, "They were in total shock." Everyone was talking at once and the meeting rapidly deteriorated until one of the leaders suggested that they meet after evening prayers.

He said, "This will give us time to reestablish our plans and possibly take new positions. The soldiers of Allah's Army left together and turned toward the banks of the Nile River. A location was found that was away from most of the visitors. The men sat quietly for a short time before one said, "We must find the ones who assassinated our brothers, the Fist of Allah. Many of the organizers will want us to target the prime minister or the president, and I say we go along with the plans until we collect expense money and get to the United States. There we should form two teams. One team of ten men will attack any target of the Great Satan—one person, two persons or 25 or business sites—no matter, we should disrupt the entire population if we can carry out our plans. Do as Fist of Allah did, and shock the citizens with our actions. The other team of ten men should quietly move in the same direction as the attackers, and it will not be long before our enemies start tracking the first team, and then we will track the trackers." A hubbub went up with many suggestions, questions and statements.

Another individual said, "Our brother has a good idea. When our enemies get between the two teams we will turn on them and bring justice for Fist or Allah. Many of us may die, but remember we will be martyrs and the Great Satan infidels will be sent to their own hell." The two speakers identified themselves as Mohammed and Ibrahim. It was decided that the two would become the team leaders and choose their team.

Mohammed stood up and quietly said, "I will lead the attackers so I need to see who would volunteer to become martyrs." All members of Allah's Army raised their hands.

The serious demeanor was broken when Mohammed continued with a laugh, "Ibrahim you can't join us because you will lead the other team"

After the release of nervous tension Ibrahim said, "All right then, I will take the first nine sitting on my right." The teams were formed and all were cautioned not to discuss the plans until Ibrahim and Mohammed had approached the leadership council of Allah's Army. The plans were accepted and applauded by all when it was announced.

After evening prayers, the meeting reconvened and each member of the Army of Allah was given money and suggested routes to the United States were discussed. Some would go by air, others by sea. They were cautioned not to become friendly with their fellow travelers. Professor Salaame suggested that they pose as students or vacationers heading for the United States. He cautioned, "My brothers, you are going to the United States of America. Leave the Great Satan name here. After you arrive you will find that the natives will refer to their country as the States, the US of A or even America. All are acceptable names, so select the one you like best and use it at all times. Also, remember, the men hold their women in high regard. Do not treat any of them as you may have treated women in the past." The two chosen team leaders exerted their authority and Allah's Army stated that the teams would gather no later than April 30. Professor Salaame give each member a telephone number to reach him and by the time of the arrival a meeting place would have been selected for them. He suggested that they not head for New York State because some may remember Fist of Allah.

The professor said, "I will meet with you after you have established a meeting place."

Allah's Army met one last time to decide how to reach the objective. Ibrahim suggested that the attack team go by air so as to be in place and familiar with the area when the tracking group arrived. The team leaders then went back to the overall leadership with the decision. They were furnished with tickets for airlines that would be traveling to the United States on of March 10 and 12 from five different airports. The sea going arrangements were for merchant and cruise ships heading for the states during the same period—three from Egypt and two from Israel. The men going on the ships would work their way across the Atlantic as a part of the crews. Each man was also given an Israeli passport with a number of dates stamped showing travel around the Mediterranean. Mohammed and Ibraham were given $10,000 for each team. The money was to be used only for transportation and lodging. The teams would be expected to furnish daily expenses. Professor Salaame warned them again not to disfigure women when they were killed. He said, "Fist of Allah made a real mistake when they beheaded the young women. The population of the country became very upset and all sorts of threats were made against the perpetrators. All of the news agencies reported the number of people killed in each raid, but the major emphasis was about the beheadings."

Allah's Army started arriving in the United States on the 11th of March.

The calls went to Professor Salaame and he furnished directions to a small farm in the state of Nebraska. A Muslim family who was supportive of the movement against the United States and Israel owned the farm. Five automobiles were bought from used car agencies in New York City and Boston. Each vehicle established contact with Mohammed, and he directed them to move independently for the destination, and he also ordered the men not to raid any businesses or kill any of the Americans while they were in transit. He said over the radio, "Our brothers will spill blood for all of us, and it is going to be our turn when we attack the ambushers who killed Fist of Allah. This is our final conversation until we arrive in Nebraska because our enemies have the capability to listen in on all transmissions of radio and telephone. We don't want them to become aware of us."

The Trackers arrived in Omaha, Nebraska, in the afternoon of April 13. The first car was the one driven by Mohammed, and he immediately called the telephone number for the farm. The contact was George Nathan Johnson the owner of the Nebraska farm. Mr. Johnson told Mohammed to start for the farm at 1600 and as the other automobiles checked in, they were told when to leave for the destination. They were greeted as brothers and the automobile was parked under a large farm building. Mohammed and George Johnson discussed the plans and agreed that the different automobiles should leave at and return at long intervals so as to not raise speculation in the community in case the neighbors noticed the traffic on the farm road.

Johnson said, "My brother, I think everything will be fine because our closest neighbor is more than a mile to the west, and the way I understand it you will be exploring to the east." They started poring over an Atlas and local maps so that the Trackers would be familiar with likely routes of the Attackers. In the discussion with their American host, it was decided that each automobile with two occupants would be exploring as far north as Minnesota and as far south as Mississippi all the time making movements in the easterly direction. The other members of the team arrived at two-hour intervals, and at 0100 Mohammed called a meeting and told them how the explorations would occur.

After the questions and comments had subsided, the leader closed the meeting with, "Brothers, let's all go to bed for much needed rest. Brother Johnson will keep watch for us and we will depart for our first exploration in two days. While we are here all of our time will be taken up with studying the Atlas and plotting our first moves. You are not to travel further than 100 miles from this place on the first day. Every road must be traveled and studied. Do not break any laws, but if the authorities stop you remember we are students and or vacationers. When you stop for food the same stories will apply. Many of these people will want to be friendly—just remember to keep them at a distance without insults." Then with a chuckle he continued, "Also my brothers, from now on you are Israelis." The meeting broke and the teams went to their sleeping places all the while calling each other "dirty Zionists Jews."

The attackers arrived at the Johnson farm and were greeted by the trackers and the Johnson family. They were allowed one night's rest and then both teams started studying the road maps and discussing the upcoming jihad. Professor Salaame also joined and suggested, that since Allah's Army had been divided into two man units, each unit would start the attacks along the axis of the east/west interstate system. The attacks would commence on April 15, and the trackers would follow their brothers but separated by one day. Professor Salaame suggested that the first attacks should be executed at the same time with plans for major casualties in each incident.

He said, "If there is a new force in America they will assume that the attacks are being carried out by Muslim terrorists. Brothers, if they call you terrorists—become terrorists. I think that the second attacks will be carried out before the enemies will be searching." He paused for effect and then continued, "When you think that the enemy is in your area, report it fast, no matter which team picks up the trail. Mohammad, the Attackers will be in the field first and it is imperative that you hit all targets across the country at the same time. After that you will be more or less on your own but before you leave here get everyone back on the maps and select an area for your daily targets. After the first day each team will make their executions at time the target for the day is reached."

Ibraham said quietly, "Allah's Army is ready to teach the enemy about terrorism."

Chapter 21

Jake rolled into Venture early in the morning before his neighbors began moving. He had a couple hours sleep when his doorbell rang. Lou Pryslybilsky grinned and asked, "Did I wake you, neighbor? I saw the car and when your light came on, I decided to check on you."

Jake responded, "Yeah you woke me. I use a night-light so I don't get scared. Come in I will try to locate a cup of coffee."

The two friends moved into the kitchen and when the coffee was poured they guardedly made small talk. After pouring the second cup Jake leaned back, and asked, "Lou, do you have something on your mind?"

The local police officer smiled and quietly answered, "Jake, I have figured out what is going on. I have been watching and listening. You were away from here for a few days a while back and the young girl from California was found in a mountain shack, two men died. Then you disappear again and something happened in Oklahoma that solved a prison riot. The only people who got hurt were four lifers who were threatening to take out prisoners and hostages."

Jake started to break in and Lou said, "Let me continue. You just arrived home after almost a month and four terrorists were cut down in a rest stop in Virginia. So Jake, I don't know who you are and but some of the things you have been doing makes sense."

After a long pause, Jake responded, "Lou, you have been reading books and watching movies. I don't know what you are talking about. But Lou, don't speculate and talk too much about news stories that may get you in trouble."

After a moment of silence, Pryslybilski said, "OK. Then let's talk about a fishing trip."

"Now you're talking my language," Jake exclaimed. Both leaned back with the coffee and you could almost hear them relaxing. The fishing trip proposed was trout fishing in one of the Canadian lakes near the headwaters of the Columbia River. Lou had reserved services of a Canadian guide and a small airplane to fly them into the lake.

When Jake asked about the landing field, Lou grinned and said, "No field. The plane will land on the river near your dock and will fly us into the lake. When you go with me, buddy, you go first class."

Jake grinned and accused his friend of setting up the transportation to get the white knuckled reaction of the passengers. Lou stood to leave and at the door he turned to Jake and quipped, "OK buddy, find your tackle box the plane will tie up at your dock tomorrow morning. In the afternoon we will see some of this fishing you brag about. You can't have a meat axe. We use fly rods."

Jake grinned and replied, "My friend, you have had it. Didn't I ever tell you about being an expert fly caster? You probably will not get a strike with me in the boat."

"We'll see," growled the lawman while displaying a big grin.

Lou turned and walked away without further response until he reached his car. He turned and called, "The plane will be here in the morning at six. I am curious to see how good of a fisherman you are. Bring your best equipment because you are going to need everything you have—and then more."

Jake laughed and called, "Better watch me. If you do you will be amazed, but you will be able to talk about a real fisherman." The next morning, Jake heard the airplane as it landed near his pier and he could hear Lou calling for him. The flight into Canada was uneventful for most—for Jake Green it was a struggle. His friends laughed when he expelled a prolonged breath after the landing was completed. The fishing was great and the fishermen enjoyed the sport and the Canadian still would not admit to defeat.

After two days of good times there was bad news from the States. Terrorist attacks had occurred throughout the Mississippi Valley. Many people had died or were wounded, and to the surprise of the lawmen because each attack was identified as a suicide mission. The Canadian hosts were the first to suggest, to Jake's relief, that the remaining days of the trip be canceled. Jake and Lou agreed and the airplane was ordered in to take out the fishermen. There wasn't much talking between the two Venture, Washington, men. Each were deep in thought—Jake was anticipating a call from Tolliver—Lou was contemplating his duty if Jake left home on another excursion. In his mind, the lawman was certain that his friend was involved in some type of operation that called death down on many people. He mused, "I approve of the actions, but the acts are criminal. I am a police officer and do not believe in vigilante justice. But what can I do? I can't place anyone at any crime scene."

Lou's final decision was to take no action because he would become a laughing stock if he spread his thoughts about a very prominent citizen.

There were two frantic messages from Tolliver about the attacks. When he answered Jake's call, he exclaimed, "Jake, get your team into the field. We have a problem because it appears that we have a wide frontal attack going on. The first attack was in Peru, Indiana. They run a car into a mini mart and gasoline station. The tragedy of the attack is that there was a busload of high school students in the mini mart. It appears that a fire team supported the suicide attack. There were at least ten victims suffering from gun shot wounds while six others are dead from the suicide attack."

Jake finally said "Slow down, partner. Where should we go?"

Tolliver answered, "Head for Davenport, Iowa, and we will try to find more information." The general continued, "There also were smaller attacks in Rock Island, Illinois, and Jonestown, Tennessee. We don't think this frontal attack will continue because the terrorists lost at least three members in the suicide explosions. The survivors will likely join together. In many ways that would be good for us."

After speaking with Tolliver, Jake called the team and told them to head for Davenport immediately. There were not many words spoken because everyone was expecting the call and were ready for a trip when provided with a destination. It took about twelve hours for all of the members to get to Davenport. They were in a motel that had been reserved for the meeting. Before all of the team members arrived, Harv and Marv started plotting the information that had been collected by the general. At first it was confusing because of the broad front covered by the attacks, but as Tolliver had suggested, the tracks were beginning to converge somewhere in Ohio or Kentucky. When Mike Stone arrived, he began his tracking exercises. There was no sleep during the night and at first light Stone predicted that the meeting would be in western Kentucky. There was no hesitation; Jake took his team into the field with two vans and headed for Kentucky. Mike Stone kept up the plot while the team was moving. Jake had linked him with Tolliver's office and the tracks ceased before they arrived at the Kentucky border. Tolliver called and said that it appeared that Allah's Army had gone to ground. He said, "Jake, you best stop and wait for more information. We are sure that they will make a move in a few hours." The teams split and went to different motels in Bloomington, Illinois.

Jake instructed everyone to stay put because, "We can't wait if we hear the location or suspected location of Allah's Army.

The Army of Allah was on the move after the two leaders talked on the radio. They were concerned about the wide front of attack. The attackers, led by Mohammed, gave up three cars and four men on the initials attacks. Ibrahim stated that his trackers would be spread too thin to be effective when the enemy was identified. During the radio conference the two leaders were talking with atlas maps in front of them.

Ibraham said, "We will be coming into the state of Kentucky on Route 24." According to both maps, they identified a highway rest stop a few miles from Fulton, Kentucky, and decided that the two teams would meet on the following Friday. Both leaders stopped on Wednesday, before the meeting to allow all of the vehicles to rendezvous before heading for Kentucky. Tragedy struck when the attackers turned onto I-24 and headed for the Kentucky town. One of the automobiles veered off the road and exploded before the two men could escape.

Mohammed called on the radio, "Brothers, don't stop. Continue to the east at posted speed. I will stop long enough to understand the damage. Our brothers are probably in Allah's arms, but we must make sure." It did not take him long to learn that there were no survivors in the blast and he called for a continued movement to the rest stop off the major highway. There they would wait for the trackers to join for the last conference before the next target.

The five automobiles with the trackers slowly moved into the rest stop and parked near the bath facilities. Ibrahim had spotted Mohammed and his driver and two other men, but there were no others of the attack team that had survived. Allah's Army had been reduced to 14 members. They gathered around a park table and spread their food to help cover their actions to the public. After a careful survey they found only two vehicles. One was an over-the-road truck with the driver asleep in the cab. The other vehicle was transporting a family of four. When the teams had settled around the park table, their first discussion concerned what should be done with the people in the automobile and truck. While they were discussing the problems, the family departed without apparent notice of the Army of Allah. It was quickly decided to allow the trucker to survive if he stayed with his truck. Mohammed led a discussion about the future of the Army. He said, "Brothers, we will only have one chance at our possible enemies because the attackers have been decimated faster they we had expected. We have had some good targets, but we lost much of our strength on the highway. I have to believe that there was an unfortunate accident which cause our brothers' deaths."

Ibrahim broke in and continued, "We should pick one important target and terrorize the world, not just the Great Satan and its natives. Let's leave a legacy for our brothers that will follow us."

"If I may," he continued when Mohammed attempted to interrupt, "When we pick the target, let us use three of the automobiles and all of our explosives for the one target." Mohammed and the others agreed and all of the munitions from the trackers were transferred to three vehicles. There was no discussion as to who would go in the third automobile. It was selected because of the close proximity of the two vehicles used by the attackers.

There were a few moments of nerves when the trucker left his vehicle and walked to the relief station. On his way back he approached the table and called a greeting and left them with good information. He said, "Friends, if you intend to spend the night in this park, you should make preparations such as putting up a tent using sleeping bags or bedrolls. Display a white signal and the state police will keep a close eye on your camp without interfering. If you don't place the flag, there will be questions when the first troopers come by."

The driver was thanked profusely and the Army started immediately constructing a campsite. Ibrahim was tying the white cloth to a tent stake when the first state car came into the park.

There were two troopers and as the automobile moved slowly past, one lowered a window and called, "Enjoy your night. We will be by every so often."

The teams broke into laughter when one of their brothers said, "How lucky we are to be in a country that will protect you when you are planning to blow them sky high."

After the camp was arranged Allah's Army gathered around the table. Four sentries were stationed around the camp and were instructed to call a warning in case a change was indicated. They were not to take actions without notice to the leaders. A decision had been made that visitors to the park would be ignored unless they became a problem by intruding. If a dangerous situation developed the leaders would decide what actions to take. No problems arose because the only other visitors were teenagers who met at the opposite end of the park. They were watched for about two hours before state troopers moved them out of the rest area. The policemen waved as they left for the highway and Ibrahim called for attention.

When all of the members except the sentries moved to the table, he said that they should decide what and where the next target would be. Mohammed stated that whatever the target, it should be high profile which would shock the entire country. One of the other members suggested a church or school, and those possible targets were placed on a list for consideration.

One of the members was looking through an atlas and suddenly held up his hand and said with an excited voice, "Brothers, I have found it. Look here in the state of West Virginia, there is a military veterans hospital in the city of Beckley."

Ibrahim interrupted and exclaimed, "The brother has found our target. This country honors the military veterans and such a target would draw world-wide attention." It was decided that the two teams would travel slowly toward West Virginia and then the trackers would go to cover and allow 10 to 12 hours to separate the forces. They decided that this tactic would give them a good chance of ambush if an enemy force appeared. Mohammed would take his team into Beckley and go quietly to a hotel and then explore the site of the proposed target and possible escape routes for the trackers. All of the automobiles traveled together as they crossed Kentucky. When the state line was reached, the trackers entered a forested area and allowed the attackers to travel toward their target.

Mohammed led the attackers into Beckley and they checked in at the Days Inn at exit 44 on I 64/I 77. All of the members were cautioned about movement and attention from the local citizens. The first afternoon in Beckley, Mohammed went alone to scout the target. He found an imposing building that had no outside security force. There were three entrances where the explosive filled cars could be rammed. He estimated that the load of ammunition would completely level the structure. After careful inspection of the outside Mohammed moved cautiously into the building. He followed the hallways and observed the movement of the hospital staff. He was pleased to see only four security guards who were unarmed. When he returned to the motor hotel the entire squad was told what had been found as the target. The soldiers were excited about the expected lack of opposition. The decision had been made to attack on the coming Monday at mid morning. Mohammed told his comrades that all would go to inspect the target and each driver would select an entrance. The leader said, "Brothers, we have two days before we will be martyrs for Allah and for Islam."

Mohammed initiated a telephone call to Ibrahim and the two soldiers talked excitedly about the coming action. Ibrahim and the trackers would start for Beckley the following morning. While the camp was being secured before leaving for the target area, Ibrahim called Professor Salaame to inform him of the plans to take the target at the expense of the Great Satan. They didn't talk long even though they were on secure telephones, but the Professor congratulated the Army for finding this very important target. The move toward Beckley had been carefully planned. The five automobiles split up and they moved independently, always waiting for signs of an enemy tracking unit. Each of the highway service areas was inspected closely, but at the end of the day none of the soldiers had anything to report. They stopped for the night in a wooded area and discussed the possibility that the attackers would not be opposed. One of the soldiers asked Ibrahim what were they to do if there was no enemy to fight. The team leader replied, "Don't become lax because I am positive that there will be opposition of some strength. We will rest two more hours and then complete the journey. Our enemy may be in place and we need to find him before the attackers head for the target."

Chapter 22

Jake's team was becoming restless being cooped up in two rooms and with nothing to do. They had been at the motels for two days waiting for news. At dinner the second night, Jake was with the Carpenters and Lydia said, "Jake, we have to do something. The neighbors are becoming suspicious with five people going in and out the same door. The waitress told us last night that some were suggesting calling the police to look in on us."

Jake replied, "Yes, I am concerned about that. Darlene Coppage said much the same thing when I called the other room this morning."

Carpenter spoke up, "Jake, we will stay if we is needed, but we ain't likely to be here in the morning. Best call your friendly general and tell 'em that."

Jake said, "He is supposed to call later. I'll tell him what we think. I'm with you. We are not sitting around here another day." Tolliver called about 1900 and was upset when Jake told him that he was sending his people home the next morning.

Tolliver finally said, "Jake, don't take any actions until you hear from me again. And I will call," he promised.

Jake responded, "O.K., I'll keep them here until Monday morning. After that I doubt if they will stay any longer. Tell the general that we have other lives, too."

There was grumbling but the team members agreed to remain until Monday morning unless more information was furnished. Sunday evening both teams gathered for dinner at a local restaurant. The conversations did not include any reasons for being in Bloomington or on the road. They enjoyed each other and the twins kept up the entertainment with stories about service life. Waseka asked Jake where he met the brothers.

Jake replied, "I'll let them tell the story. They are evidently accomplished liars, but whatever they say is OK with me." The other members offered rapt attention as the mountain rescue story unfolded. There were many questions, and Jake would not answer until someone asked if it was a true story.

He caused general laughter when he said, "I warned you about those two being good liars. Well, maybe I should make that good storytellers. They found me in a weak moment and we did a good job for those people." The party broke up about 2200 and everybody noted that they would be leaving the next morning.

Carpenter left them with smiles when he muttered, "Yeah, we jest don know which way we is headed."

Jake was still talking with the Carpenters when the telephone rang. It was Tolliver and there was excitement in his voice. He said, "Jake we have ourselves a problem. We have found the Army of Allah, but maybe too late. They are in Beckley, West Virginia, with the Veterans Hospital as their target. Our information indicates Monday, mid-morning, and you are about 500 miles away. Do you think you can get to Beckley in time?

Jake answered, "I doubt it. That is an eight to ten hour drive. I suggest we call the FBI and maybe we can make it for support. Let me make the call that will keep you away from the Feds."

"Do so," Tolliver said. "Keep us informed as best you can."

During the conversation Lydia called the other hotel and when Jake ended the conversation both teams took to the road. I 64 was their route and the drivers were instructed to make it foot to the floor until first light, then set the speed 10 mph above the posted speed limit.

Jake dialed the Washington, D.C., FBI Regional Office and asked for Special Agent Walter Swackhammer. The operator was hesitant in calling his boss, but Jake convinced him with, "My friend, I suggest you call him and mention my name—Jake Green. If you don't, he will have your ass tomorrow when he gets the message."

About 15 minutes later the telephone rang and when Jake answered he heard, "Jake, this better be important because this line is restricted to our personnel. How did you get this number?" Jake answered, "Lighten up, Walter T.. We have a problem. I have information that terrorists have targeted the Veterans Hospital in Beckley, West Virginia, on Monday morning. That's all the information I have. If I find something else I will call you."

"You aren't kidding are you, Jake," Agent Swackhammer asked. He continued, "Where are you, by the way?"

"There is no kidding, friend. I am leaving Bloomington and will be in Beckley in about 10 hours. We are in two brown vans, so don't shoot us if we get there in time," Jake responded. Swackhammer ended the conversation with word that he and two other agents would start for Beckley immediately. He said another special agent just happened to be in Beckley with one other officer. After about an hour, Tolliver called with important information—the terrorists were thought to be in three automobiles and were checked in at a motel on I 64 in Beckley. Special Agent Swackhammer acknowledged the information and informed Jake that he was already on a flight from Reagan International Airport to the Beckley airport.

Walter Swackhammer was a little steamed as the executive jet leveled out for the short hop to Beckley. He was mad because he had to argue to get the plane that had been scheduled for hop to Bermuda. He had threatened to go to the Director—the plane was being denied because Walter would not identify his source.

The crew had made a call to Beckley and Walter said to Special Agent Carlos Ramirez, "Carlos, I am sorry for the early call but I have some disturbing information. Get your people on the street. There are three cars packed with explosives with the Veterans Hospital as the target. We think they are checked in at a motel on I 64 and they are posing as Israeli students. That's all the information I have and I'll be in Beckley within 30 minutes and will rent a car. If I hear anything more I'll call and you call me if you get lucky and find those autos."

Ramirez said, "Walter, there are only two of us here. Should I call the local police?" He was told to use his own inclinations on that aspect, and he decided to call the chief of police and explain what was going down. The local policeman and the FBI special agent started making plans to unobtrusively search the motel parking lots. They agreed that this task could be dangerous if the terrorists were with the cars. The plan was for unmarked cars to cruise the entire length of the interstate system in Beckley with all parking lots coming under scrutiny, especially the motor hotels.

Agent Swackhammer was to say later that the flight into Beckley from DC was the longest flight of his career and it only took about 45 minutes of flying time. The local police met him at the airport and took him directly the chief of police, Ben Ruggingham. The chief informed his visitor that he had four cars touring the interstates bisecting Beckley. They decided to conduct a combined operation with the local enforcement conducting the search with strict orders not to take unnecessary actions. The FBI agents teamed with the

Beckley police and all agreed that Special Agent Swackhammer was in overall charge on the operations. All parking areas along the major highways were being toured with two officers per car. Special Agent Ramirez with two men, was covering at the hospital. Shortly after 0800, one of the patrol cars reported a possible contact. They had spotted three automobiles parked together at Days Inn and each vehicle was registered in a different state. No occupants were observed and the officers were instructed to leave the area but to stay in visual contact until other patrols arrived. Chief Rugginham instructed the patrolman who spotted the targets to run checks on each license plate. In a few minutes and excited policeman reported, "Chief, two of the cars have been reported as stolen—one from Alabama and the other from Tennessee. The third car is checking clean and has a Georgia plate. They are parked at the south side of the parking lot."

The police and FBI moved in slowly so as not to draw attention. They were to late for one of the cars. No one had noticed that it was occupied until it started and sped out of the parking lot. Walter Swackhammer called Special Agent Ramirez and said, "Carlos, heads up. One of our suspects has left before we knew what was going on—we missed the occupant of a light blue Plymouth with a Tennessee license plate."

Carlos calmly answered, "I think he just pulled into the front lot. Yes, he is parked and appears to be surveying the front entrance. We will wait for a few—he's getting out of the car! Walter, I'm going to take him out. He is not carrying anything in his hands that we can see."

Walter answered quietly, "Carlos, he's your target. Do what you need to do. Oops, here come our boys, we think. There are three of them. We will take them before they get to the autos."

He turned to the chief of police and said, "Chief, assign a target to your men. We, the FBI, will shoot all three. With that many shooters there should be no problem unless a bomb is detonated." Chief Rugginham did not reply. He keyed his radio and quietly assigned targets to his men. The FBI agents looked surprised when he told at least three men to take each target. Swackhammer looked at the Chief, smiled, and give thumbs up. The three terrorists were almost to the automobiles when one of them probably realized people were waiting. He shouted and turned back to the motel. No one made it, as they sprinted back to possible cover each one was hammered by four shots. Swackhammer shouted, "Chief, secure those cars. We are going to the hospital."

At the hospital Carlos and his assistant stood up and fired at the terrorist, and they immediately drew fire from behind other cars parked in the lot. One FBI agent fell and two city policemen were hit. The terrorist had been hit but was crawling back to his vehicle. He had the door open when one of the city cops ran toward him firing. There came an explosion as the wounded man evidently blew himself up and that explosion set off the explosives that had been wired to the automobile. The devastation was terrible with people and nearby vehicles had been flattened. The policeman going toward the terrorist was blown up and over three burning automobiles. Meanwhile, the unexpected fire was keeping the surviving officers pinned down. Carlos called Swackhammer with the new information and, about the same time, the chief of police called also that he had men down and was receiving fire from three surrounding vehicles. It was apparent that the terrorist group was well organized and the attacking force had been under the cover of the next group. The leading officers had a hurried radio conversation and it was apparent that the attack was coming from four or five different automobiles. Three were identified at the motel and at least one was at the hospital.

Swackhammer said, "I think there are at least two here, because the fire is coming from different directions." The firefight continued and each time a person ventured into the fire area, they were immediately gunned down. The downed officers were all killed by multiple shots.

The chief of police put out an emergency call and was immediately answered by the state police; the barracks informed the chief that they could have two patrol cars in the area of Days Inn within a half an hour.

While they were talking, the line was broken with, "Walter T., what's going on? I am approaching from the west—should be in your area in a few minutes."

Before Swackhammer could respond, the police demanded that the line be cleared for emergency traffic. Walter broke in and said, "Chief, these are friends. They probable can bail us out of this mess." He continued, "Jake, police are pinned down at Days by three automobiles. You can get more information from Chief Rugginham. Chief, talk to these guys, they are friends."

Jake broke in and called the police chief and they exchanged information. Five or six gunmen had pinned down the police and they were using a green Plymouth, a green Chevrolet and a black Ford.

Jake said, "O.K., Chief. I am sending in a brown van and all of the people will be wearing black, so don't shoot them." Then he said, "We are two miles from Days Inn, Walter T. What is happening at the hospital?" He whistled when the

FBI agent explained the situation and said that the other brown van would be closing in on the hospital in approximately 20 minutes.

Marv Whiteside called the police at the Days Inn. He said, "Chief Rugginham, we are turning into the driveway of Days Inn. Which way should I go?"

The chief answered, "Your best bet would be to go to the left and circle the motel. As soon as you make your second turn, the green Plymouth should be about 100 yards ahead and in the right parking lane. The green Chevrolet and the black Ford will be parked alongside the building."

Marv responded, "Roger. We see them. Watch for us, we will be coming in behind the Plymouth. We are all in black and some will be departing the van while it is still moving. Tell your people to watch for us." Mike Freeland and Seaman stepped out of the van and expertly tumbled and were on their feet moving in a matter of seconds heading for the Plymouth. Waseka and Lydia dismounted and closed the Ford. Marv drove the van and blocked movement of the Ford and Chevrolet. Mike and Seaman surprised two shooters and took them out immediately. They turned toward the building and with only a couple of steps, Seaman went down. Mike grabbed her and pulled her to the cover of a parked vehicle. He ducked down because bullets were hitting all around and he realized the fire was coming from one of the police units.

He yelled, "Marv, we have one down from friendly fire. Tell those clowns to hold their fire or I am going after them." In the meantime, Waseka and Lydia had taken out two terrorists at the Ford and Marv had captured one man hidden in the Chevy. Chief Ruggingham had heard the friendly fire call and was trying to stop the firing. The fire kept coming in before Marv and Waseka stood up and demolished one of the police cars. After that, an eerie quietness surrounded the area before the officers started assessing the firefight. Five of the terrorists were down with one captured. Two police officers were down; another was wounded along with Darlene (Seaman) Coppage.

When the van was about two blocks away, Harv Whiteside pulled to the curb and said, "Jake, I think we had better do some recon work. Mike, you and I will scout ahead and let these two old men take it easy."

Everyone chuckled when Carpenter mumbled, "Old guys, huh? We will pull you kids out before you shit your skivvies."

Jake said, "Marv, hold up a sec." The he said over the radio, "Walter T., what's going on?"

The FBI agent relayed the location of two of the gunmen who were using a motor home as cover and at least one more gunman had not been located. The two scouts started slowly and kept to cover along the street full of parked automobiles.

Harv spoke up, "We have the two at the motor home. How about seeing if you can draw some fire. One of the city policemen jumped up and ran behind a pickup truck. There was immediate fire and the Mike Stone said quietly, "I have them. One is behind the flower bed with the red leaves, the other is in the oak tree in front of the building."

Jake said, "O.K., lets do it. Carpenter you get the guys in the flowerbed and tree and I'll take the two behind the motor home. You others shoot at anything that isn't dressed in black. Walter T., give us some fire and then keep your head down. Harv, stay with me. Mike, go with Carpenter. The FBI and police immediately started firing and the terrorists started reacting and in a few minutes the firing ceased. The four terrorists were down, one policeman was wounded, and one of the FBI agents was dead.

Jake called Special Agent Swackhammer when he was told about Darlene Coppage being hit and needing immediate attention. The FBI agent agreed to look after her and agreed with Jake that she should not come under the auspices of the local police.

Walter said, "Jake, we need to talk. I need information for my people and I don't even know who you represent."

Jake said quietly, "Walter, you do not have the need to know. We are on our way now and will be gone to ground before you guys get your reports made. Take care of our friend, friend."

Swackhammer said, "Depend on it. Who do I say she is?"

Jake answered, "Give her good cover, buddy. See you one of these days." The team abandoned one of the vans and headed for Cincinnati, Ohio. Jake called Norman Olson and told him to come immediately to Ohio and have space for eight people. A short time after arriving at the airport the team was on the way west.

The nation and the world were swept by the breaking story about an attack at the VA Hospital in Beckley, West Virginia. The FBI and the local police did a good job in handling the media until someone mentioned that one observer reported a SWAT team that was involved in the fire fight. One of the news reporters speculated, "This SWAT team reminds me of other reports that a mysterious fire team had shown up at different location. They either are the attackers or supporting other forces, and no one knows who they are. If you remember the story out of Virginia that four young men were assassinated at a rest area and had been identified as members of a new terrorist group called Allah's Army." No one could or would add to the speculation. The massed coverage went on most of the following week before the disgruntled news teams were recalled with no information about whom the so-called SWAT team represented.

Chapter 23

Jake pulled into his garage at almost 0300. The people in Venture were not moving so he closed the garage and didn't turn on any lights. His purpose was to be well rested before having to face neighbors. As he stepped in his secure telephone was ringing. Tolliver had good news. First he said, "Jake, you did a great job. The FBI is singing praises to an unknown swat team. We also have learned that your colleague was secretly moved to Bethesda, Maryland, and admitted to the Navy Hospital. She is stable and the prognosis is good—a complete recovery. There will be no problems with the cost for her care." Then he continued, "Also, we have located the control agent for Allah's Army. He is a university professor and has been taken into custody. We think, though that there is a support depot some where in this country, but we have no idea where it is located. We'll keep you advised." After finishing the conversation Jake went to bed and did not rise until almost noon.

He turned on the television after getting coffee started. The noon news opened with a report from Beckley, West Virginia. The scene was the front entrance to the Veterans Hospital. According to the reporter, the damage looked worse that in really was. The local experts were talking about how fortunate the hospital had been because the automobile had been parked over 100 yards from the front entrance. There was some speculation that if it had been directly in front of the building, the entire structure would have come down. The reporter corralled chief of police Ruggingham and asked him to explain what had happened. The policeman shrugged his shoulders and said that not much background had been uncovered.

He said, "First, we have found that this terrorist group is called Allah's Army. To my knowledge that is a new organization. Then, we received a call early yesterday from the FBI. They warned us to be on the lookout for the terrorists who had targeted the Veterans Hospital. The Beckley police located and identified a number of suspect vehicles in the Days Inn parking lot. FBI agents joined us, and three automobiles were captured. All of them were wired with explosives." He paused and then continued, "One car escaped and was exploded at the Veterans Hospital. We think all of the perpetrators were killed. They evidently were in two groups. Three cars were loaded with explosives and four or five vehicles with shooters." The reporter broke in and asked about the rumor going around that an unknown swat team had been in the area. The chief suggested that the FBI be contacted, because the Beckley police didn't have extra officers on the scene.

Jake smiled when Walter Swackhammer was cornered. The special agent was uncomfortable in front of the cameras but led the reporter through the event from the time he received the call from an outside caller. He said that the fire team in question was not FBI and no one had claimed any knowledge as to who they were. He said, "Whoever they were, they pulled us out of big trouble, and we think that they were trailing the terrorists."

The reporter said, "Mr. Swackhammer, one of the local policeman said that a member of the mystery team was wounded. What happened to that person?"

Walter said, "Yes, one was hit by gunfire and was taken to the hospital. It was a woman and I am informed that she has been removed to an unknown location." The speculation was running rampant, and the idea of an unknown fire team was leading the story.

When the television was turned off, Jake sat for a few minutes and mused, "How in the world did the general get there so soon? It had to be him who could get Seaman out of the local hospital and to Bethesda that fast." He was pouring the first cup of coffee when the doorbell sounded. Jake went to the door and was greeted by Bill Wharton, who acted as caretaker when Jake was out of town. He delivered mail and accepted the invitation for a cup of coffee. That was surprising because he had never accepted before.

When they were settled he said, "Jake, I may be out of line but Lou has been bringing people onto your property. I know he is the copper, and he told me to mind my own business when I asked for an explanation."

Jake responded, "Bill, you are not out of line. Thanks for telling me. I will talk to our top cop about bringing visitors to see me when I'm not here. Thanks for holding the mail." They both chuckled when he continued, "If there are any bills, I'll give them back to you."

After having lunch, Jake went to his pier and boarded the boat. Everything was all right except it was little musty. Jake smiled as he said to himself, "It won't take long to get it aired out when we hit the river." He lifted the hatch to the engine to make sure the compartment didn't have a buildup of fumes. While he was checking the equipment he heard voices in the boathouse.

Before he could make his presence known he heard Lou Pryslybilski say, "This is his cover, in this area he is known as The Fisherman and he does do a lot of guide work, both fishing and hunting. But he is gone much of the time without explanation and I ..."

Jake surprised his visitors by breaking in, "Lou, who are these people? I don't remember inviting anyone to this pier." There were three strangers with the Venture policeman. Jake continued, "My friend, this better be a duty call, because you are not here legally unless it is police business. I hear that you have been bringing other visitors while I've been away."

"Take it easy, Jake, these are visitors and I am showing off the community," Lou said with an embarrassed grin.

"Well, introduce me to your visitors." Jake responded. Then he turned to the strangers and asked, "Where are you people from and what is it you are looking for?"

No one said anything and after an unpleasant silence, Lou said to the three men, "Let's go. We will talk some other place."

Jake called as they turned away, "Lou, be careful who and what you talk about." Before anyone could respond Jake entered the cabin and started the engine.

The boat cleared the pier and by the time it turned up river Jake was relaxed and smiling. "Who cares who they are," he thought to himself. The afternoon was spent trolling, catching and releasing fish. Just before sundown he brought in a nice size river trout for dinner and decided to spend the night on the river. The anchor soon splashed in a cove on the eastern side of the Columbia. Darkness fell and brought with it the klaxon calls of the night creatures on both the water and on land. While Jake was cooking the fish he heard a noise on the bank and eased out into the shadows that had fallen on the boat. The noise came again and he watched three deer daintily step into the shallow water and drink the cool, clean Columbia River water. They raised their heads and listened to a distant coyote singing his lonely song. Jake watched the deer as they bedded down for the night. He stepped out into the light, and the buck raised his head, looked toward the boat, snorted and lowered his head for a night rest. For the first time in almost two weeks Jake was at home on 'his river' and immediately fell asleep lulled by the lap of the water against the boat and the night sounds of the other creatures around him.

Lou Pryslybilski caught the line Jake tossed when he came alongside the pier. Neither said anything until the boat had been secured which included Jake pointedly stayed on board and slowly cleaned and swabbed the traces of the fishing from the boat.

Lou slowly said, "Welcome back neighbor. We need to talk."

Jake nodded his head and said, "I think we do, too. What are you looking for, and who are helping find what you are looking for? This place is my place. You are always welcome but don't start bringing strangers around here when I am gone."

The chief of police bristled and said, "I do my job the way it should be done. Everyone comes under my eye, and that includes The Fisherman."

"That's fine, Lou. Do your job the way it should be done," Jake responded brusquely and continued, "But why me? What have I done to come under your scrutiny? If you have something to say, be man enough to say it."

The lawman snarled, "O.K., my friend. You are under suspicions about the unknown SWAT team that is operating with no authority. And since you have asked, the Attorney General, the Marshal Service, and the ATF are the ones I have been showing around."

Jake said, "The next time you come, Lou, have the search warrant available because you are speculating. You don't know the first damned thing about anything. So don't travel into harm's way."

Pryslybilski said quietly, "Jake, I don't listen to threats…"

Jake broke in and said as quietly, "Lou, you don't have to listen to threats, but you better pay close attention to informational statements." With that, Jake turned for the house and Lou went to his car, neither had further words.

The town fishing pier was run by one of the elders of the village, and when Jake visited for the first time, Charlie Stillwell said, "Sure glad to see you, boy. Here people want to go fishing and you are gallivanting around the country." Jake accepted a sheaf of messages and accepted a cup of coffee. While they were at the table, he started leafing through the stack of telephone messages, and as one was put down, Charlie would tell him what the caller was wanting. According to him, "there were fishermen and there were boat riders."

They had a pleasant time telling about 'fish stories,' river sightings, and camping along the river. When they parted, Charlie called and said that the town had had a lot of visitors in the past few days, and before Jake could answer, the old man had turned away. Later, when Jake started returning the calls he understood what the pier owner had said. The fishermen were given open dates and the boat riders were told that the calendar had been filled, and Jake had been warned of unexplained visitors. The river routine soon returned and most days and some nights, the river had bait and tackle being cast. Jake and Lou had no association except for greeting with a nod when they happened to meet, and there were no unexpected visitors. The Fisherman decided to take himself fishing one afternoon and as he put out his rig, he heard on the radio, "Jake, your friend is being discharged on Friday. When you see her, let her know that her bank account will grow at the end of the year as has been noted. Hope you are catching the big ones. Out." Jake smiled and started reeling in the tackle. He had recognized Tolliver's voice and wondered how the brigadier knew that he was on the river alone.

On Thursday evening Jake arrived at the airport in Ellensburg, and Norman Olsen met him grinned and said, "Hurry, hurry. My co-pilot is heated up and is ready to go."

The flight was non-stop to Reagan International Airport in Washington, D.C. The crew was instructed to be back and ready for the return flight at noon. Jake called Tolliver and accepted an invitation for a visit.

Tolliver said, "Hurry up, man. My wife insists that I call her George when your name is mentioned." The visit was enjoyable, with Little George entertaining all of them. Later in the evening Tolliver invited Jake to take a stroll and indicated that he had found a bug in his house the night before. The sweep showed a clean house but they were not ready to take a chance. After a short walk they moved into a city park and occupied an empty table.

Tolliver said, "Jake, what do you know about Canada? Do you have any contacts up there? Nothing is for certain yet but there are indications of mountain hideout that we would like to explore. The Canadian government will not allow any of our organization to operate under the mantel of secrecy. They are insisting on going before the legislature before allowing us to come in—the FBI has given up."

Jake chuckled and said, "General, old buddy, tell me when and where. One of the people that was in West Virginia is a Mountie doing his night job."

Tolliver laughed and retorted, "The general, how did he know? He said last night that you would know someone from our northern cousins—but a Mountie—are you kidding me?" He continued, "We don't have real information yet but put your people on alert, especially that Royal Canadian

Mounted Policeman." They went back to Tolliver's home and Jake accepted an invitation to spend the night.

Jake walked into the hospital room and complained, "Shucks, I wanted to get here while she was in that gown that opens in the back, and here she is dressed."

Darlene Coppage didn't look around and responded, "Shoot, you couldn't stand a sight like that."

They were both laughing as Jake took her in his arms and asked how she was doing and when he was assured that the wounds had healed he said, "Let's go home."

Darlene answered, "Jake, the FBI will be here at 1330. They want to interview me again."

"Ha," he grumbled. "We will be halfway to Porter Lake by 1330. The FBI can wait. We don't have time to mess around. The co-pilot is chasing the pilot and he is anxious to leave at 1200 while he still has the strength. So grab what you want and I'll take it out of here. The doctor has already signed your release."

They stepped out of the door and a third-class Petty Officer in Navy dress blues saluted and said, "I have a car waiting and they are waiting to take the lady down in a wheelchair."

He grinned when Jake said that she was too old to walk. The nurse's aid took them to the main entrance and the Navy sedan was waiting. When they arrived at the airport, Norman Olsen was there and took them to the plane that was ready to fly. It only took them a few minutes to turn to the northwest. After about an hour into the flight, Darlene said quietly, "Jake, I'm through. I love you as a friend but not your work."

Jake put his arm around her and said brusquely, "What do you mean you are through? You are fired, of course I'll hire you back anytime you want to come back. My boss said to tell you that at the end of your year the money in the secret account will be transferred anywhere you want it and taxes will be paid."

The plane landed in Boise and Jake rented an automobile for the ride to Porter Lake. A direct route was taken to Darlene's home because she didn't want to talk with her neighbors until she was rested. Jake told her to go directly to bed and he would stay the night to keeps the wolves away. She came out of the shower with her hair up in a towel and wearing a robe. She had hardly sat down before the telephone rang. She grimaced, shrugged her shoulders and answered the call. The grimace turned to a smile as she spoke quietly to the caller. Jake didn't want to eavesdrop so he went into the kitchen for the coffee pot. When he got back she was still on the telephone and said, "Yes, he is here with me now. How did you guess that?" She looked at Jake with a big grin and handed him the telephone.

"Yes," he answered and immediately recognized the voice and said, "Walter T., how did you find this number? Don't tell me you forced Seaman to give it to you."

Walter Swackhammer laughed and said, "No, she forced me to take it in case she needed protection from guys like you, and it sounds as if she had the right idea. I knew that is was you who checked her out of the hospital. Some of these people are steaming because they didn't get to question her after she left the hospital."

"That's too bad," Jake, replied, "They know all there is to know about her. By the way, Walter T., have I missed something?" He raised his eyebrow at Darlene before continuing, "She acted like she was glad to hear from you. I can't imagine why. She's a pretty girl and you are just flat butt ugly."

The FBI agent laughed and said, "You are not only ugly, you are dumb. Let me talk to her again."

Darlene listened and said, "That's great. We will see you tomorrow afternoon." She grinned at Jake and continued, "Oh, he'll be here. I'll make him stay. Bye, sweetie."

Jake found that the "sweetie" had been developing over the time that she and Walter had known each other and had peaked when Walter started visiting at Bethesda. Jake explained to her that she could not, he emphasized, could not tell Walter about her involvement with Jake's operations. She assured him that there would be no talking about her recent past. They discussed what would happen when her year in service had past.

She said with a big grin, "That's great, Jake, but ask your boss how I explain how I suddenly become a very rich woman."

Jake laughed and responded laughingly. "That's your problem, sweetheart. We didn't cover any of that in our training, but," he continued, "I am sure you will have an iron-clad explanation."

She yawned widely and Jake said, "Bring me a blanket and get your butt into bed. You have to be fresh and rested when Walter T. gets here." She brought out a pillow and blankets and made a bed in the pull-out couch. She kissed him and turned for the bedroom, looked back, smiled and waved. He returned the wave and pulled up his blanket.

Walter Swackhammer settled in the seat of an executive jet that he had hitched a ride from one of his supervisors. It was scheduled for Denver but the FBI official smiled and said that if Walter talked the pilot into going to Boise, a lot of information from a certain young woman would be expected. The Agency wanted to know exactly who she worked for and where they would be located. "We owe them a big debt of gratitude for what happened in West Virginia. We would like to know about that SWAT team, also. According to your report they moved in, did the work and left with no one knowing where they went. The real mystery is how the girl was moved from the local hospital and admitted to Bethesda without a referral. We sure want to talk to her, but one of her friends walked in the hospital, checked her out and left in a military sedan."

Walter grinned at his reflection in the window and mused, "Jake Green had to be the one who checked out and took her home. He's not going to talk and I doubt that Darlene will answer any questions about her recent past."

Jake Green was another puzzle to the FBI. Swackhammer had met him the first time when all agencies were trying to protect the man scheduled to become Premier of China. The Chinese official had died as he boarded the plane to take him to China, and the shooter had never been identified. Agents from all jurisdictions in the D.C. area surrounded Jake and his crew, and that included members of the Chinese secret police. After the incident, Jake had moved back into the 'house down by the river' in Venture, Washington. These thoughts were going through Walter's head and then he and Jake became associated when the agent asked for help in the Okalahoma Federal Prison. Four convicts were threatening to kill other convicts and captured personnel if certain conditions were not met. The four men were killed with head shots from the prison wall and the shooters had escaped without a sighting from anyone. The case was still open. The Swackhammer brothers knew about the shooting because they had helped to arrange the operation—so no talking came from them—even between themselves. The FBI agent continued his thoughts about Jake Green. He had showed up again in Porter Lake, Idaho, and the area lost a drug ring and a group of White Supremacist in one operation. This was when Walter had met Darlene Coppage, and Swackhammer soon realized that she was an associate of Jake Green. The FBI agent was wondering how she would respond to questions about her past.

Darlene was waiting at the door when Walter left the car and walked toward the house. His thoughts were, "How will she greet me?"

The answer came quickly and very special, she kissed him and said. “My favorite G-Man. I thought you would never make it.”

He laughed and hugged her tightly and they kissed again. Jake was waiting and shook hands with Walter and said with a grin, “I don’t know nothing about nothing and refuse to answer questions about anything.”

They all laughed and Walter quipped, “Shoot, man, I know how dumb you are about nothing. So I’m not going to ask you about anything.”

They visited for the balance of the afternoon and no questions were asked until Walter turned to Darlene and asked, “How long have you known this guy, sweetheart?”

She responded quietly, “I have know him since I was in the Navy. He was one of my instructors at the survival school.”

The next question came, “Do you trust him?”

The answer, “With my life.”

The FBI special agent said, “Well, that’s all. My superiors told me to grill you, so consider yourself grilled.” He turned to Jake and said, “Speaking of grilling, I’m hungry. Let’s all go down to the restaurant and I’ll buy.”

Dinner was enjoyable and three of them had no questions except about the trout down in the lake. George Strong, the local newspaper editor, walked in and joined them without invitation. He said, good naturedly, “There has to be a story here. One that is always looking for the ‘big one,’ an agent of the FBI, and the chief of police of Porter Lake and one of them has a story to tell. Chief, I’ll start with you. Where did you go and how did you get hurt?”

Darlene laughed and replied, “I went all the way to Washington, D.C., had an accident and spent time in the hospital.”

Strong said, “I heard about all those things, except I couldn’t find you in a hospital. What kind of accident did you have?”

They broke into laughter when she answered, “Oh, just a run of the mill gunshot wound. You know how things are in our nation’s capitol.”

Strong joined in with a chuckle and said, “O.K., O.K.” Then he continued with a question that almost surprised them, “When were you last in Beckley, West Virginia?”

Walter Swackhammer was fast on the draw, “George, I was there during the shootout with the terrorist and the Days Inn and the Veterans Hospital. I might be able to answer some questions about that, but let’s do it tomorrow. Darlene needs rest.” With a wink, he continued, “And I have too keep her away from Jake.”

The friends talked for a while, but after the second cup of coffee, Jake said to the publisher, "George, stay on Swackhammer. He's got some good stories." He stood up and continued, "It's time for me to go. I want to get back to the Columbia River where you can always find a 'big one." He turned to Darlene and Walter, and said softly, "Good luck, you two, I couldn't be more pleased. Walter T. you be good to her or I'll be looking for you. Seaman, standup because I'm going to kiss you. And call if this cat causes any problems." All of them suggested that he stay the night because it was in the early evening and he would be driving all night. He declined and Darlene kissed him and said, "Stay in touch, because you are one of my favorite people." There were tears in her eyes as he turned for the door.

Jake was soon on the route to Boise. He was planning to turn the rental car in and get another to be returned to the owner in Washington. After leaving Boise on I-84, he drove steadily to Hermiston, Oregon. He was planning to drive through the night and smiled as he mused, "O.K., general, what's next?" He and the team had been busy during the first few months of the year. At a rest stop, his mind turned to Walter Swackhammer. The FBI agent probably was the closest to the truth of the general's operations because he had been involved on two occasions. One was when he called about the Oklahoma prison problem, and then his being called about the raid in Beckley, West Virginia. The Oklahoma mission had nothing to do with the general except for the personnel involved, but in West Virginia, Jake had called the FBI. There were no second thoughts about the communications, but should the general be told?

At midnight the trip was interrupted for rest and fuel in Hermiston. He decided to check in at a motel for a few hours sleep. Before going to bed, Jake called Tolliver, and when the telephone was answered by Mrs. Tolliver, Jake laughed and said, "George, I need to talk to your old man."

She advised that the Brigadier was with the general in North Carolina.

Jake grunted, "Huh. What are they plotting now?"

She laughed and said, "Your name is probably being used and I'll give him your message."

The next morning Jake was on the road early. He had picked up I-82 and crossed into Washington near the tri-cities area. He stopped in Richland for coffee and looked at his map. His plans had been to stay on I-82 to Ellensburg but after perusing the map he decided to take Washington State Highways 240 and 243. He would stay alongside the Columbia River until reaching Venture—then to the big house down by the river.

A siren wakened Walter Swackhammer at about 0500. He dressed and peeked into Darlene's room. She was burrowed into the covers and he didn't call her and eased out the front door and walked to the restaurant at the pierhead. George Strong, the local editor, was already in a booth and he waved Walter over and indicated a seat. Walter sat and they talked of mundane subjects until George took out his notebook and started asking questions about the FBI duties. Walter answered all questions without hesitation and answered fully, except at points that could injure the agency. Strong didn't question the right of the non-answers. Then he stopped and turned a page in his notebook and said, "Now tell me about Jake Green."

Walter laughed and answered, "George, you probably know Jake as well as I do. We met a few years ago in Washington and he was working for a U.S. Senator. Then I didn't see him until I was sent out here after the raids on the drug traffickers and the KKK. And of course you already know that he called a warning to the FBI about a possible raid on the Veterans Hospital in Beckley, West Virginia. I haven't talked to him about the report and my bosses haven't decided about questioning him." Walter laughed and continued, "George, I have told my people that if they decide to question him, just call and he would agree to a meeting, but if they are planning to take him in, they would have to find him."

Walter left the restaurant and walked down the pier. The fishermen were beginning to gather at the boathouse and the lying was being strongly spoken. Everyone had caught the ' big 'un,' but for reasons unknown the stories couldn't be verified, so each of them took the story teller's word as truth. A few of the boaters invited Swackhammer to go fishing and he refused but told them that he fully intended to show the locals how to fish. This brought up laughs, hoots, and words not spoken in mixed company. All of the hilarity and good spirits ceased when they put the boats in the water. Each of them headed for 'the hole.' Some hoots and hollers could be heard up and down the lake when the first strikes were made after sunup.

Walter started back up the pier when a new thought entered his mind, "I can retire next year—and wouldn't this be the place to call home? I am going to ask her to marry me and if she says yes, Porter Lake will be my home." With the thoughts his pace quickened and as he turned in the driveway he could see her waiting at the door.

She called out, "I hope you didn't eat because I've cooked..."

She didn't finish before she was grabbed and kissed, and her special guy said, quietly, yet excitedly, "Darlene, I love you. Will you marry me?" Before she could answer she was swept back into his arms and was kissed again—this time lingering.

She pushed him away and said, “Before you come to your senses, I was going to ask you to marry me. YES—YES!!! I’ll marry you.”

During dinner, Walter said, “You had better call Jake about this. He might not like hearing it from me.”

She chuckled and said, “Jake will approve. He likes and respects you.”

They both broke up when he grumbled, “He’d better or I’ll arrest his ass.”

Chapter 24

Harv and Marv Whiteside, the recon marine and Navy SEAL, finished packing the RV and secured the tow car to the hitch before having breakfast. They entered the kitchen and Harv said, "Take a seat, swabbie. You can't cook. I hope you like scrambled eggs from last night and a piece of dry toast."

During the meal, the twins discussed the telephone call from Jake Green. He had told them that some Cajuns in Bodie, Louisiana, needed help. About six months before, three brothers, John Don, Billy Frank, and Jimmie Lyman, had come in and began terrorizing the peaceful little bayou town. According to the information, which had been smuggled out by boat, the three had set up a drug operation and were running roughshod over the community. Two of the local citizens had been shot in cold blood in front of the post office for no apparent reason except to frighten the community. The local sheriff had seen the shooting and took no actions because he was afraid of or in cahoots with the Lyman brothers. Jimmie Lyman had raped two girls and bragged about it. The local population was up in arms before the sheriff arrested three locals for threatening to kill Jimmie Lyman. Three men, fitting the description of the brothers, had robbed a bank in one of the neighboring towns. Two people were shot at the bank because they did not respond immediately to a command to get face down on the floor. One was a 50-year-old man trying to help his 80-year-old mother. The people of Bodie were being forced to help in unloading, transporting and storing the drugs that was coming by airplane. The entire community would be turned out to load the contraband when trucks would come in during the night. Two women were shot because they would not take part in loading a truck. The community was locked in the vise grips of fear, and the local authorities would not take any action against the outlaws.

The Whiteside twins stopped for an overnight stay in a roadside park and reported to Jake of the arrival in the target area. The first action they took was to become familiar with the terrain where they would be operating. The atlas showed that the park was 75 miles from Bodie and there was only one road in and out of the small community. The surrounding features offered warnings about swampy ground, flooded creeks, and reptiles. In most of the published material about Bodie, Louisiana, offered the warnings about water snakes and alligators—some which had grown to be very large creatures. They decided to leave the RV in the park and travel separately to the town. Harv grinned and said, "Brother, since you are a Navy SEAL, you can swim into Bodie and I will drive the car. I know that Navy SEALs are not afraid of snakes or alligators. By the time we join up the entire community will have been checked by the best recon marine anywhere in this country."

His brother responded with a Bronx cheer through his fist and then growled, "Jarhead, you will be lost when I leave the car. You Marines always go in the wrong direction and here you only have one road to scout. Send up a flare or call me on the radio when you admit that you are lost."

They spent some time preparing for the move into Bodie. While they were packing the equipment they made plans for their movements. Harv would take the car and slowly make his way into town and explore the neighborhood after leaving Marv close to the mouth of Bluefish Creek. The SEAL would swim the creek trying not to bring attention to his movements, but he would take two knives and four grenades in case the denizens of the swamp threatened him. They were on the road before sunrise and stopped at the creek bridge for the SEAL to make his departure.

He grinned and waved to his brother who quietly said, "Little brother, don't take any chances with the gators and snakes. If they become a problem, get out of the water and call me. I don't want to have to tell Mom that you become gator bait."

The swimmer entered the water a few feet from a large alligator. There were no movements from either that would be threatening. The big reptile snorted one time and swished his tail as if too warn the stranger to leave the territory. At sunrise Marv checked all equipment and estimated that there was another five miles to the southern edge of the town. Meanwhile the automobile was slowly closing on Bodie from the north and had only met one automobile. Harv waved but the man in the car didn't respond. The visitor parked in front of the one café in town and no one would answer his greeting. The people in the establishment studiously ignore the stranger. Only the waitress spoke when she brought the menu to the table, and she only asked, "Want coffee?"

Marv swam slowly up the creek and on occasions, he would have to pay attention the bayou reptiles. There was only one point of real concern; he met three very large snakes that he decided were cottonmouth moccasins. After they passed, he mused, "Do they have cottonmouths down here? I'll have to check it out because I know my brother would like one for our birthday." He investigated all parts of the harbor and anchorage. Most of the boats were small and appeared to be fishing crafts. There were three boats that didn't go with the neighborhood. One was a high-speed craft on the order of a cigarette boat. It could go at fast speeds in very shallow water. The other two were very large airboats that could navigate most areas of the region. These boat were not tied at the rickety town pier, they were anchored out in the middle of the creek. The swimmer moved away from the pier and in a few minutes realized the creek was running into a small lake. He thought to himself that this was the point of debarkation for the drug traffic they had been warned about. After a familiarizing tour of the lake, he turned back and surprised some town people when he surfaced at the foot of the pier. They watched quietly as he changed to shorts and a shirt that he had packed in his diving satchel and stowed the diving equipment under a bench. None of the town people said a word nor would they answer his questions. He sat without talking for a while and soon began to think that he noted fear in the eyes of the fishermen. He asked if there was a place that he could get some food. After some moments of no action one of the young boys stood and pointed uptown.

As he approached the small café, Marv saw his brother step out the door and they did not acknowledge each other. When he entered the café he noticed a table sitting alone and made his way toward it. He was sure that it was the table that Harv had used. This became factual when the waitress stopped and asked, "Want anything else?"

No one had noticed that there were two different people. Marv answered the waitress while indicating the used dishes, "Yeah. I know I have eaten enough for two men, but I want some fried frog legs."

No one would respond to his attempts at talking. He was eating the first frog leg when three men entered by slamming the door and walked straight to the table. One of them snarled, "Who are you and what do you want?"

The ex-SEAL leaned back and said quietly, "It is none of your business who I am and I have what I want—these frog legs." He knew that he was talking to the Lyman brothers and slid further away from the table with his hands concealed. The three men started to move toward him and he said once more quietly, "Don't come any closer or I'll blow two of you away before you take another step, and I'll take my chances with the other one."

They stopped and one of them snarled, "Oh yeah, we have seen that movie many times. I'm betting you don't have a gun, so I'm coming to see you." He took a step and a bullet broke up the floor between his feet. Marv smiled and said, "Yeah, I've seen that movie too and decided to take the bluffing out. You still have two guns with fourteen rounds ready to end your misery for being outsmarted in front of your friends. So get your asses out of here or sit down where I can see you before I use three more rounds."

The Lyman brothers backed away and as they started to take seats, the oldest brother said, "My name is John Don Lyman." Pointing to his brothers he continued, "That's Billy Frank Lyman, and that is Jimmie Lyman. The next time you see us, check the eyeballs of the one that shoots your ass." Marv laughed and said, "Before you mess with me, let me tell you, you and your brothers will think that an army is firing if you make a dumb move on me." There was a lot of scowling and glaring but no further word came from the Lyman table. Marv laughed once more and brought both hands up and started eating the frog legs.

The people in the restaurant were looking at the stranger with appraising eyes and the waitress come to fill the coffee cup, she turned her back to the other table and mouthed, "Be careful."

He smiled and nodded slightly to answer her warning. Marv made a show out of pushing back from the table and leaving money to cover the check and handed the waitress some bills as a tip. He stood up and pulled his coat back to offer a view of an automatic weapon and rapidly made his way to the door. His brother came up with the automobile and Marv jumped in and said, "Get out of here." The car was moving when the door slammed. He looked back and the townspeople were watching, some with broad grins and elbow nudging. One of them muttered to an agreeing friend, "I didn't think I would see the day when John Don Lyman would turn away from any fight, but none of them wanted any part of that stranger."

After getting back to the RV, the two brothers spent a number of hours, telling and retelling what they seen. The maps were changed to meet the new knowledge and the big difference was the lake. They agreed that this was the likely spot for the illegal drugs to make the entry into the region. Harv laughed and said, "They have seen both of us but they don't know it. Let's keep it that way for a day or so. When one is in town the other will stay out.

Of course you are the one that pulled a gun on them, and they will have to do something to hold the local people in their grip. So, both of us better be ready at anytime."

Marv drawled, "I pulled two guns on them and I wasn't bluffing so, big brother, you better have two pistols that they can see." It was decided that the exploring would continue for the next day—except Marv said that he wasn't going to swim the creek any more. He would make his way to the landing and start his dive before the fishermen arrived. His next mission would be to explore the airplane moorage in the lake, and Harv would be scouting for the locations of the storage spaces, and each would take a supply of plastic explosives in case they found some need for it.

Their day started very early in the morning and they arrived outside town before anyone was visible. They spent all morning with the scouting and plotting possible targets. The locals had not spotted either brother and they left town without being noticed. The SEAL had taken another swim and explored the aircraft landing site and buoy. While there he decided to rig a booby trap and placed the explosives from the anchor to the mooring links just under the surface. He wired a trigger to the buoy just above the surface of the water that would be hard to spot after he covered it with marine growth from the lake. Meanwhile the recon marine was looking for a storage area that would hold any contraband. He made his way slowly through the town. As he turned down one path at the edge of town he observed a young boy who waved and pointed down a trail. When the marine turned toward, him the boy ran and disappeared into the swamp. Harv cautiously started down the trail and soon found a camouflaged warehouse. After breaking in, he found a room full of bales and bags. The marijuana smell pervaded the area and explosives charges were placed around the entire building site. When they returned to the RV the new information was plotted and they agreed that it was time to disrupt the Lyman's hold over the people of Bodie.

After talking to the twins about Bodie, Louisiana, Jake was satisfied that they could find a way to settle the problems of the small bayou town. He went to the restaurant in Venture for the first time since arriving back to his town. The regulars called him to the table and drew up another chair. None of them asked about his movements since being away—this was one of the things Jake liked about his neighbors—they tended to their own business.

There were always exceptions because after he had ordered Lou

Pryslybilski walked in and the first words were, "Here is our old friend Jake Green, back home from the wars. Where have you been, Jake?"

The table laughed when he answered, "I been here and there, somewhere, everywhere and nowhere, and it only took a short time to do that. You should try it, Lou, especially to somewhere." The policeman joined in the laughter but his eyes were not mirthful when he looked across the table at Jake. Their eyes held until Lou dropped his with a frown.

Jake watched him and mused, "We are going to have problems my friend, and that's too bad because I like you when you are minding your own business."

The next morning the ringing of his secure telephone awakened Jake. He answered it with, "OK, Brig, what do you want?"

Tolliver laughed and answered, "Jake, don't you think I could call without wanting something?"

The answer was, "Nope."

They both laughed before the brigadier continued, "The general wants us to meet him in Bremerton, Washington. He will be at the Oyster Bay Inn on Kitsap Way and asked that we be there on Wednesday, two days from now. He says to meet him in the restaurant at noon. That's just a hop skip and jump from you, isn't it?"

"Yeah, just a couple of hours on the freeway and a ferry ride. I'll see you there," Jake responded. He got a late start from Venture on Wednesday and decided to press his luck. The cruise control was set for 85 miles per hour and his luck held. The first policeman was encountered after he approached slower traffic entering Mercer Island. The traffic was moving at 60 miles per hour so he didn't lose that much time. His luck had held because he was one of the last automobiles on the 1030 Bremerton Ferry from Colman Dock on the Seattle waterfront. Jake became a visiting tourist and enjoyed the views from Puget Sound. He almost rocked back on his feet as he turned down the port side of the ferry. Mt. Rainier was standing stark against a blue sky and appeared to the sightseer to be near the water's edge. But he knew that Rainier was well back in the Cascade Range about 100 miles from Seattle and is also the highest peak in the lower forty eight states. The local population refers to Mt. Rainier as "The Mountain" when discussing it with visitors to the Puget Sound area.

The ferry docked in Bremerton at 1130. Jake decided to go to the Oyster Bay Inn and wait for the general. When he arrived at the restaurant he asked for General Sheffield's table. He was escorted to a table that had been set for three and was at a water view window. While he was admiring the view he felt a presence and found Tolliver approaching. The two old friends sat and talked of old times and recent news. Neither said a word about the general. They knew that he would arrive at 1200 and sure enough he made his appearance right on time. They enjoyed visiting until the food arrived. Jake and Tolliver looked at each other with grins—no one had ordered yet, but the food arrived within a few minutes after the general had taken his seat. When the meal was finished, he told the waiter to bring a pot of coffee and there would be no need for further service.

"Jake, what's going on?" the general asked.

Jake settle back and said, "Bodie, Louisiana, should soon be in good hands. Two of my people called this morning and reported that they had arrived in the bayous and were exploring the area."

Tolliver leaned forward and responded, "Jake, you think two men can control that situation? I figured that you would take at least four people because the hometown perpetrators are three bad-assed brothers plus their henchmen."

Jake chuckled and said, "I sent more than four people—one of those guys is a Navy SEAL and the other is a recon marine."

They all laughed when the general asked why so many people were going after only three hoodlums. He said, "A SEAL and a recon would be able to take on the entire state of Louisiana."

"Now," he continued, "We have some decisions to make. This is a prime area for a terrorist attack against the military because all of the installations can be approached by land or water. Tomorrow we will have a guide show us all of the possible targets. Now let's go to my suite and discuss what should be done immediately."

After getting settled in the suite, the general looked across the table and said, "Jake, this is going to be a tough call. If you don't want to do it, I'll understand and will never mention it again. Frankly if you try it, you probably will not survive."

He stopped and Jake nervously chuckled and responded, "General, you are scaring the hell out of me. Quickly, tell me what you are looking for. If you waste anymore time I might run."

Tolliver broke in saying, "You won't be running alone."

There was a continuing silence for a few moments before the general smiled at both and said, "I've never seen you two run from anything. If anything, you run toward it." He paused and continued, "Jake, there is going to be a parade in Gaza City in about two weeks. They are introducing the Army of Allah. This group is becoming stronger, and as you already know they are willing to kill anyone at anytime. Last word we have is that they have adopted a red headdress. They will be easy to spot and not be covered by the surrounding crowd. There will be a crowd because Hamas has ordered it. What we would like is for the Army of Allah to be taken out in public during the parade. The only support you will have is a young woman hotelkeeper. If you make it, she will arrange for you to be taken off the beach at the edge of the town."

After a few moments of silence, Jake said, "General, there will be three of us going in and three will be coming out. I want another chance at Allah's Army because of the Veterans Hospital. After we leave, I will call a meeting of my people and plans will be made for this mission. Either or both of you are welcome to attend. Just remember at a meeting like that, I am the boss."

There were grins exchanged by the two generals and Tolliver retorted, "If you're the boss I am not coming. My wife says if I ever go with you again, I will get whipped, and you know her—she means it."

General Sheffield also spoke, "I can't make it, either, Jake—and you don't need us there. Just keep the brigadier in the loop with your plans and information."

Jake continued the conversation, "Who is this woman and how do I find her?"

Tolliver responded, "Her name is Leila Shawa and is well known in Gaza. Her hotel is known by her name and it's located on Ahmed Orabi Street on the waterfront and is about one half mile from the city center. She calls us, we don't call her, and so you will have to make contact after you arrive in Gaza City."

Jake replied, "OK, that's it, then. Let me know when you know the date and time of the parade and give me as much notice as you can. Getting into the Gaza Strip will be the hardest part of the mission, if, of course that woman can get us out."

The general said, "That's all I have, unless you have something else. Meet me at the restaurant at 0800. Stop at the desk—there are room reserved for you." Without further words, Tolliver and Jake left because they knew they had been dismissed

The Gaza trip was not mentioned again and at breakfast the general explained that he had been asked to make an unofficial threat analysis of the Navy installations in Kitsap County, Washington. He asked them to observe all the bases during the tour and come up with the best plan to penetrate the different sites. He said, "Just make casual observation from the car and when we stop."

The trip started at Bremerton Naval Base, and the tour included Puget Sound Naval Shipyard. Their guide was a Navy lieutenant commander and he included most of the streets within the locations and would stop when one of the passengers asked him too. The longest part of the tour was along the waterfront in the shipyard. The guide drove out to, and entered the submarine base, Bangor, and took them for a tour of all the acreage around the inside perimeter. They did not approach the off limit areas.

The Undersea Warfare Center at Keyport was the smallest base and it only took about half an hour before the general said, "That's it, commander. Take us back to the hotel." They went to the general's suite and spent the balance of the day discussing their observations. They arrived at a consensus that people who had the capability of forging Department of Defense or Navy identification cards could enter the Navy Base, Bremerton and Undersea Warfare Center, Keyport, through the regular gates. At each gate there was a notice of a hands-on inspection that turned out to be a casual touch of the gatekeeper. This procedure was improved at the submarine base—the guard actually took the cards and compared them to the holders. The two marines were saluted, but Jake had to produce two pieces of identification and the general vouch as to his identity. They decided that the best way to penetrate Bangor would be to go through the perimeter fence, which would take preparation and observing the patrol patterns. Jake ended the conversation by adding, "The shipyard looks to be vulnerable from the waterfront. If I were running the show, I would follow the local ferry and when she entered the slip, all attention is directed at the arrival and debarkation. That would be the time to go through the yard perimeter."

The general conclude with, "It would probably be tougher to get aboard the bases than we have said, but I plan to make this report to higher authorities."

"Shucks, General, I've always said you were the final authority," Jake said laughingly.

Both marines joined the laughter, and General Sheffield said, "Well, I let them think they are in charge. Jake, good luck." He looked at Tolliver and continued, "Brig, let's get out of here. We have to catch an airplane."

Chapter 25

Jake spent another night in Bremerton and attended a stage show at the Admiral Theater on Pacific Avenue. The show was entertaining but most of his thoughts were about the coming trip to Gaza. He considered all of the team and decided that the Canadian Mountie and the marine sniper would be asked to join him for the mission. That posed a problem if Lydia Carpenter insisted on going with her husband. If she insisted, there would be only two of the team available to the general, and those two, Waseka and Mike, were the least experienced of all the team. Jake decided to ask Lydia to head up any other actions by and for the general. He would have to get to her fast before she heard of the coming action because she had made it plain that wherever her husband went, she would be there, too. He shrugged his shoulders and mused, "There are almost two weeks to get things settled, and I am not going to take more than two to Gaza—more than that would be too unwieldy to be extracted on the water front. When the show was over, Jake returned to the Inn and over a seafood dinner he tried to imagine how a young woman in a man's world would be able to take on the task that would be confronting Laila Shawa. The general had made it plain that he didn't know her background but with available information she would have to be trusted.

The next morning Jake took the early morning ferry to Seattle. It was only a few blocks to I-90 East. He decided on a leisurely drive to enjoy the scenery through the mountain passes; there he would be engulfed in the Cascade Mountain Range of western Washington. The difference between eastern and western Washington is abrupt. The eastern side of the state is a high plains desert with most reclaimed for farming operations. The reclamation project occurred by using the Columbia River as a water supply. In the middle of a dry arid looking community would be lush growths of produce or orchards. To the west high mountains and greenery was in evidence. Some people will tell you that the forty days and forty nights of rain from the Bible makes an average rainfall. This is bragging though, it may rain every day for a month, leaving three inches of rain, but of course there will be days that 10 inches of water will fall.

He was enjoying the drive but was busy thinking about the coming mission and took a break in Ellensburg. After coffee, but before leaving, he made telephone calls to the Carpenters and Mike Freeland and invited them to visit on the weekend. He spoke to Lydia and said, "Pretty lady, I am going to ask for a great favor from you. Carpenter and Mike will go with me to the Middle East, but I need for you to stay and possibly run a mission. I would like to furnish your number to Brigadier Tolliver as the one to contact for any work while we are gone. You will be alone with Waseka and Mike Stone, and they don't have much experience. I wouldn't do this because I know you want to travel with Carpenter, but Harv and Marv Whiteside are on another mission as we speak."

She hesitated for long moments before answering, "OK, Jake. One time—but don't make me your executive officer because I want to be with my husband when there is danger." Jake told her that he understood and promised he would not put her on the spot if he could help it. At about 1100 on Wednesday, he rounded a curve and there was the bridge over the Columbia River and the next exit would be to Venture.

Jake spent the next two days researching all he could find about the Gaza Strip—and especially Gaza City. He spent one day in Ellensburg at the university library. He found a reasonably good map of the city that showed the major points of interest. The beachfront was not to far from Ahmed Orabi Street, which paralleled the waterline. With any luck he felt that the seaside extraction could be done with little notice. Of course he realized one small distraction, such as people walking the beach, would delay the vehicle that would be the used for the escape from the oceanfront. The big question without an answer was the parade route and the trustworthiness of the woman he was to contact. There was no way that he could make even a qualified guess. He closed all the books and thought with a slight smile, "We can do it." He knew that Carpenter and Mike Freeland would be capable team members and he was ready to trust them to do what was needed without questions. He regained the car and started the short drive home and continued thinking about the mission. As he took the off ramp to Venture, he mused, "Well, you can't live forever."

With a laugh the tension was relieved with the thoughts about the number of times he had heard that phrase. Captain John Silvers had coined the phrase in Korea and it had been used many times during the following days surrounding the actions of Jake Green.

Jake was just coming in from the river when the Carpenters drove into the driveway. Lydia looked at Jake sternly and said, "One time!" She was referring to his request for her to stay behind and be ready to carry on team business as dictated by the general.

She chuckled as she hugged him and he responded, "OK, Ma'am."

Carpenter picked up the bags and snarled, "No more talking until I git some supper."

Jake led them into the house and got them settled and said, "I don't have anything to eat so I'll buy. Please don't eat a lot—just a little bit."

Carpenter grunted, "Huh, jest lak a swabbie that ain't prepared fer nothing." As they walked out, Mike Freeland drove up.

Jake yelled, "Leave everything in the car—we're just going to dinner." After Mike greeted everyone, Jake took them to the town restaurant. Many of the people called a greeting to Jake as his party took seats. They ordered coffee and asked for the menu. Jake watched Lou Prysylbilski come toward the table.

He stopped and said loudly, "Is this some of your gang, Jake? Where are you headed this time?"

Jake replied, "Lou, it is none of your damned business and I resent the way you talk about my friends."

Before he could continued, Carpenter broke in a snarled, "Mistah, I don know who you is, but git this, I ain't no member of a gang and neither is my wife."

The lawman started to sputter and Jake said, "Drop it, Lou, before you embarrass everyone, including our neighbors."

Lou looked long and sternly at Jake before turning and walked out of the restaurant. The café had gone very quiet and it took a few minutes before there was a nervous laugh and conversation returned. No one made a comment to Jake.

After the orders were taken, Mike Freeland asked quietly, "Jake, who was that and what's his problem?"

Jake answered, "He is our chief of police and he has decided he knows what I do. He has done a good job putting things together about our operations and my absence from home. He was a good friend but he has brought outside agents to look me over. I'm afraid that he will have to be handled because the questions are becoming direct." Carpenter held up his hand and quietly said, "Want me to talk at him?"

Jake answered with one word, "Might."

After dinner they all returned to Jake's home. He didn't let them get settled before he suggested an evening boat ride. They were soon in the middle of the Columbia River and the engines were cut and the boat turned gently down stream. After everyone got settled with something to drink, they started discussing the upcoming mission. Jake brought out the map of Gaza City and discussed the information he had found in the research. After studying the map for a while, they started talking about the possibilities that would have to be faced. If the parade followed the seashore there would be a problem of finding suitable firing points for the three to operate simultaneously. They were in total agreement that for the mission to be successful they couldn't operate independently. It would have to be a team effort or they would abort the mission. There was a long discussion how to operate in case of death or capture of any member of the team. Mike Freeland caused a pause in the considerations, he said, "If one of us gets hit or captured the other two should leave unless there was a definite chance of rescue and escape from the enemy. We can't let them win by getting us all."

Lydia said quietly, "If anyone can carry out this mission, the three of you can. And I want to see all of you back here, so knock off the crap about dying."

The tension was broken when Carpenter responded, "Yes'um."

The remainder of the evening was just a fun night drifting down the river and hailing and answering the other folks on the river. After returning to the house they decided to leave for Egypt on Tuesday, hoping that they could complete the travel by Thursday. The touchy times would be getting to, and entering the city—then to find the woman contact, Laila Shawa.

Jake called Tolliver while the others were having breakfast. The brigadier told him that there would be tickets waiting for Mr. Black, Mr. White, and Mr. Blue when they arrived at SeaTac International Airport, Monday night. The first flight would be a 'redeye' out of Seattle to New York with a connection on Egypt Air for a direct ten-hour flight to Cairo. Jake joined his guests and told them the plans to get to Cairo. He also told them that the travel to the Gaza Strip would be arranged through a contact at the International Airport in the Egyptian capitol. He said, "Let's be careful here. We should not appear to be associated except for being from the States and traveling in the same direction."

They assumed names that had been agreed upon during a training session; Jake would be Mr. Blue, Mike would be Mr. White, and Carpenter would be Mr. Black. Lydia remarked that such names on one airplane could draw attention if someone was investigating the incoming passengers at both airports. This was considered for a few minutes until Carpenter said, "We has to trust someone an' I trust The Gen'al."

The others nodded in agreement. Lydia suggested that she drive the travelers to SeaTac International and then return home. When all the talking had been completed and the breakfast cleared away, the Carpenters stood without a word and walked toward the river. It was apparent that they wanted time alone so Jake and Mike started planning a fishing trip for when they returned from the mid-east.

They arrived at SeaTac International at 2200 on Monday night. Jake and Mike left and took individual routes to the check in stations within the airport. The Carpenters were left to themselves. Mike was already in line when Jake joined the travelers. Carpenter showed up a few minutes later and within a half an hour they took seats in the loading area lounge. Mr. Blue smiled ruefully as he looked over his ticket to the cabin area of the airplane. When the flight was called, Mr. White stood and grinned at no one and started for the first class cabin and Carpenter smiled and left for his business accommodations. In cabin, the flight was crowded and Mr. Blue mused, "Well, at least I have a window seat."

That helped, but a bickering man and woman joined him. Neither would allow the other to have the last word. The argument continued as the plane loaded and didn't end after take off. One of the flight attendants finally came over and suggested that some of the other passengers were trying to sleep and were complaining about the noise. This inflamed the situation until Mr. Blue said, "Shut your damned mouths. We don't want to hear your crap." There were two insulted grunts and applause from the surrounding seats. With this the couple turned away from each other and an onion breath was directed at window seat. When the flight landed at JFK in New York, the man started to scold Mr. Blue, and was told quietly that if he didn't shut up his pencil neck would be without an eraser.

The 'redeye' out of Seattle connected very closely with Egypt Air to Cairo. This flight commenced loading about an hour after the passengers cleared the overseas departure counters. The airplane was a wide body Boeing and it was not fully loaded so there was room to maneuver in the cabin. Mr. Blue had a seat alone at a window and there was a pleasant hum of contented voices to be heard, and he was asleep before the takeoff. Before leaving New York, the team had paused briefly at a newsstand and spoke a few words. They agreed that rest would be needed on the long flight because the coming few days would be very busy with high adrenaline flow. Each member of the team later reported at least eight hours of sleep on the remaining portion of the trip. Mr. White bragged later about how he was treated in first class and Mr. Black indicated that he had enjoyed the business. They were very concerned about how the cabin may have hindered the reliability of Mr. Blue. The concern was expressed with wide grins—even Mr. Black offered an unaccustomed smile.

At 1900, the pilot announced his intention to start descending into the Cairo airport, and by the time the plane landed, Mr. Blue was ready to leave because he was expecting some type of contact that would lead them to the route to The Gaza Strip. He had asked the flight attendant to allow him off before any of the others passengers left the airplane. Upon the point of landing she came back and told him to meet her at the door and he could disembark before any other passenger left. The senior flight attendant asked all of the other passengers to remain seated until the plane was ready for disembarking. There were some grumbles when Mr. Blue was allowed to move to the door, but that was stopped when the attendant looked at him with a smile and announced he had an emergency waiting at the airport. When the door slipped and began to open, the young attendant suddenly found a hundred dollar bill in her hand. She tried to refuse but Mr. Blue ignored her and left the aircraft. As soon as he stepped into the waiting area he heard the word passed for Mr. Blue to go to the nearest service telephone. One of the attendants took him around the first door and pointed to the telephone.

He picked it up and heard a dial tone, before he could react he heard a voice saying, “Don’t look around I am standing on your left side pretending to use the telephone. By the way who sent you? The brigadier said that you would offer a name. Now I must have that name before we go further.”

Mr. Blue thought for a few seconds and responded with a question, “Have you heard from Sheffield?” The answer was in the affirmative and an invitation to follow was given. It was a young man who had spoken with a mid-eastern accent and looked as if he could be an Egyptian.

As they approached the exit gate, the young man spoke quietly and said, “Signal your friends to join us, but don’t act as if you recognize them.” Mr. Blue looked over his shoulder and spied Mr. Black and Mr. White and gave a slight nod. The guide worked it so the three men could pass through customs together without offering the fact anyone was recognized. When they cleared customs, the guide started walking and the team followed, but without paying any attention to the other passengers. They cleared the baggage gate just in time to see three taxis roll up with the passenger door open. Mr. Blue noticed that the young guide had disappeared and with a shrug he entered the cab.

The driver spoke into his mike and then turned and with an unaccented voice said, "Welcome to Cairo, Mr. Blue." He grinned and said that he had grown up in Detroit and would be the agent to get the team into Gaza City. He said, "Don't worry the other cabbies are with me and we all three have permission from Cairo and Gaza to make this trip. You are a college professor researching for a textbook on the Middle East. Your friends will also have like cover." He pulled the taxi to the front entrance of the Moevenpick Hotel and said, "Each of you have rooms and be ready to leave at 0600 tomorrow."

Chapter 26

After a light breakfast, Mr. Blue stepped out front of the hotel and was surprised when the taxi pulled up and the young guide ran around and opened the rear door. The passenger looked around and hesitated to enter the automobile until the young man said quietly, "They will be along but at different times." The move from Egypt was without any problems, and at the Gaza Strip the border guards casually inspected the taxi. They appeared to know the driver and soon waved him through. After clearing the gate Mr. Blue was advised to relax and enjoy a desert drive with no air conditioning. The driver took a number of turns at different points of interest. He would get out point out different sites and Mr. Blue would take notes as the tour made the rounds of the area. At noon they entered Gaza City and Mr. Blue was driven to the Laila Hotel situated on the waterfront. The driver took the baggage to the desk and a beautiful young woman shook his hand and walked him to the door where he turned and waved to his passenger. The woman came back to the desk and said, "Welcome, Mr. Blue. Your accommodations are prepared and the porter will take you there." She turned away without further conversation.

The new tenant inspected the room thoroughly and could find no listening or transmitting devices. There was a washbasin and a pitcher of water on a night stand; there he saw the direction to the bathroom at the end of the hall. He freshened up at the basin and walked downstairs to the restaurant. He was seated by a window facing the beachfront and was surprised with the menu. One page looked like any XYZ Café in the United States. There was fast food cooked mid-eastern style. The other page was written for the natives in the Palestinian language. He ordered French Onion soup with a small loaf of the local bread. The bread was very good and he smiled when he thought that no one could spoil the soup. A surprise was forthcoming, he ladled the first spoon of the concoction and could faintly taste the onion inter-mixed with the hottest preparation he had ever experienced. It took the entire loaf of bread to clear the effects of the spices. When he looked around the natives were laughing at his actions. The young woman from the lobby stopped by with a smile and inquired about the soup. She led the laughter when Mr. Blue replied that he couldn't talk.

While she was there she reached across the table with a water pitcher and whispered, "I am Laila, and the other colors have arrived. You may meet in my room after 2300. The door is to the left of the desk. Tap three times and hear two taps from inside. If you do not hear them do not remain because I will not be available. The others will be instructed, so don't attempt to meet outside my room."

At the appointed time he tapped lightly on the door and heard the response. The door opened into a darken room and he entered, fully alert. When the door closed a single light was turned on and she was a beautiful sight to behold. She led Mr. Blue to a sitting area, and went back to the door. In a few minutes Mr. Black entered followed by Mr. White.

When they were comfortable around a table Mr. Black mumbled, "Sho will be glad to git outta this Black stuff."

Mr. White responded laughed and said, "I'm not to much into colors myself. I have almost forgotten my name."

Laila joined and quietly said, "This is Thursday and the parade will be at midday on Saturday because that is the Sabbath for the Israelis. The parade will form in the Ashar Gardens near the campus of the Al Ashar University. The plans are for them to proceed to Rashad Shawa Cultural Center along Victor Hugo Street."

Mr. Blue leaned over and spoke quietly, "Laila, you have a known name—are you involved with the cultural center?"

She smiled and said, "Rashad Shawa was my grandfather." There was a moment of silence but she didn't continue.

Mr. White asked, "Is there a good location for our mission on Victor Hugo Street?

She said, "I believe you will find a location just about anywhere on the street. I would guess the best site would be about midway between the park and the center. There are three houses taller than the other structures." They discussed the plans for a couple of hours and decided that each would spend Friday taking in the sites of Gaza City. They were told that it would probably be best if they stayed away from the hotel as much as they could. Laila suggested that everyone should be off the street by 1600 because the police were more likely to stop visitors late in the day.

They moved to the door and Mr. Blue hesitated as his two comrades left. Laila hesitated but then closed the door. She said, "You should leave, too, because the hotel is closed for the night and it is not safe to be found."

He responded, "I will leave in a few minutes but first, are you safe here?"

She considered her answer for a few moments, and then replied, "I am safe until I get caught. So far I have been lucky and I have been here for two years. There are times when I think someone is watching me."

Mr. Blue put his hand on her shoulder and quietly said, "I think you should leave with us. The one who sent us told me that you were in danger."

She did not resist as he drew her closer, but whispered, "I have to stay because I am needed here. This is my home or it has been for a long time and my family is buried here." She moved away and said, "Now, you must go." Her eyes were moist when he leaned closely and kissed her softly on the lips.

As she opened the door, he said, "I think I have just found you and don't want to lose what I have found. Think about going with us. I can arrange for you to stay in my country and you will be safe."

She pursed her lips with "Shhhh. Be careful and good luck."

Friday morning, Mr. Blue came to the restaurant at 0800 and ordered breakfast. He ate slowly and leisurely read two papers with his coffee. While he was sitting there Mr. Black and Mr. White entered the establishment and ordered food. They each offered brief nods but no one spoke or paid more than passing attention to anyone. Mr. Blue asked the waitress to summon a taxi and when it arrived he nodded slightly to the others. He asked the driver to take him to the Rashad Shawa Cultural Center. Before entering the cab he told Laila his destination. His voice was loud enough for his team to hear. At about 0900, Mr. White asked for a taxi and asked to be taken to Ashar Gardens, Mr. Black walked out and turned toward downtown Gaza City. The cultural center was open when Mr. Blue arrived and the taxi was dismissed after payment. The morning was spent reading, talking, and taking notes because some his plans were to enhance the cover story of being a visiting researcher in Middle East culture. Mr. White toured Ashar Gardens and visited the University. Mr. Black wandered through the city as if he was out for a leisurely walk. All three of them were observing the people and traffic patterns. Each stopped for lunch in different cafes or food stands.

In the afternoon the team spent most of the time on Victor Hugo Street.

When their paths crossed, there was only a casual greeting. It did not take long for them to identify the three taller buildings. One was a housing unit with an outside stair to the roof. The other two were businesses on the opposite side of the street. It took some exploring to find a way but each member made the roofs of all the buildings and looked for the best spot for the shooter to observe the street. Mr. Black had a nervous moment when he was seen on the roof of the apartment unit. The observer called out, but Mr. Black ignored him and walked slowly down the stairs. Two young boys surprised Mr. White on one of the roofs and threatened to call the police.

He told them that he would pay them a dollar if they wouldn't do that. But they said, " That isn't enough. It is going to cost you twenty bucks."

Mr. White didn't have that much money, and the kids called the cops. Mr. White scrambled down the alley and disappeared into a doorway. In a few moments, the two boys saw a stooped old man walking down the street. They ran by the old man and asked if he had seen someone going up the alley. He told them that a young man had walked hurriedly around the corner. Mr. White smiled as the boys took off after their target because they had not recognized him. On the way back to the hotel most of the transit time was observing traffic flow and looking for route to use after the mission was complete.

At dinner Laila seated all three at the same table that was surrounded by other western visitors. There was a steady hum of conversation in English and a smattering of romance languages. Mr. Blue said, "After we eat, we will meet in Laila's suite. There we will be able to make plans for tomorrow with the information we now have."

They finished the meal at different times and made their way to the meeting place. The host invited all of them in and served coffee and left a pitcher of water. Mr. Blue started the conversation, "Do you see any problems with the mission that are not expected? I went to all the buildings and only foresee a traffic problem after the mission is complete. There will probably be a panic and that should give us a chance to get back here. To be successful, we have to get back here as fast as possible, but the only running we should do is while the panic situation is in control."

Mr. Black said, "Ah don see ennythin that will stop us. You covered the big prob'lm about gittin back heah. We has to be here with no sweat other than what is normal."

Mr. White broke in and said, "There is one problem I see; how do we dress and where do we get the guns? Then what do we do when we get back here?"

Mr. Blue responded, "We should be back, relaxed and sitting in the restaurant because you can bet that there will be a search of every building in Gaza City. If you have any thing that cannot withstand a search get rid of it tonight. We will dress in the local fashion and we will have weapons with a fifteen round magazine. This material will be in Laila's storeroom off the lobby. Mr. Black, you are the best shot, so take the second building the parade will pass. Mr. White, you go to the first building on that side of the street and I will be across the street over the apartments. Now, all of us better be on our toes because security forces may be on the same structures or we may have visitors. We don't want to kill more than our true target but if we do, we have to do it quietly. The weapons will have silencers but try not to waste ammo. Mr. Black when you take your first shot we will empty the magazines and drop the weapons and beat it out of there. Our major targets are the ones in red headdress—the Army of Allah. On the way back try to get rid of the native dress without drawing attention. Any further comments or questions?"

Mr. Black said "Yeah when can I change mah name. I don't know no Mr. Black."

The next morning between 0930 and 1000 anyone watching could have seen three men in local dress casually walk out and take routes down town. They did not appear to be in a hurry because the parade would not move until noon. One at a time, they casually turned up Victor Hugo Street and it was apparent that the population was planning for the festivities. A large majority appeared to be heading for the assembly area at the University and the Ashar gardens. The team didn't cause any suspicion as they turned purposely into the individual buildings. Mr. Blue greeted a family that was heading for the parade route. Mr. White had to wait until the shop in the building front closed, and Mr. Black strolled to the next building without meeting anyone. As they approached the different roofs each was confronted with like problems. A security policeman had taken up position on each building. The immediate problem was when and how to take the watchmen out. Each man waited until the parade could be heard. Mr. Black and Mr. White used knives, and Mr. Blue hit his foe with a piece of lumber across the back of the neck, killing the man instantly. As the team gained control of the buildings, they found their comrades and acknowledged each other with a slight motion.

The parade could be heard as soon as it left the Gardens. The marchers and watchers were calling and talking loudly to others. The parade members were firing their weapons into the sky when Mr. Black stood and shot one of the leaders. The silenced weapons were emptied and the marchers completely routed in less than a minute. There were about twenty men in red headdress and none could be seen standing as the shooters dropped the weapons and made their way to the street. They joined the panic driven crowd and hastily beat a retreat to the planned escape routes. Each of them stopped running as they cleared the street but walked hurriedly toward the waterfront. As they moved they casually dropped the local clothes and soon became three tourist walking away from the noise in the down town area. They walked into the hotel and Laila took them into her room. She had washbasins, towels, and fresh shirts for each of them. When they finished the washing and had clean shirts she led them out to one of the tables among the other westerners. On the way, her hand sought Jake's and they hooked fingers for a few steps. Many of the hotel guests were talking about the disturbance in the city. Some of them said and others agreed they were glad that they had heeded the suggestions not to go to the parade route. Word soon came that terrorists had shot many of the parade participants. It was not long before the police arrived at the hotel. Laila was questioned closely about her clients. She adamantly replied that all of the westerners had remained at the hotel all morning. It was also pointed out that service had been provided for the guests. The police were efficient and took each person into the lobby to be questioned but did not find anything out of line. Most of the guests breathed a sigh of relief when the officials left for another hotel.

As the afternoon shadows lengthened, there had been no word about the recovery nor did the team have any idea what would happen.

After dinner they made their way to the rooms and Mr. Blue whispered, "Howdy friends, my name is Jake."

They all laughed and Mike Freeland responded, "Shoot, big guy, I knew it was you all the time."

Carpenter broke them up when he drawled, "I don' ever want to see Black agin. I didn' even know myself. Ah'm jest a poor old mountain boy." They all stopped in with Jake and they were talking about leaving the hotel.

Mike said "Jake, if something doesn't happen soon, I think we should get out of here. Those cops will be back, you can bet on that."

Carpenter spoke, "Yeah, we cain't wait too long because these color names will soon make someone ta take notice." Jake said, "Let's not get to rushed. I can't believe that the general forgot about getting us out of here. I'll go down and see if Laila has any information for us."

Mike chuckled, "You been wanting to go down there all day and probably yesterday."

Jake grinned and said, "Go to your room and be prepared to leave on a moment's notice. If she knows anything I'll be right up. If she is waiting for a word, I will wait with her."

Jake raised his hand to tap on her door and it opened before he made contact. She smiled at his surprise and simply said, "I was waiting for you."

He took her by the shoulders and said hoarsely, "If you have any information tell me before I kiss you." She smiled and moved against him and initiated their first kiss. They sat on a small settee and held each other without speaking. They only action between them was kissing and stroking each other.

She stopped with a deep breath and whispered, "I want to, but we don't have much time left. Get the others and I will take you to the landing area on the beach. There will be a boat coming for you."

He breathed deeply and whispered, "I want you to go with us. When we disappear you may be in danger." She responded slowly and also whispered, "I can't go. I am needed here and I will be all right. The police have questioned me many times. When they come back I am going to be furious and tell them that you left without paying me for your room and service." He handed her one of his cards that only had a telephone number and said, "If you need me, I'll be at the end of that line."

She led them down to waters edge and they settled in to wait for transportation. Laila said, "I have to leave. Good luck to you. Your friends should be here at anytime, they will be coming from the sea."

Jake walked with her for a short distance and she stopped him and said, "You must stay."

They kissed and he turned back and joined with the team. Mike said, "She is some lady, Jake. Don't lose her. When you come for her and need help, let me know."

Carpenter said, "Me, too." In a few minutes they heard the mutter of an engine coming from the sea. Jake flashed a signal and in short order it was answered. The signal went on and off for short intervals and the engine sounds were becoming louder but still muffled. A small flotation craft ran up to the shore but before it grounded the three men were in it and the cox'un had it backing down before hitting the land. He saluted his passengers and shoved his throttle forward. The craft picked up speed but was immediately challenged from the beach. Lights were flashing and loud hailers were squawking and the cox'un looked back with a grin on his face. They were soon taking fire but he expertly maneuvered from side to side and none of the hot rounds hit the boat. He yelled to his passengers, "Get down low, there is a boat chasing. I doubt if we can out run him but we may be able to take him by surprise when he comes alongside." The chaser was spewing white water as the bows cut the smooth sea. He ran around and closed from seaward and there was an explosion that took him out of the water. The flotation craft had to make a hard turn to keep from entering the area of the foundering boat. As they put the scene behind them the cox'un grinned and pointed to seaward. The explosion had originated from a submarine that was running slowly with decks awash. A submarine? The general had done it again.

The next morning before day break, the team was roused and told to prepare for leaving the sub. They went topside on invitation from the captain and he pointed out a small freighter. He told them that the ship would take them to Athens, Greece. The submarine crew launched the small rubber boat and took them to the ship that was waiting with a Jacob's ladder hanging on the port side. Jake and Carpenter didn't have any problem getting up the ladder, but they had a good laugh at the Mountie when he lost his footing and fell back into the water. Everyone including the victim laughed and the tension was reduced. The captain of the ship invited his new passengers to the bridge and briefed them on the plans. Upon debarking in Piraeus they would be met by others to speed them on the journey. He told them that he planned to enter port at dawn the next morning.

The ship docked during the early dawn, and before the new guides arrived, Jake received a call from Tolliver who said, "Great job, Jake. The news media all around the world is reporting this story. You took out most of Allah's Army and the Palestinians are fuming. They are trying to blame the Israelis and the Jews are denying but goading the government of the Gaza Strip. Now, Jake, get out of town. The people that were to meet you have disappeared and we don't know what is going on. Get to the Athens airport as soon as possible and take the first flight to Europe. There is a flight at 0900 your time heading for Rome—if you can make it there are three first class tickets made out to you and your team under your real names, the colors have faded away."

Chapter 27

The town of Bodie, Louisiana, sweltered and with the heat index the temperature would reach 120 degrees before noon. This was a daily condition and the people had adjusted to the atmosphere. No movement would be seen in town between 1000 and 1600 except around the restaurant and the boat landing. Even then no work would occur; but the Lyman brothers had broken this routine. The natives would be called out anytime that a load of contraband would arrive. On most occasions by boat, but other times a floatplane would land on the small lake outside of town with the contraband. When the Lyman brothers would send a load out of town, the work would be done day or night, and on occasions the people would have to work 20 to 24 hours with only a few breaks for water—no food. Marv and Harv Whiteside observed this routine for a number of days. Generally the aircraft would come in on Sunday morning, and the boats arrived late on Saturday evenings. When these events coincided, the trucks would come in to be loaded for transportation of the contraband to off loading destinations in the Midwest and Northwest regions of the United States. The twins kept a low profile and were not seen together by the local people; therefore it was a great surprise when they walked into the restaurant one Sunday afternoon. It caused a big stir among the Bodie population, and within a short time the restaurant was filled with unexpected guests.

No one was talking or talking very little—every so often there would be a whispered conversation at the bar or one of the tables. All of this shut down when the Lyman brothers entered. They rocked back on their heels in surprise when they saw the twins.

Billy Frank recovered first and walked up to the table and snarled, “So it takes two of you to do a man’s work. We should have known there was more than one wise guy in town. What do you want from this town?"

Marv spoke up, "The only thing we want out of this town is you."

There was a pause until Joe Don spoke, "Well you are not getting us out of town because you are the ones that will be leaving. We don't care how—you either get up now and split or you go out feet first."

Harv interrupted him, "Joe Don, you have got it wrong. Don't you remember my two guns, now there are at least four for you to consider. There are two pointed at you now—look for my brother's hands. Now just sit down or we're going to lay you down—right here—right now."

They hesitated and Billie Frank said, "You pulled that on us last time, but when we walked in I saw all your hands so I know there is a bluff now." There was silence and glares when Harv moved back from the table and bumped the edge of the table with his two handguns.

Marv drew his two and said quietly, "Get on the floor or we blast your guts all over this fine eating establishment."

He continued to the town people, "You folks move back out of our line and you won't get hurt." There was a scramble for the door or the sides of the room. He then turned to the Lymans, smiled and said, "Since there is room at the tables you don't have to take the floor, but get your ass into a chair. Now before you do, empty your pockets especially those handguns you don't have nerve enough to go for."

When they did not start unloading their pockets one of the twins' guns barked and the round hit a chair close to Jimmie Lyman. He immediately started emptying his pockets and his brothers did the same with grumbles and curses. Marv stood and slapped Joe Don alongside the head with an automatic and said menacingly, "O.K., big brother, take that hideaway out and slide it over here."

"I don't..." he started and was slapped again, this time bringing blood before he leaned over and took a gun from an ankle holster. The other patrons of the restaurant had moved away and Marv said, "We are not looking for trouble and we want to be good partners. You guys have had it too easy with these Cajuns, so we want half of your organization."

Joe Don wiped the blood off his forehead and said, "You have the drop on us, but no way are you taking over our business. We have a plane and two trucks coming in and there is no way you can take all of us."

Two trucks pulled up and Jimmie laughed and boasted, "Now you bastards are in for it. These guys carry machine guns, and I believe I hear the airplane, he has a .50 caliber machine gun on that plane."

Harv looked over and said, "Brother of mine, I think we should cut this visit short." They backed away toward the rear door of the building among laughs and ribald remarks from the Lyman's.

When they had cleared the restaurant building Marv said, "Let's take them this afternoon." His brother nodded and turned toward the storage facility and Marv headed for the waterfront where the diving equipment was stored. There were two men on the pier when he pulled on the diving gear.

He looked at them for a long moment and said quietly, "Maybe you should go home for a while." One of them gave a thumbs up and both took off in the direction away from the down town area. Meanwhile, Harv started down the path toward the contraband storage and saw the young boy who had pointed toward the facility during the scouting moves.

Harv stopped and said, "Son, you should not stay here and don't allow your friends to come down this path, and if there is a loading crew, get word to them to clear out as soon as the work is done. The others—let them come. Do you understand me?"

The youngster had a face-splitting smile when he said, "Aye, aye, sir." He turned toward the edge of town. The Whitesides went about their chores and with care installed firing circuits to the previously planted explosives. Harv was not interrupted, but when Marv broke the surface of the lake he immediately spotted a lookout on the airplane. He was sitting on one of the skis with an automatic pistol. The SEAL slowly, so as to not make ripples, sank back into the water. He moved toward the airplane from another direction and this time when he surfaced, the lookout was busy tuning a radio. When the Spanish music started, the SEAL came to the surface and hauled the man under water before he could make a sound. There was a brief struggle, but the unfortunate guard sank slowly to the bottom of the lake. After completing their work, the brothers joined up on the waterfront and took cover in the bait shack.

Shortly after 1400, two semi trucks rolled into town. One was parked while the second one was backed down the path to the storage facility. The Lymans brother went to their cars and started blowing the horns. This was the signal for the workers to start loading the first truck. The Whiteside brothers counted 15 men and women that came slowly out of the houses and walked down the path as the truck was backed down to the buildings used for the storage of the contraband. It took an hour and a half to load the semi and as it moved back into town, the 15 workers went into the restaurant and another work party followed the second truck as it backed down the trail.

The recon marine whispered to his brother, "Cover me, I am going to booby trap that truck. No one is guarding it, so I should be back in a few minutes." He took half of the remaining gel explosives and two electric fuse boxes. He applied half of the explosives under the engine and cab of the truck and the other half was attached to the gasoline tank. When the work was finished, he returned to the bait shack. They were standing back from the window, watching the trail when the door opening with a hinge squeal startled them. They separated and went to the floor with weapons at the ready and faced one of the villagers. He stopped short and as he recognized the twins, smiled, and backed out, closing the door. The brothers watched for overt moves but the man walked slowly to the restaurant and in a few minutes he and others walked out and started a cooking fire behind the building. The brothers chuckled and one of them said, "I do believe we are going to have some crawdads for supper."

The second truck moved slowly back into town and parked behind the other vehicle. Joe Don was heard saying, "Let's go in have some coffee and settle all of the bills from this afternoon. The trucks should wait for at least another hour before moving out. The plane will be safe for the night and the crew can spend the night with us. We may be invited to a crawdad feed." There were laughs of derision from the entire group.

One of them bellowed, "You mean to say our work force will feed us after a hard days work."

They turned and went into the restaurant and Marv said, "My turn." He took the remaining explosives and booby-trapped the second truck. When he returned, Harv quietly said, "OK, little brother, lets start the show. Take out the plane and the three boats out in the creek."

The SEAL used an electronic trigger to set off the charges he had attached to the airplane and then rotated the switch to three separate settings and the large boats in the creek were completely destroyed. There was a shocked silence from the townspeople and they did not approach the piers. Joe Don Lyman led a rush out of the restaurant and headed for the pier. They had covered about half of the distance when the storage shed was blown. Everyone stopped in confusion and was mowed down when the two trucks exploded and started burning. The Whiteside twins moved from the bait shop and headed through the carnage to the restaurant. The villagers moved toward them yelling and laughing. Everyone wanted to shake hands but the twins did not stop until they picked up the moneybags left by the smugglers. It became quiet as the villagers saw the two strangers opening the bags full of money.

Then the celebration started again as the greenbacks were split among the Bodie residents.

Harv said, "When the law gets here, hide that money."

Excitement exploded and Marv said quietly, "Big Brother, let's choose up sides and get the hell out of here."

With that, they walked to the car. The Bodie people had not noticed that the visitors were gone until the tires squealed and the Whiteside brothers raced out of town toward the main highway. As they cleared the marshes and had four lanes of traffic, the FBI and the DEA were called and a vague story was related about the happenings in Bodie, Louisiana.

Chapter 28

The team met at Carpenter's mountain home, the hosts extended the invitations with an explanation that it would be more private than other areas. Everyone was in attendance, including Darlene Coppage and Walter Swackhammer. Jake said that it was great to see them but they should explore the farm when special meetings were called.

They understood and caused some laughter when Darlene said archly, "That's OK with me, because I've been wanting to take this city boy into the woods."

Walter grinned and went with banter by saying, "Jake, don't let her do that. I'll quit my job and go to work for you. I'll do anything to stay out of the woods." They spent the first day visiting and listening to an excited news media. The furor had been going on for three days and there was no sign of it dying down. The stories were told over and over again and retold more times than that. The reporters were frantically attempting to uncover the specifics of the two incidents.

The foreign news teams were reporting the Gaza City story and all known organizations were named as possible perpetrators. The Israeli secret service was denying any involvement but would slyly smile and express admiration of the ones responsible for the take down of the newest terrorist group known as the Army of Allah. The Gaza story was tied to the terrorist attacks earlier in the year by this organization that also used the name of Allah's Army. Media outlets in the United States were all reporting an incident that had gone on in Bodie, Louisiana. According to sources, this small bayou town had been under the iron grip of a smuggling ring that brought in contraband mostly described as a drug operation. There also were some reports that people had been smuggled through Bodie. FBI and DEA agents were still in Bodie trying to piece together what had happened on Sunday afternoon of the previous week.

The federal agents were not talkative; their only comments were, "We don't know what was going on and the local people will not talk. Our only information came from a fisherman from a neighboring village." He had told the agents that a family of three brothers kept the Bodie citizens under hard-fisted control and actually forced them to do the labor needed to transfer the different items being smuggled.

After visiting during the first day, Jake called a meeting for the next morning. After breakfast, the chores were finished and the team followed Carpenter up the river. Jake remembered the site as the location where Long Ball Qwong was discussed when it was decided he should be executed. When everyone had settled down, Jake asked the twins to relate their experiences in Bodie, Louisiana, and any recommendations for future operations.

Marv took the lead and told of his work in the water ways, he said, "First I went under the water in a creek and had to swim around moccasins and 'gator to get to the town." He told them that the lake was not that bad but having to guess when and where the explosives could be set off was a concern. Harv took over and said that working on shore was easier than the water but he still had problems scouting the area under the eyes of the local citizens.

He said, "If it hadn't been for a young boy, I probably would not have found the stash house as soon as I did." During the discussion that followed the reports, it was decided by the entire team that a lookout should be employed in all missions. The Whitesides said that they had been at a big disadvantage without a scout.

Jake asked Mike Freeland to make the Gaza Strip report and the Mountie said; "We were lucky because we did have an outside member." He told them of the help and support that had been supplied by Laila.

He related stories about their initial scouting and selection of fire zones that would offer some protection for the innocent bystanders. "The actual mission was fairly simple," he said and continued, "We had made plans to only use one magazine of ammunition before departing the area."

He related with some hilarity about the fast trip back to the hotel and having to wait for the authorities.

Carpenter's bit was, "Huh, don' ever jump in a boat on the strand and go on a sub ta git outten the area." Jake asked for questions—none was forthcoming.

He said, "OK, that's it. Let's go back and eat Carpenter's food and drink his whisky."

The host muttered, "Huh, all you bin doin since ya bin heah ennyway."

When they arrived back to the house, Jake called and left a message for General Tolliver, of the team's location. It was only a few minutes later that the call was returned and Tolliver's first words were, "Congratulations, my good friend, you made many folks very happy. Not the CIA or FBI because they can't find the anti-terrorists. The CIA is fuming because no one warned them of the attack in Gaza City; likewise the FBI is trying to uncover the people who were working in Bodie, Louisiana." Jake called the team together and put the Brigadier on a speaker. He congratulated each one by name and they were surprised at that because they had been assured that no one would know their individual names.

Mike Freeland and Harv and Marv Whiteside questioned that fact, and Tolliver chuckled and said, "The general gave me your names and I think that guy knows every name in the country."

Tolliver went on to advise them that many people were thinking that Allah's Army was passé because most of them had been liquidated. They were also told that the FBI had arrested a farmer from Nebraska who had been assisting a number of terrorist groups other than Allah's Army. They had also arrested a college professor who had been the control agent for the same groups including Allah's Army. In the meantime, the FBI had been led to the Bolivian suppliers for the Bodie Louisiana operations. The brigadier finished by saying, "The general says for you to lay low for a while and relax. He says the next operation would be a couple of months down the road."

The stay at Carpenters' lasted until after the weekend. On Monday, Charlie Daniels ferried everyone to the airport in his helicopter, and they went their different ways. Jake and Mike Freeland had seats on the same flight to Seattle but did not stay together. The only byplay between them happened when they reached the destination. They gave a two-fingered salute at the baggage racks and turned toward other interests. Jake didn't spend any time in the big city; he walked from the terminal to the nearest rental agency and was soon on I-90 East. He had set a speed of 70 miles per hour until he saw the sign for the Venture exit. His speed went up and in just a few minutes he had to brake to take the off-ramp. There was only one stop before going home; at the restaurant he paid two of his neighbors to return the rental car to the agency in Seattle.

After getting settled in his home, a call was made to the neighbor who looked after his place. In a few minutes the mail was delivered and Jake enjoyed a quiet afternoon catching up with the news and listening to a radio talk show, that was still talking about the Gaza Strip and Bodie, Louisiana. Jake smiled as one of the callers disputed and castigated one of the show's guests. The guests were retired from law enforcement agencies—one was for the actions and the other supported the efforts to find the so-called anti-terrorists and bring them to justice. The host was making sure they kept arguing their sides and the callers were responding rapidly. It appeared the a large majority of the callers were lined up behind the idea of taking on such organizations as Allah's Army and the Lyman brothers' smuggling operations and destroying such organizations. One caller said, "It's about time someone took on those outlaw jerks. Who ever wiped 'em out, I salute them."

A few mornings later, Jake went to the restaurant for breakfast. He was greeted at The Table when he took a seat. All of the storytellers were in full voice and he just sat back an enjoyed all of the tales. He was finishing his breakfast when Lou Pryslybilski joined the group. He only offered Jake a casual nod that was returned in a like fashion. The lively talk continued and no one appeared to notice the tension between Jake and the Policeman. After a final cup of coffee Jake took leave and before he was out of the door Lou left the table. They passed in the parking lot and the policeman would not look at Jake.

On his way to the house there was some thought about the situation that led to musing, "Lou, what's with you? If you don't stay away, we may have to travel in a direction that I don't want to go."

Lou didn't stay away; later that day he drove up and joined Jake at the boathouse. As he approached the pier, Jake stepped aboard the boat and motioned to a seat when Pryslybilski boarded. They sat for a few minutes with silent appraisals, and Jake broke the tension by going into the cabin and brought out two cups of coffee.

He sat down and each took a sip before Jake spoke, "OK, Lou, if we have baggage between us let's take a look at it. I am tired of the attitude you have introduced between us. I think it's time for us to clear the air, and I have already said that I don't make threats, only statements." The policeman leaned back in his chair and his face had reddened.

He took a sip of the coffee and said quietly, "Jake, never mind the statements. I see them as threats, but having said that I am going to take a strange and hard trip for me. I apologize for some of my actions. When the story broke about the Gaza Strip and Louisiana I said to myself, 'Jake is at it again.'" He paused and leaned forward and continued, "Jake, I like what you are doing, but as a lawman I can't believe that you are not breaking the law."

He hesitated again and then, "My friend, I am going to resign my commission as police chief, and I would like to be invited to do some traveling with you." There was a long silence before Jake stood up and offered his hand.

When Lou took it, Jake said, "I am glad to hear you say that buddy. I'll see if I can get you an invitation sometime in the future. I am not alone in whatever it is that you think I'm doing." Both men chuckled and shook hands again. Lou turned without another word and left the boat. When he got to the car two, two finger salutes were made simultaneously.

On the river again—the lifestyle of the surrounding area was pleasant and fulfilling for Jake. He settled down and when he left, it was by boat up or down the Columbia River. Fall was approaching and with it, the leaves on the trees were beginning to take on color. Overnighters required heavy covering during the night and during the day warm clothing was required. The river trout were running and most days he went to the river as a guide for visitors. Word of mouth travels fast and on the river, "Go fishing with Jake Green and you will get your limit" was the message which spread across the region. On the weekends he could not fill all requests and would send the prospects to other guides. Times were good in Venture and its environs. The only disquieting problem was the steady reports of unrest in the Gaza Strip and the thoughts of Laila Shawa. The memory of her stayed close to surface of his consciousness.

Jake and Lou had become friends again and did not mention the conversation about the policeman joining some of the trips made by The Fisherman. On one occasion while talking to General Tolliver, Lou was discussed and Jake was told to use his own discretion about adding new people to the team. One afternoon, the telephone rang and he was invited to the wedding of Darlene Coppage and Walter T. Swackhammer.

Darlene said with a chuckle, "You have to come or Walter will arrest you, and I'll put you in my jail, and you will never see the light of day again." In a serious tone, Jake told her that he would come because he didn't want a hassle with a broken down FBI agent or a hick town chief of police. He was pleased to hear that the team had been invited and all had accepted. The wedding was a very nice affair and the team took a few minutes all together. They waited until the newlyweds had left among good wishes and teasing comments, and then Jake asked them for any comments about the work they were doing. Everyone got a chuckle when Waseka complained about not going on a mission. Jake furnished new telephone numbers and radio frequencies to call if needed. He made it a point that they should not be used on casual calls. Mike Freeland took Jake aside and asked for a ride and said, "We need to talk."

They left Porter Lake early on Monday morning after having breakfast with the members of the team and saying goodbye to some of the town people. When the freeway was gained, Jake said, "O.K., Mr. Mountie, let's talk."

Mike chuckled and said, "We have a little situation going on up in the north woods. A smuggling ring has been set up, and they are bringing in an estimated 25 people each week. A few are caught at the border by the Mounties or the Border Patrol, but you folks here in the states are gaining citizens by an estimated average of 15 per week. No one has been able to crack this operation. Oh, we know who they are, but can't prove anything. Do you think the big boss will allow us to visit Canada?"

Jake hesitated for a few moments and replied, "Let's not ask him—just tell him. I'll give them a call tonight and you get everything set up and let me know when to visit. I haven't been to the north woods in a long time. I'll bet some of our friends have never been up there."

Mike said, "OK, that sounds good, but what if he says no to the plans?"

Jake grinned and said, "Why, shucks, we'll do it on our own. I don't anticipate any problems."

Later that evening, after convincing Mike to spend the night, Jake called Tolliver.

His wife answered the call and giggled when Jake said, "My goodness I am talking to George and she is too far away to run my ass ragged. Let me speak to your hubby, honey chile."

She responded laughing and said, "You call me honey chile again and I will go to your place and start some training exercises." Then in a serious tone she told him that the brigadier had not come home but he was expected.

After about a half an hour, Tolliver called and Jake broached the subject of going to Canada and looking over the smuggling situation. His answer from Tolliver was a laugh and, "The general is in Canada at this moment. I don't think he would object, because that is becoming a sore spot for all of us—Canada and the U.S."

Jake said, "OK, we will do it and will keep you informed. It may be a couple of weeks before we go."

Mike Freeland went back to his work with the Mounties, and he called Jake every evening at 1900 with all the information he had gathered on the smuggling ring. Two couples, Tom and Mamie Lom and Rex and Sylvia Sellers, operated it. They were all Canadian citizens and had been in the smuggling business all of their teenage and adult lives. Their fathers had been smugglers in all kinds of contraband. The young couples decided to launch an alien smuggling ring and had been successful for a number of years. The Mountie relayed that the authorities knew all about the business and the site locations needed for transporting the people into the United States. A number of raids had been made and the smugglers were back on the street before the paper could be completed. It was evident that the operations had a direct line to the authorities—high enough to quash the charges and release those arrested. Mike Freeland said during one of the calls, "My troop is refusing to make any arrests but are watching and tracking the situation." He paused and then continued, "Jake in a few more days I will have all of the local information we need for our mission. These guys are going back through all of the past operations and are plotting all the info they can gather." Jake responded by telling Mike that what was needed was locations and time of the operations.

Jake had called and warned the team to stay available because of the likelihood of a mission. He also approached Lou Pryslybilsky in the restaurant parking lot and said, "Lou, I may be taking a trip in a short time—do you want to go along?"

The policeman hesitated for a long moment and then said, "Sure I want to go along—when and where are we going?"

Jake chuckled and replied, "I don't know when, and I'll tell you where when we get there."

With a laugh, Lou asked, "Why won't you tell me? Don't you trust me?"

Jake answered with a grin, "Of course I trust you but this is a need-to-know business and you don't need to know. All you need to know now is that you will be working with a highly trained team."

There was no response from the policeman and Jake continued, "And Lou, once you join the group, you are tied to us. If you or anyone talks about the operations we carry out, they will not hold many more conversations. Now, before you start, you will be paid more money than you will ever need." Before any answer could be made, he opened the door and entered the restaurant. He could tell that Lou was straining to say something but Jake did not slow down until he took a seat at The Table.

He grinned as Lou took a seat across the table and heard, "OK, Jake, we need to talk again." He received an affirmative nod and both placed their orders with the waitress. After eating, they walked out of the establishment together and Jake said, "OK Lou, maybe this will clear up some of your question. We do clandestine operations that often kill people—all bad, we hope. If you join us, you will be required to not talk to others about us. If you do talk, you will probably end up like many others—dead."

They walked a few more steps and Lou said, "That clears up a lot of my questions, but I still don't like to be threatened."

"OK, Lou," was Jake's response as they parted.

The smuggling information came from Mike Freeland. He called and said, "Jake, we have word that a major effort will be made in a week or so. They are thinking about the weather because we will be getting snow before long, and according to our information there are about 50 people to be taken across the border. Our government is like other governments; something has to happen to make things happen. We don't know where and when the crossings will be, but the bosses have all appeared in Revelstoke and have set up at the Best Western Wayside Inn. That is pretty close to the border and we know that they have some cargo. One shipment came in on the Powell River and we almost caught them in Sullivan Bay. We did intercept nine people, and one of them told us that five others had already left when the raid happened. There are always passengers traveling the Alcan Highway." He paused and then continued, "Jake, they are close enough for our people to get together."

"I'll call them together and wait for your word," Jake replied. Then he continued, "Mike, I want you to stay at your place until we know for sure where the actions will be. Now, do you think its possible to involve your people in some way? I know we can't get them for the first part of the operation but maybe we will be able to leave some folks for them to find."

The Mountie said, " I like that idea because some hard work has gone on this case. Let's think about it and see if we can involve them in some way."

"Before you go, do you think we could go to Revelstoke without causing too much stir? There will be eight or nine of us," Jake said.

Mike replied, "I don't see why we can't get to Revelstoke. It is not a very big place but there is a lot of hunting and fishing action so we won't cause any unnecessary stir."

Jake began calling the team as soon as Mike Freeland had broken the connection. The first call went to the Carpenters. When Lydia answered, Jake said, "Hello, pretty lady. Get that ugly lazy husband of yours out of the house and make your way to Revelstoke, Canada, and check in at The Hillcrest Hotel. As soon as you get there call me on the radio—and watch for Mike Stone."

The other calls were made with the Whiteside brothers to go to the Super 8 Motel and to watch for Mike Freeland. Waseka Stone was told to go to the Best Western and wait for Jake and Lou Pryslybilski. There was some concern about the Venture police chief because none of the team knew about him, and he didn't know any of them. After the calls were made, Jake went to the restaurant and was soon joined by Lou. They took a table away from the others, knowing that they would not be disturbed.

After ordering, Jake quietly said, "Lou, arrange for some days off if you want to go on a trip. We should leave by the end of the week and pack for outdoor work."

Lou took a moment and replied, "OK, Jake. Where are we going and what are we going to do?"

Jake smiled and said, "We are not going very far—just to visit with our neighbors to the north, and we are not quite sure what we will be doing—if anything."

Jake would not answer any further questions until Lou said, "OK, but I will need to know what we will be doing."

The reply was, "Lou, this is a need-to-know situation and you don't fit that position yet. When we get instructions, you will be told along with a team of nine people. That nine includes you and me."

Later in the day, a call came from Tolliver. He related that the general was still in Canada and that he approved of the team going after the smugglers. Tolliver said chuckling, "Jake, I've run across some information that may help you. This informant says that some smugglers will attempt to cross the border at Kings Gate, near the Idaho border. Also, they will make the attempt at Newgate, near the Montana border, and another attempt will be made from Grand Forks near the border with Washington."

Jake said, "That's great. Where did the general come up with this information?"

Tolliver replied, still chuckling, "My informant suggested no one should know the source of this information."

As soon as the call with Tolliver ended Jake called Mike Freeland and related the information that had been received from an anonymous source.

The Mountie asked, "Where did you get that information? That's the one item we have not been able to come up with, but we do know that the run is planned for next Saturday night from outside Revelstoke. There will be three guides available to help us get to any location the fastest time possible. These three people can be trusted to get us into position, but they should not be allowed to participate further. One of them will probably try to egg his way into the action." Mike laughed before continuing, "He is known as Digger Davis and according to Digger Davis's stories, he used to be a smuggler in his own right. His contraband was cigarettes and booze for you folks in Washington state. He was caught and sent to prison, and according to legend he started digging an escape tunnel the first night he was locked up and was gone within the first week."

The team was in Revelstoke by Thursday evening and Jake called a meeting for the next morning at one of the nearby parks. The Carpenters had arrived before the others and had a fire going and coffee perking for the meeting. Jake had brought a bag of goodies, as did Mike Freeland. The meeting site was a three-sided, covered mountain cabin. The first item of business was the introduction of Lou Prysylbilski. When everyone had settled in with the coffee and whatever, Jake told them what the mission was about. He then turned the meeting over to Mike Freeland. Mike had to take some kidding about the Mounties needing help to catch "their man." He told them about the background of the problem and why the police had not been able to get the smugglers. There apparently was a leak somewhere in the command structure of the police forces. This leak became apparent after three or four raids come up empty because the smugglers had been there and gone by the time the first forces arrived. The entire operation was known but no one could come up with real evidence to break the operation. Some arrests had been made, but the suspected perpetrators were back on the street in a very short time. When he paused and opened for questions, Lou Pryslybilski immediately said, "I am new to this organization. How do we operate if we catch some of the smugglers?"

Mike replied, "There is open season on everyone that opposes. The escorts will be members of the rings. It is likely that the drivers of the carrier vehicles will be locals trying to pick up a dollar. If they do not oppose you, tie them up and leave them for the authorities."

Lou wasn't satisfied, he retorted, "Are you telling me that all hands are to be taken out unless they surrender?"

Carpenter drawled, "Yep, or you are likely to catch one from a hidey gun."

Jake broke in and said, “There are three more people that you watch for. Mike told me that they would be guides to get us to the action sites as soon as possible. They are not to get involved in our mission. Anything further, Mike?”

Freeland shook his head and Jake continued, “OK, then, we have information of where the aliens will be moved to the States. When we leave here start making your way to the sites—be sure you take the radios. Carpenter, you take Lydia and Mike Stone and head for New Gate, that’s over on the Montana border. Mike Freeman takes, these two boots (he indicated the Whiteside brothers) to Kings Gate over on the Idaho border. Waseka, Lou and I will take the leaders here at Revelstoke and then head for Grand Forks near the Washington line. OK, don’t be too obvious about the departures and good luck to all of us. The guides will check in with you at or near the sites. They will be guarding the radio frequencies.”

The Carpenters and Mike Stone left that afternoon because they had further to travel than the other two teams. Saturday morning the second team left for Kings Gate after having breakfast with Jake, Waseka, and Lou. When they left, Jake said to his team, “Let’s go for a walk.”

They left together and went to a city park and discussed their missions. Jake told them that they would take care of the ringleaders. He pointedly told Lou that the four people would be killed. Waseka accepted the plan but Lou tried to argue, and was stopped by Jake when he said, “Lou, you asked to come on this trip, after your theories of what we were doing. I also told you that we would likely get into a fire fight.”

The policeman said, “Two of those people are women and I don’t shoot women.”

Waseka broke in and said, “Those two women carry guns, too. If you won’t shoot them, they will shoot you.” In an insulting voice she continued. “Leave the women to me and then you can watch Jake hit the men.”

Lou was speechless for a few seconds but before he said more, Jake said quietly said, “Lou, it’s now or never. Are you with us? We have to know for our own protection.”

The policeman grumbled, “OK, I am with you on this mission but I may leave after we finish here in Revelstoke.”

Jake stood up and stared at his friend for long moments and then replied, “Waseka, watch him. If he moves wrong, shoot him.”

The young woman said, “OK.”

Lou did not make any other statements but he was upset and red faced.

On the return trip no one talked and as they approached the motel Jake stopped and asked, "Lou do you have any questions? I have to know, because this a dangerous business."

He responded, "OK, Jake. I'll be there when you want me."

Jake said, "Good enough, pal, watch yourself. This isn't Venture." They stopped at the desk and found that the targets had reserved a table for an early lunch at 1100. Jake told his team to go and get ready for travel and they would meet at the restaurant at 1045. At the scheduled time, Jake stepped out of the elevator and joined Waseka at the door. She told him that she didn't trust Pryslybilski and was told that he would probably be a good teammate but he would have to be watched.

The focus of their discussion stepped out of the elevator, closely followed by the Lom's and Sellers. They passed with a nod and entered the restaurant. Waseka preceded the men and took a table across the room from the target table.

Jake leaned over a said quietly, "OK. Let them get their orders and as they start to eat, we will take them. Waseka, move over toward the check stand, and Lou go to the front window as if you are taking in the scenery. I will go directly to our targets and, as they look around, you two head for the table. No hesitation. We take them out and leave through the front door. The car is just to the right on the curb. No running, and drop your guns to your side. Try not to startle anyone by flashing it. All attention will most likely be directed to the target area."

After drinking a cup of coffee, the targets were served a meal and Jake nodded to his team. Waseka walked casually toward a card rack by the check stand, and Lou stopped at the window. Again, Jake nodded and the team moved on the targets, and when they became alert, three weapons appeared and a hail of fire took out the breakfast table.

Jake said, "To the car, have it running when I get there. I will make sure we did the job." It only took a casual look to see that there were four headshots along with the extra rounds. Jake started for the door and was pointing back toward the bodies and he was sure everyone followed his direction rather than looking at him. Waseka was at the wheel and the engine was turning. Lou was sitting in front and as Jake got in, the car left before he could shut the door. They left town at a leisurely pace until they cleared the downtown streets, and then took on speed toward Grand Forks and the Washington border. A radio call confirmed that the other teams were at or near the target areas.

Lydia Carpenter made the report from the New Gate/Montana site. They had established contact with the guide and he led them to a small clearing alongside Highway 93. Before he left, he pointed out that both directions could be watched and that the Montana border was just a few miles down the road. When they were settled, in the guide departed after saying, "Good luck. I ain't seen you, I don't know you, and I don't want to know you. But, my friends, be careful and good hunting."

The report was continued with Lydia saying, "Jake, we have some information that we can expect our visitors around 2200. We don't know who generated this information so we are keeping it at arm's length. Let us know if you hear something like that."

Mike Freeman reported from the Kings Gate/Idaho site. His team had reached their lookout area earlier in the afternoon and without a guide. They couldn't establish radio contact with anyone so they had made their own way to an area that Mike was familiar with. They were so early that the car had to be hidden and lookouts concealed alongside Highway 95 that joined U.S. 95 at the Idaho border. The Mountie could not explain the information reported by the New Gate team concerning the time to expect the targets. He said that he would make a landline call to a friend at the Revelstoke Station. In a short time he reported that someone in one of the restaurant made the statement about the night plans and was rushed out the front door before he could say anything further.

Waseka Stone relayed the information from the Grand Forks/Washington group. Her message was cryptic as she relayed the information that the head of the smuggler organization had been decapitated. She said that the guide called for them rather than waiting for a call. She chuckled and said, "His name is Digger Davis and so far we haven't been able to get rid of him. Jake has finally convinced him to go back toward Grand Forks to give an early warning if sees the expected vehicles."

Jake came on the line and warned everyone to be alert for outside efforts. He said, "I'm suspicious of the information received at New Gate. Someone may be worried about someone with similar plans as ours."

Waseka continued, "Everyone hunker down and try not to get surprised. We need radio silence until the first target is hit. When you complete your mission—get out of Canada and don't look back until you are safely in the United States."

Jake had assigned Waseka to help with the escort car and its occupants. She assured him that she would be able to take on anyone coming her way. She grinned and bragged, "Even at night, I can hit 'em in the eye."

Lou would take care of the driver in the contraband vehicle. Jake told him that the ones in this vehicle would be captured and restrained unless they put up some opposition. "Lou, if there is any reason you can't go through with this operation, take one of the cars and leave. If the people at your station put up any show of disagreement, they have to be shot for the protection of all of us."

There was a long hesitation before Prysylbilski answered, "Jake, I asked to come on this trip so you can depend on me to do what has to be done."

"Thanks, friend," was the only response. The team settled in for a long wait because the smugglers were likely to try after midnight. That didn't happen. A few minutes before 2200, a racket was heard with doors slamming and horns blowing and Digger Davis yelling, "Here they come. A station wagon is in the lead with a large passenger van following close behind."

As had been planned, Lou turned one of the cars across the road and they waited quietly without moving. Engines could be heard as Lou regained his position, and the lead vehicle was running with bright lights, and at a high rate of speed, the blocking car was hit by the skidding wagon. The passenger van was stopped before entering the pile-up. Four men came out of the wrecked vehicle with guns at the ready. As Jake opened up, he heard the fire from Waseka. The escorts were taken down with only a few shots and on inspection; Waseka had not hit the eye but had made four headshots on two men.

When the firing ceased, Lou called, "I have two prisoners and the van is full of people." They made sure that the people in the van were not hurt and then locked inside the vehicle. Waseka spoke to them and asked, "Do you understand English?" One of the men indicated with a nod and she continued, "You will not be hurt. We will be leaving in a few minutes and the authorities will soon be here to help you."

The guide came up and said, "Get out of here and I will call the Mounties. You will have a 30 minutes head start before anyone is notified. Boy, if you need more help up the road, let me know."

Jake offered a two-finger salute as they headed for the border. They were casually observed at the Canadian station and waved through on the U.S. side. Jake mused, "Someone gave us a hand here."

The other sites didn't go as smoothly as the Grand Forks interception. At Kings Gate, the smugglers were not recognized until they had passed the ambush site. Mike Freeland and the Whiteside twins started trailing the targets on Highway 95 and came to the border and found the Canadian Border Agents pinned down by the smugglers. The U.S. Border Patrol could be seen moving toward the fire-fight. The gunmen took positions alongside the passenger vehicle that appeared to be a covered two-ton truck, and neither side of the law enforcement agents could return the fire from the enemy. From their position, the Freeman team could see two Canadians down and one of the U.S. Border Guards had been dragged out of the fire zone by his comrades. Mike Freeland moved to a point where he could see the right side of the covered truck as Harv Whiteside took up the left side. Marv slipped across the Canadian border until he could see all of the different units. Upon signal from Mike, Marv fired twice and two of the tires exploded. This caused confusion among the smugglers that was multiplied when the other men started taking down the enemy gunmen. It only took a short time for the sharpshooters to decimate the smuggler gunmen. Quiet reined for a few minutes with the three teams attempting find a way to close out the issue.

Mike Freeman stood up and called, "Mates, you have not seen us and we don't need any publicity. There are three of us, and if you will turn away from the road we will cross the border and head south." The U.S. Border guards were the first to move.

One of them stood up and called to the Canadians, "Sergeant Wheatland, if it is OK with you, we will come over to your side and see if we can figure out how we succeeded in taking down these outlaws."

The Canadian called back, "Sounds like an idea, Yank. Come on over a join us for a cup of coffee."

When the patrols went into the station house, Mike ran the border at a high rate of speed. One of the twins questioned him about the speed, the Mountie said, "I know Wheatland and he was not turned away from the road—you can bet on that." There was no pursuit and the speed was lowered to the speed limit on U.S. 95.

At the New Gate site, things really turned bad. The smugglers were stopped and ordered out of the vehicles. The four doors on the escort car slammed open on both sides and a withering firestorm occurred. The New Gate team was expecting two guards, but six machine pistols were putting out a steady stream of projectiles. The Carpenters were pinned down and the truck crew came out firing at Mike Stone. Mike was in a position where he was able to take out the truck crew and then turned attention to the escort vehicle. With Mike's fire through the back windows, Carpenter was able to move to a better position and opened up through the windshield. Lydia had not been heard from and the sniper started working his way toward her. The firing stopped and he found his unconscious wife. She had evidently been hit as the firefight started. The front of her shirt was covered with blood and he did not hesitate to use his knife to get it off. The sniper breathed a little easier when he located the wounds high on his wife's right shoulder. The blood was flowing freely but it was not from an artery. The blood was soon stopped and she breathed deeply upon regaining consciousness.

She smiled weakly at her husband's concerned face and softly said, "Pookie, take me home."

Without a word he picked her up and started walking south. Mike watched as they left the scene. He wanted to go, but knew that he still had a job to do. He went to each of the outlaws and made sure they were dead. Then he called to the riders in the truck and told them that they were no longer in danger and someone would be along to take them out of the vehicle. Mike took one last look around and then speedily left the scene. He soon overtook the Carpenters and settled the wounded comrade in the rear seat. When they crossed the border, none of the guards held them up. They were waved through and Mike called Jake and told him the situation. Jake said, "Mike, go to Kalispell and I will send transportation to you. The airplane will take you anywhere you want to go."

When Jake finished with his instructions, he called Norman Olsen and told him to get the plane to Kalispell, Montana as fast as possible. He said, "Norman, don't ask any questions after we hang up. Your passengers will be two men and a woman. The woman is hurt badly and her husband will not put up with much talk."

Olsen asked where he would go after Montana, and Jake answered, "Go where they want to go. I anticipate that they will head for the Ozarks. The two men will know any landing sites that will take the aircraft." The conversation ended when the pilot said that he could take off within 15 minutes. When the airplane landed in Kalispell, the co-pilot jumped out and ran toward the operations building.

A young man met her at one of the doors and asked, "Did Jake send you?" She only nodded and headed back toward the plane. She heard the running feet behind her and she pulled the ladder down and allowed the passengers to enter first. As she pulled up the ladder, she heard the pilot say, "Thank you,

Kalispell. I'll see you one day and we will have a drink."

There was a chuckle from the radio and the co-pilot said into the mike, "Kalispell, we are rolling. Thank you for all your help."

As the radio calls came in, Jake advised everyone to get home as soon as possible and be natural but lay low. He assured them that there would be no problems but warned that many people like to put two and two together and come up with five. Jake had accused Lou Pryslybilski of this when the policeman was questioning the trips Jake had been taking. Instead of returning to Venture, Jake called Norman Olsen and asked to be picked up in Spokane. The pilot was grinning when they met at the information desk near the general aviation departure gates, and quipped, "It has been so long since you called, I was afraid I had been forgotten. Where we going, Boss?"

"Take me to your last landing spot," Jake answered.

The pilot laughed, "No, no, no, not me. I will take you to Popular Bluff, Arkansas, that's only about ten miles away." He continued with a grin, "Jake, you have some strange friends—but interesting. I landed this bird on a two lane highway and in some fashion—I don't know how, but a helicopter was waiting for us."

Jake laughed and said, "OK, if you don't have the nerve for a second landing, call that helicopter pilot and tell him to meet us at the airport."

Charlie Daniels was waiting when they arrived and in a few minutes they were on the helicopter heading into the Ozarks. After many turns in and around the terrain Jake had no idea where they were and Charlie just smiled and reported that they would soon land. They circled a farmhouse in one of the many valleys of the area and landed near the house and a woman stood on the porch waving.

Jake asked, "Who is that ugly redhead on the porch?" Charlie laughed and threatened to tell his wife she had been called ugly. Doreen O'Halloran Daniels met them with a hug and kiss for each man. Then she took Jake's arm and led him into the house to find Lydia sitting in an easy chair.

"My goodness, look at that gorgeous hunk of woman lazing away in a chair." He knelt beside her and said gently, "Sweetheart, I am sorry, so sorry. Are you hurt badly?"

She smiled her beautiful gentle smiled and answered, "I'm in good shape, Jake. Don't blame your self; we all knew that something like that could happen. The doctor says that in a couple of months I will be fully recovered." She grinned and said, "Except for a few bragging scars that will be left."

Jake leaned over and kissed her again and heard, "Git away from my wife or I'll make you a drink from a jar of good likker,"

The sniper was smiling when Jake took the offered hand. Later in the day Jake was told that the house and location was the home of one of the mountain doctors that reported only what was needed.

Carpenter took him back into the room with Lydia and softly said, "Jake, don't call us any more."

Before Jake could respond, Lydia said, "Jake, we don't blame you for this but we decided before the mission that it would be our last one. We don't want you to call for a side trip but we expect you to visit—and visit often."

Chapter 29

Jake returned to Venture, and to his surprise heard that Lou Pryslybilski had resigned as chief of police—then left town. He had not spoken to anyone and the signed resignation had been left in the mayor's box at City Hall. This worried Jake because Lou had always been potential problem, and he had expressed some reservations about the conduct of the mission into Canada. The mission was completed without Lou having to fire a shot. He had captured the van driver and escort, and had handcuffed them to the vehicle for the authorities to find and appeared to be relaxed on the trip south.

The reports out of Canada said that the transport vehicles had nineteen aliens that were being smuggled into the United States and unknown agents had killed at least twelve smugglers. In both countries the news media was on a feeding frenzy because of the operation had been carried out and neither Canada nor the U.S. officials would admit knowing who carried out the operation. Some tried to make a new story about the ambush of the two well-know couples in Revelstoke. The Royal Canadian Mounted Police helped squash that story because they made a statement that the Loms and Sellers had been suspected for many months, but no agency had been able to come up with sufficient evidence for an arrest. In the statement, the Mountie Officer said, "We do not approve of this type of operation and we will investigate and try to detain the perpetrators. The Canadian law makes no allowances for anyone to take the law into their own hands. The perpetrators broke our law and we will prosecute when they are arrested." The authorities on the U.S. side of the border made similar statements, but many people in both countries smiled and nodded when someone would say that both countries should thank them for ridding the northwest of a real problem. As the days passed, with no comments from the investigating agencies, the story shrank from front-page banner headlines to an occasional Letter to the Editor. Likewise, the television crews packed up and returned to their respective headquarters.

Life in Venture returned to its normalcy as a quiet, peaceful river-front town. At The Table, the suppositions concerning the missing chief of police were dropped after a few days of discussion. Some of the people appeared not to know that Jake had been gone for a few days, and he let it drop in that fashion. There was little talk about the takedown of the smuggling operation in Canada. One of the older members at the table suggested, "The world is better off without them people, and I hope the next bunch gets the same." There was no argument from any of the patrons of the restaurant, and the talk turned to hunting and fishing.

In Venture, this was the important subject in life around the entire community. As in any small town, many items would come up for discussion but somewhere along the line the river and its environs, such as the mountains, would be mentioned. Jake returned to a daily routine of either working on the boat or going up or down the river. One of his favorite past times was to go up river for about five miles and then cut the power and allow the boat to drift down stream until he was ready to go home. On a few occasions he would stay overnight somewhere on the river. One night as he was settling in for the night, after dropping the anchor at the river's edge, Tolliver called on the radio. He told Jake, that the general was pleased with the operation in Canada. Jake said with a chuckle, "Yeah, I could feel his presence as we crossed the border with hardly a notice."

They discussed Lou Pryslybilski in depth. Both of them were concerned as to what Lou's actions might be. Jake told the Brigadier that he was fairly certain that there would be no adverse actions taken but did note that Lou had reacted in a negative fashion even after he had agreed to take part in the Canadian operation. "We didn't require him to shoot," Jake said. "But he captured and secured the driver and escort to the passenger vehicle, so that will put him right in the middle of the mission. I think he will consider all those things and keep quiet."

Before the conversation ended, Tolliver said, "Well, I will call the general and run this by him." Then with a chuckle he continued, "Find your boy's location in case the general wants to send him a message. I'll let you know how the boss reacts to all this."

Jake reflected on that comment for some time. He mused, "Where did Lou go, and what is his state of mind? I hope we don't have problems because, in the most part, he has been a friend. Oh, well. We'll see what happens." Jake made a few calls asking for Lou but couldn't find any trace of the ex-policeman. He dropped the exercise because too many calls would likely draw someone's attention.

Later that evening, Tolliver called and said, "The general says not to worry about your past chief of police. We know where he is and he seems to be relaxed." Jake started to interrupt, but his friend cut him off with, "Don't worry about where Pryslybilski is located. You will be informed if he starts making wrong moves."

Jake took off one day in his boat and no one saw him for a week. He had worked his way into the landward side of a small island and dropped the anchor. There was no work except for catching and making meals, and he caught up with his reading list and spent many hours thinking about a beautiful long-haired woman from Gaza City. He remembered, with pleasure, every moment they had spent together. There were times that he worried about her because of the double life she was living. Laila Shawa lived with danger lurking over her shoulder twenty-four hours a day. Jake had spoke to her a couple of times and always asked her to come to the United States, but she demurred and would say that she was needed at her present position. He was insistent on one of the calls and she cut him off with, "Jake, I will call you if it is needed, but please don't call me again because it is too difficult for me to refuse, and I must stay here. I hope one day I will be able to come to you, but that time is not now. Dear Jake, I must go." It was a hard task but he did not call her again and she was constantly in his thoughts.

The remainder of the year was uneventful. Jake did not hear from the general and didn't mind at all. When the general called, everything went into high and fast action and at times became nerve-wracking. It appeared that the team members were doing OK with staying at home. One night he finally told him self, "Buddy boy, you are getting too old for this life. You may have to do some talking to a couple of marine generals about this type of thinking."

The hunting season opened in the middle of October and there was not much rest because the calls for a guide began in September. Jake made trips to the potholes in eastern Washington and to the mountains in both Washington and Idaho. His prowess as a guide was well known, but most of the memories from the hunters was something call 'innards stew' because that concoction was a favorite in the evening camps high on the mountain side or in the prairie of the eastern section of the state. The old timers would tell the new hunters about innard stew and then act mysteriously about the ingredients in the pot. The cook always went along with the mystery by saying, "Can't tell you. That's an old family secret handed down by Grandma Green."

The stories around the campfire were many and varied. One night someone said, "Jake, you are always speaking of Grandma Green. Tell us about her background."

Jake thought for a few minutes and then started the story, "Her name was Mary Caison and she was born and raised on Crusoe Island in the upper reaches of the Waccamaw River in southeastern North Carolina. The Crusoe people were, and still are, very strange in their approach to life. Grandma was the community storyteller and I sat at her feet for many hours, listening to the tales. My favorite was her story about her great grand father, Jacob Green—so now you know where my name came from. After finishing all of her stories, she would warn her audiences about "The Curse of Jacob Green."

Chapter 30

The hunting, fishing, story-telling, and innard stew came to an abrupt halt in March. A brutal attack by some of the Muslim organizations had gained worldwide attention. The Palestinians ignored the warnings emanating out of Israel and started taking actions against anyone who was not Muslim. According to the media, the city had become a bloodbath. The Israelis and Palestinians were fighting on almost all street corners. After about a week, the Palestinians began closing down the city by massive arrests, with people being taken into custody or put under house restraints with constant guards. World opinion came into play and the Israelis withdrew and set up a wide perimeter around the landward side of Gaza City, constantly patrolling on the seaward side with gunboats. They would not allow anyone to cross the perimeters in either direction, but the unrest didn't slacken in the besieged city. The United Nations sent a peacekeeping force, that sat off-shore on a ship, and neither faction would agree to let them land. Jake was surprised to hear that the major force of Muslim fighters were from Allah's Army. This group had not been heard from since his team had attacked the army in Gaza City. The commander of Allah's Army challenged anyone from the non-Muslim world to come to the Gaza Strip.

He said forcefully, "We were ambushed during a peaceful Gaza City parade. The terrorists who did this cowardly deed are invited to try again." He looked into the camera lens and continued, "We want you to come back, you infidel dogs who ambushed the freedom fighters of Allah's Army."

Jake watched the news clips and smiled as the diatribe was delivered and couldn't resist calling Moise Bernstein, a television reporter from Tel Aviv. The reporter was told about the cowardly attack referred to by the commander.

Jake chuckled and told Bernstein, "Get the word to that guy, in public if you can, that his parade unit was taken out by a three-man team.

Moise laughed and asked, "Jake, do you have a story for me? Where did you get that information? Do you know that the story is true?"

Jake chuckled and replied, "Whoa, partner. No story. Can't say. Yes, it's true." It was the first time that Jake had leaked such information, but he couldn't resist after watching the bombastic, self-righteous Muslim terrorist. It didn't take long for Bernstein to get the word out across the region that more than twenty of Allah's Army were taken out by only three men. There was much speculation as to the originating point of the shooters. Sure enough, the commander of Allah's Army took the bait. He claimed that there were more than ten terrorists who had ambushed the parade. Then he went on to say that the Army had identified the shooters and they were executed.

Moise Bernstein went on television and disputed this claim. He said, "It's funny that all of them had been executed, since I recently talked with them. No one in that organization has been hurt. By the way, why would the so-called commander of the so-called Allah's Army put out a challenge for them to return if they had been executed? I challenge Allah's Army to prove me wrong—all he would have to do is to show the world evidence that the people were executed."

After that quietness reigned in Allah's Army, the reporter called Jake, and said, "Jake, you owe me one." He was assured that the debt would be paid.

Tolliver called and said, "Buddy, you have been talking, haven't you? The international lines are open trying to figure that was responsible for the raid against the Gaza City parade. The Mousaud is especially interested, because many say that they are responsible. One of our contacts in Israel told us that Mousaud is somewhat upset that such a show could be put on under their noses without them knowing about it."

The two friends enjoyed talking about the fracas and agreed that it was not time for the news to be released. Jake said, "I hope no one will be upset, but when the time comes, I want Moise Bernstein to break the story."

They talked for a few more minutes until Tolliver, said quietly, "Jake, I have some disturbing news. Laila Shawa has been put under house arrest, and word has it that she will be brought to the court and tried as an enemy of the Muslim world sometime soon. We have no word on the actual schedule."

After a long silence, Jake responded, "I am going to get her. There will be no negotiation, I am going to bring her back."

His friend replied, "The general said that you would react in this fashion.

He says to inform you, that you will have to make it to Tel Aviv. If you can do that, there will be a helicopter that will get you to Gaza City and furnish papers for all of you, including Laila."

Jake said, "Tell the general that I appreciate his help, and that I will be in Israel by Friday. If everything goes right, we will be out of there no later that Sunday night. There will be four plus Laila coming out."

Jake set up a conference call to Harv and Marv Whiteside and Mike Freeland. After the greeting were over and after a few moments of small talk, Mike Freeland asked, "Jake, what are we here for? It's always nice to talk to you chaps, but a conference call? Are you in trouble?"

Jake chuckled and replied, "No, I am not in any trouble, but I want to take a few days for a trip to Gaza City."

Harv Whiteside said, "Oops. We got ourselves a problem if Jake wants to go on a vacation."

Jake chuckled and said, "Yes. One of my friends is in trouble and I am going after her. Would you guys like some excitement?"

Mike quipped, "Oh boy, I went to Gaza City with this guy one time and we had to be taken out by submarine."

Then, with a serious voice, "Jake, if it is Laila, I have already said that I would go with you."

Marv Whiteside broke in, "I don't know anyone named Laila, but if the Mountie says yes—then I say yes."

Harv chimed in, "Me, too. I've always wanted to go to the Gaza Strip. Jake, we have a friend there, also. Want us to call him?"

Jake said, "No, not right now, but remember this offer because we may need some inside help. Laila is under a closely guarded house arrest. What are your friend's qualifications, and is he a Muslim?"

Harv, responded, "He is a Muslim and one of the best high explosive operators I have ever seen. A few years ago, he and four other guys did some training with the SEALs and Recon. We can depend on him. His wife is from Rhode Island and according to him she whips him quiet often."

Mike Freeland laughed and jibed, "Never mind him, but let's get her."

Jake ended the conference call with, "OK then. Mike, drive over here to my place and we'll pick up these boots on the way to the Middle East. I estimate we will be over there for a week or ten days. Our weapons and necessary papers will be provided when we get to Tel Aviv. Mike, be over here by next Monday and we will leave for the Ozarks during the night directly to Popular Bluff, Arkansas."

When the conference call ended, the next call was for Norman Olsen. There was an intercept with a sweet female voice stating that no one was available for a conversation. Jake surmised that the co-pilot, Martha Hawkins, had assumed other duties. Less than an hour passed before the pilot called.

Jake asked, "Norm, can that bird make it to Tel Aviv and back? If so, file a flight plan that would appear to be a leisurely trip—but not wasting time."

"You bet we can make Israel with no problem," Olsen replied, and continued, "Martha is from Israel, so we can take her to see her family. How many people will be riding with us?"

Jake told him that two would fly from Ellensburg to the Ozarks and pick up two more passengers. All of the riders would be traveling light and should have no problems gaining entry into Tel Aviv. He was instructed to be ready to leave in time to be in Tel Aviv by a week from the coming Thursday.

"We will have to do some heavy planning during the flight," Jake said. "Make the flight plan so that we can travel as long as possible without a dangerous fuel situation arising."

Norman finished the conversation with, "It will depend on the weather. If we find good weather, this plane can go for eight to ten hours and still have fuel to land."

The flight lifted off from Popular Grove, Arkansas, with the first leg of the flight plan to be a fueling stop at Presque Isle, Maine. From Maine, the plan called for stops in London, Nice, Naples, and then into one of the Mediterranean Islands—probably Cyprus. Before leaving the Med, all plans would have to be in place, so Jake called Tolliver and told him that the Israeli help would be needed by Thursday of the next week.

The brigadier gave all the information that would be needed. He gave them a radio frequency to contact the expected helicopter service and warned them that the entry into Gaza City would be the most dangerous part of the trip. Tolliver explained, "The four of you will have papers that identifies you as a television news crew. Your identification will have the strength of being issued by a well-know middle-eastern Muslim cleric. To make things easier, this person will be unavailable for calls, but you will have to be on your toes until you get on the ground in Gaza City. Then it should just be a matter of carefully carrying out your mission. The helicopter should be available for your extraction." He paused and finished, "Jake, that is far as we can go. If the plan does not come together, you're going to be on your own. Good luck. Call me when you are extracted and on your way home."

"Thanks, Pal," Jake answered to finish the radio transmissions. He turned to his team and said, "There you go. You heard the scoop. What do you say now?"

Mike spoke up, "Sounds like a snap to me. Let's make sure we get on the ground in Gaza. My concern will be getting off the ground, 'cause we will probably be in a hurry. If we get sidetracked for any reason, there may be real trouble."

One of the twins growled, "Huh. I have been in trouble ever since I met this guy," as he grinned and pointed to Jake.

The flight across the Atlantic went off easily and was enjoyable to Jake and his team. Sometimes the talk was just visiting, but mostly the conversations concerned the coming operations. Mike Freeland was the first one to mention how to carry out plans for taking on the Army of Allah. He said, "We went in there the last time and three of us took out the operating forces of the movement. At that time it was a new group, but now they will be fully organized. Jake, how do we handle it?"

"Like we did the last time. We go in expecting trouble, not waiting for it. If someone gets in the way—take 'em out or they will get you," was Jake's answer.

Harv Whiteside asked, "When did we take on Allah's Army? Where were big brother and I?"

Mike responded, "You guys were on vacation down in Louisiana while we were slaving over there in the desert."

"Vacation!" snorted Marv, "When was the last time you went swimming with big snakes and bigger alligators? I had rather see three soldiers from Allah's Army than one of those bayou bandits we went up against. Now those were some mean people."

They spent the night in London and made a big deal out of checking out and operating the TV news equipment. A special trip was made into the Arab community to establish the cover for their trip. It was expected that the events would find the way back to the Middle East. The cover started taking shape when their guide introduced them to a Muslim from Gaza City. They questioned him closely about his home and he was pleased to be singled out. He give them detailed descriptions of the city and Mike Freeland spent a lot of time asking detailed questions about the Gaza City waterfront. One question was worked in quietly and seemly with not much attention to the answer. Mike asked about the waterfront—the best food—the best lodging—if a helicopter could be landed on the beach—the best clothing—the best swimming area—and if a helicopter could be landed, where would the landing occur. The answers came freely, the best food and the best lodging would be at Laila's Hotel, and a helicopter could be landed about one block north of the hotel in a police parking lot. The clothing and swimming area was also discussed at length and nothing more was said about a landing site for a helicopter.

The trip continued with one night in Naples, where the news crew hit the streets again. Problems did not occur until the landing in Cyprus. They were searched, researched, and searched again with continuous questioning about their mission. During this time the Greeks and Turks were cooperating, because the two factions would question and compare, but the team held the story of being a TV news crew with permission from one of the leading clerics of the Gaza Strip. They were kept under house arrest for three days. On Wednesday, Jake decided to clear the air or the mission would have to be scrubbed if they were not allowed to leave for Tel Aviv on Thursday morning. He demanded to see the officer in charge of the situation.

A Greek Army major received him with a sneering aloofness until Jake said quietly, "Listen, Major, and listen closely. If we are not out of here by early morning this island is going to be invaded by American officials and Muslim Clerics."

The officer tried to talk it down, by saying, "No one knows you are here and under close guard."

Jake smiled, "Major, don't make the biggest mistake in your life. My people know where I am at all times. I am supposed to be in Tel Aviv tomorrow. If I don't make it, your boss is going to skin you alive. As a matter of fact, you should call your boss now and tell him what I just said."

The major glared across the desk for long moments and when Jake would not break the eye lock, the major nervously dialed the telephone and talked for a few words and then Jake could hear a tirade over the phone. Red-faced and furious and with threats from the Greeks and Turks, Jake and the team were released on Wednesday afternoon. Everyone laughed when the Turkish commander haughtily told Jake to leave by 0500 on Thursday morning.

Norman Olsen and his co-pilot had the airplane in the air and heading for Israel at 0430. Jake had decided not to create any confrontation with the local officials. The frequency to contact the Gaza City transportation was dialed in, and Jake made the call. He was told that the transportation would be ready for flight when they arrived, and permission to fly out of Israel had been obtained. The requests for landing in Gaza City had been sent but no answer had been received. Jake suggested that the permission papers from the Cleric to enter the Gaza Strip be mentioned on the next contact.

"Don't harass them," Jake said, "but make sure they understand that we will be landing in Gaza City this afternoon." During the last leg of their journey the team discussed what they would have to do to have a successful mission. The Whitesides were to take over the outside area of the hotel when Jake and Mike Freeland made the move to rescue Laila.

It was understood by the team that no one would be allowed to hinder the operation. During the discussion, Jake said, "When we get to the hotel, we will check in and then contact local officials for plans to do the television broadcasts on Friday.

Harv Whiteside asked, "Are we actually going to do any TV work?" The following discussion had everyone agreeing that the cover story would have to be used to subvert any questions from the local authorities.

Marv suggested, "Let's go into town on Friday morning and actually shoot some film."

He looked at Jake and continued, "Jake, I think you should stay at the hotel to keep an eye on Laila, and the three of us will put on a good show for the Muslims." Before any objections could be made, Harv and Mike had agreed to the plan.

Mike grinned at Jake, and said, "You are too old for this kind of stuff. We younger guys will take over the hard work." Then in a serious note, he asked, "Jake, how are we going to get out of town with that girl?" After a short discussion they agreed that nothing could be planned until meeting with the helicopter crew.

The Tel Aviv tower was apparently waiting for the flight. Norman Olsen called back, "Jake, they are ready for us—you must have some pull somewhere. We have been instructed to land away from the terminal and they say a helicopter is waiting and ready for immediate take off."

"OK, Norm, call the chopper and tell them when we will set down and that there will be four passengers." The co-pilot came back and said that all messages had been received, and then she told the team what to expect on the landing. Israeli officials would be waiting and no one was to leave the plane until clearance has been issued. The landing was smooth and as soon as the door was opened and steps released four men entered the cabin. One of them said with a grin, "Welcome to Tel Aviv and I don't want any names. There is a helicopter waiting for you and it's cleared for your entry into the Gaza Strip. The pilot and two crewmen are Jordanians and the co-pilot is one of ours. All of them have been instructed to take orders from you. You will be taken to landing zone near the Laila Hotel on the beach." With a wider grin he said, "The landing zone, by the way, is a police helipad for the Gaza City police helicopters. When you leave, head straight north after you get over the water. More than likely they will try to intercept you with helicopters, but we assure you that they will not catch you. Your helicopter crew has not been briefed on their part of the mission other than getting you into Gaza City and waiting to take you out. Don't ask me any questions because I don't have any more answers. These men will give you any equipment you need. As soon as you are equipped head for the chopper and good luck."

The equipment was in a carryall setting next to the helicopter. Each member of the team selected a machine pistol, a handgun, and a knife. They were offered an armored vest but it was agreed that a vest would be very noticeable and they did not want to draw any undue attention. The helicopter pilot was waiting in the cabin when the team took seats and strapped in. He said, "I need your letter of permission to go on this trip. The people in Gaza said they have to see it before you will be taken to your hotel." Jake was expecting that request and handed the pilot the papers. He did not look at them and in a few minutes they were in the air. The flight moved off shore and headed generally south. The team worked for the first few miles securing the arms that they had been issued. Each weapon was checked to make sure all movements were in order and the crew was startled when they fired out of the open hatch to check the firing mechanisms. All the material disappeared into the different bags that a well-equipped TV news crew would have on assignments. The co-pilot came back and told them that a Gaza City helicopter was on the way to escort them to the helipad. He told them that it was a normal procedure and no problems were expected. They all laughed when the news that the two pilots knew each other very well, was relayed. In a few moments the escort moved into view and told the visiting pilot to trail at one half mile. They headed directly toward Gaza City, and there was a large contingent of policemen and forty or fifty soldiers wearing the red headdress of Allah's Army.

Mike Freeland smiled at Jake and pulled his visor lower on his head. Jake shrugged and said, "I doubt if any of these people have seen us." They all chuckled as he pulled his cap lower over his eyes.

The helicopter was surrounded as soon as it touched down. The city policemen were on the inner circle and the members of Allah's Army were about ten yards behind the policemen. A quick count by the Whiteside twins came up with at least sixty armed men standing ready as the inspecting officials walked toward the aircraft. The pilot came back and told the passengers to belt themselves to a bulkhead ring and sit on the deck. Steps were placed at the open hatch and the crew started opening all the bags as two officials entered. Both took appraising looks at the visitors and studied the letter from the cleric. Jake nodded when they were asked to identify the leader of the news crew. No one had spoke until one of the officials said, "Who are you and why are you here?" Jake responded, "I think the letter you are holding answers both questions."

He surprised the two men with the direct and challenging statement. They bristled and the second man snarled, "We want to hear it from you and don't try to lie because I am from the Great Satan."

Mike Freeland snarled back, "We don't identify with your Great Satan, but as the letter tells you we are here to do stories about your problems. If you don't want the truth sent to the outside world, get off this aircraft and we will leave." The officials appeared to be nonplused at the response that had been generated. The team held a collective breath while the luggage was searched. The contraband had been hidden well except for each man's pocketknife. They had not been hidden nor had they been declared. Jake explained that the trip was taken on in such a hurry they had forgotten about the personal knives that would be used only during the filming.

He said with the first smile, "You don't know how much junk we have to cut during a film run." The senior official smile weakly and said, "Very fine, the policemen outside will take you to your accommodations."

Harv Whiteside stood up and asked the one who had brought in the comment about the Great Satan, where in the states had he lived. The man replied that he had been reared in and around Monterrey, California.

Marv said quietly, "I won't ask you how in the world did you get over here and why."

The man stared for a long moment and said with some heat, "You wouldn't understand, and..." The brothers shrugged and started repacking the equipment without paying further attention to anyone.

The ride to the hotel was a short one, but the entire team carefully surveyed the terrain from the helipad to the hotel. They were escorted to the check in desk, and the clerk was ordered to call the owner. Jake held his breath when Laila walked into the room and stared at the guests while the official was explaining the situation. Jake noted that a woman escorted her to the desk and he had spotted a man that he was sure was another guard. The breath was released slowly when her inspection was complete. There had been no indication that she had ever seen any of the news crew. When she started the check in procedure, there was a hint of a smile when Mike Freeland stood in front of her.

When Jake stepped up she gave a full smile and said, "We are glad that our place of rest has been chosen as the base for your work. If there is anything you need, please ask."

Jake returned the smile and replied, "Thank you for your kindness. If it is possible we would like adjoining rooms so your other guests will not be disturbed by our movements in and out of the hotel."

"She said, "I will show you to your rooms." On the way up the hallway the two made contact by hooking fingers momentarily. When she started back for the lobby, Jake was sure that her eyes showed excitement along with anxiety. He watched her as she walked away and sure enough the escort was with her and the man was casually standing near the exit sign and waited until the two women started down the stairs. He quietly followed.

The news team was on the streets by 0800 on Friday morning. Jake stayed with them until noon and then made his way back to the hotel. There had been no undue attention and the street people, complicated the team's action, because they wanted to be on television. Before he left Jake suggested that the streets would be a good place to work so the officials could relax. The children were lined up for a still shot and then allowed to play before the camera. It was working because everyone seemed to relax and were laughing and talking about the actions of the kids. Jake got back to the hotel after the lunch hour. Laila and her escort seated him at one of the windows that offered a view of the beach. When they came for his order, there was no opportunity for them to talk. He noticed that she was taking time to write the order. She handed him the paper and he waited until the two women were back in the kitchen area, then he casually opened the paper slip and she had written, "NO." in large letters. Later when she got to his table without the escort, he smiled and said, "Yes."

The escort was coming toward the table and he turned to look out the window and said, "Be ready at any time."

Her face betrayed no emotions but her eyes were smiling. After eating, he went to the beach and started toward the police helipad and was taking notes for all to see. He stopped at the helicopter and walked around it until he reached the pilot. Then in a casual conversation he asked if there would be anytime that the engines could be started without arousing attention. The pilot appeared to ignore Jake and walked a few steps toward the nose of his aircraft and said quietly, "The only time we can start the engines is with permission from the police. So far they have allowed the engines started at 1600 each day for thirty minutes and after that we have to deliver the keys to the police station."

He then assured Jake that he had enough fuel for the trip back with a few gallons to spare. "Jake turned away, and said quietly, "OK, be ready at 1600 on Sunday for an immediate take off, and we might need some help with the police." When he got back to the hotel, he made a number of trips in and out and around the building and spotted four people that he considered as house guards. If they remained in place, the team would have to face five people with the female who escorted Laila.

They stayed away from the hotel all of Saturday. The local authorities were eager to appeared on camera and berate Israel and the United States. Jake interviewed the commander of Allah's Army of the Gaza Strip. The soldier was raging about the Great Satan and the lackeys of other nations when Jake stopped him with a question, "Commander, is it true that someone has wiped out a number of units of Allah's Army—both over here and in the States?"

The official went into a tirade about lies being spread across the world. Marv Whiteside kept the camera aimed and film rolling, and all were surprised when no one confiscated the film. The mayor of Gaza City finally led the commander off the street, and Jake watched Marv hand the film to his brother who disappeared into the crowd and thought to himself, "There are going to be some people who will love to have that film." The work for the day was over and the team walked back to the hotel, and Jake related the conversation to the chopper pilot. He mentioned the people that he suspected of being house guards at the hotel and where they seemed to be stationed.

Mike Freeland said, "Let's spend all day tomorrow tracking these people because when the action starts there will be no time for guessing. Jake, if you can ask Laila to take out the female guard. In case you cannot get the word to her I will take out the man who sits in the hall and the girl. You be ready to get to Laila and get her out of there. We will be able to cover the beach as we make for the aircraft."

Sunday morning dawned bright and clear. The team had been hoping that it would be raining or foggy. They spent the morning walking around the hotel complex and at noon they discussed the observations. It was agreed that the police had five guards on Laila. The woman was the one who caused the most concern because she was with the target.

Mike Freeland asked, "Jake, do you think Laila can take out the woman? If she can, get her out of the way, these boots and I can get the four men."

The twins grinned at the descriptive 'boots' and nodded in agreement with the Mountie. When the check was being paid, Jake slipped Laila a note asking if she could take out her guard. He received a thumb up when he turned at the stairs. He saluted, making sure she could see four fingers and hoped she would understand it as the time for the action to begin. For the next couple of hours, the helicopter could be heard at times. The crew was doing their part to hold off any suspicious movements. Jake and Mike walked by the guard in the hallway at 1545. They stopped outside Laila's door and made a scene by arguing. The hallway guard came up and demanded to what was going on. Jake took him by the arm and started talking. When the room door opened Mike took the man out with a blow to the side of his head. They pushed him into the bedroom and he joined the woman guard on the floor—both were dead. Mike made for the front of the building and Laila guided Jake down the back steps.

When they stepped into the first floor hallway, three coughs from silenced weapons were heard. The team members had the other hotel guests sitting at two back tables. Harv Whiteside said sternly, "Don't get involved in this and stay in those chairs. If you follow us out or raise an outcry we will shoot you. When the authorities come in, answer all questions truthfully and you will probably be OK." They left the hotel at a brisk walk and when they heard the helicopter engine rev, all of them broke into a run. The co-pilot and crewmember were outside and threw Laila and the four men into the cabin. When they yelled, the pilot jerked the machine into the air. A hail of bullets could be heard with some hitting the outside frame. The team stood to the doors and sprayed the beach with bullets. A number of the policeman were taken out and the others went to ground or run for cover by the building.

The pilot turned out over the water and after about 20 minutes, the heading was changed to north. Everyone was beginning to relax when the pilot yelled and abruptly changed course and commenced a dive. When the machine gun rounds started hitting, it was apparent that they were under attack by another aircraft. The pilot was throwing the aircraft all over the sky, but the intruder could outmaneuver because of more power. Then disaster almost struck, the attacking aircraft pulled up alongside and over the radio demanded that they return to Gaza City.

All attention was on the attacking helicopter when the co-pilot drew a gun and ordered the pilot to obey the order or he would be shot. The turn was started and Marv Whiteside took a hand. He had stood up behind the co-pilot and chopped him across the forearm and the weapon fell and the co-pilot screamed in pain. The Navy SEAL had broken his arm, and the Marine threw a line around his neck and snapped it.

The pilot asked, “What do I do? We cannot fight this one, he is too good for us.” Jake quietly said, “If we have to go, let’s take that guy with us.” He turned to the pilot and said, “Ram that guy.” There was no answer, but the helicopter was brought up abruptly and turned to the tormentor. The team stood up and charged the weapons and started firing out the doors. Then it happened, the attacker exploded in front of them and they were thrown to the floor by the moves of the aircraft as heading and altitude were changed to avoid the falling debris. Before they could recover, a fighter aircraft that was flying low and rocking his wings buzzed the helicopter. The northerly heading was regained and the engine was firewalled by the pilot. No one spoke for a while until Laila asked, “Where did the fighter come from?” The question could not be answered, because the action had only taken seconds and in a few moments the savior aircraft disappeared over the horizon. Jake called Tel Aviv and sent a message to Norman Olsen to be ready for takeoff within an hour.

Chapter 31

The remainder of the flight to Tel Aviv was quiet. No one was talking, and it was obvious how tightly they were wound. This was understandable, because of the pressures of the last three days. Laila and Jake were sitting together and were lightly holding hands.

When the pilot called and told them to fasten their seat belts, Laila belted in and said to all of them, "I can't thank you enough for you have done for me. The authorities were going to charge me tomorrow and my days were numbered. Thank you. Thank you." Jake squeezed her shoulders and the other team members appeared to relax listening to her.

Harv responded, "Shucks, ma'am, hit warn't nothing."

They all chuckled when Laila smiled and said, "I don't know what he just said."

Harv answered again, "Miss Laila, we are happy to have you out of that town."

The others agreed and began laughing and talking as the helicopter came in for a landing. Jake looked out the open door and could see the airplane close by and Norman had the engines lit off. It only took a few minutes for them to transfer from one aircraft to the other. As soon as the doors were closed, the jet started rolling and there was no hesitation when they turned onto the runway. The plane rotated as the co-pilot said, "Thank you, Tel Aviv, maybe we'll see you again one of these days."

As soon as the airplane leveled on its cruising altitude and speed, the tension of the crew and passengers lessened and laughter and talking could be heard throughout the cabin. Even Norman Olsen left the cockpit and was kidding all of them by telling how much he suffered on the ground in Tel Aviv.

He laughingly said, "Those Israelis are like a bunch of Jews, they know how to eat and drink." A hand reached out of the cockpit and the Jewish co-pilot swatted him.

Laila spoke up, "I cannot tell you how great I feel. Thank you all for coming after me. The prosecutor was intending to charge me with treason on Monday morning. According to my guards I was to be there by 0800."

She laughed delightedly when Norm spoke up, "My sweet, you will be in Syracuse, Sicily, at 0800 Monday morning."

He turned to Jake, and continued, "When we leave Sicily, we should be able to get to Heathrow without stopping. If the weather holds, we have clearances to head directly there. Someone has arranged for us to fly outside the normal flight routes, with distant escort most of the way. Boss-man, you really have some connections somewhere."

Everyone chuckled and agreed. Laila leaned into Jake's shoulder and captured one hand with both of hers. She whispered, "Jake, how can I ever thank you for rescuing me?" He chuckled and responded quietly, "Just stay as gorgeous as you are now and whisper in my ear when you want something." She giggled and rose up and kissed him on the ear and breathed, "How was that?"

"Makes me quiver—let's bail out of this plane and then we will be alone," he answered, faking a breathless state of mind.

They spent the night in Syracuse and left at 0500 on Monday morning. During the evening, Jake asked the co-pilot to take Laila shopping for a change of clothes. She came back dressed in jeans and a tee shirt and enjoyed all the whistles from her new-found male friends. The news from Gaza City was a steady torrent of complaints and threats from the official family of the Muslims. They didn't know whom to blame and cursed the Great Satan and its outlaw friends from Israel. The Israelis were laughing and disclaiming any part of the raid on Gaza City. One of their news reporters suggested that a private organization had gone in and rescued Laila Shawna because the government was ready to try her on trumped up charges. One of the television reporters from the United States suggested that the Army of Allah were the real outlaws.

She said, "It appears someone or some organization has the number of this so-called army. We have reliable reports that since the inception of Allah's Army someone has been tracking them—taking them out as fast as they can train a cadre." This caused a storm of protest until someone asked the commander what happened during a parade in Gaza City and who stopped terrorist attacks in the United States. There was an in-depth story about the two incidents. No one saw the commandant of Allah's Army after that news broke nor were there any more tirades on the television stations.

At Heathrow, the flight was directed to a small hangar for general aviation aircraft. The site was near one of the gates, and the passengers were allowed to leave the airport without going through customs. They all checked in, as previously directed, at a hotel near the airfield. There were seven rooms available but only five were used. The aircrew took one room and Jake insisted that Laila check in with him. She was hesitant until he said, "I am not leaving you alone until we are sure you are safe, and besides I want to take you shopping for a full wardrobe. I like that white tee shirt, but these other guys do, too."

She blushed, as the others were enthusiastic about the get up. When they reached the room, Jake took her in his arms and said gently, "Don't worry. It's going to be tough, but one of the beds is yours and the other is mine."

She smiled and said, "It will not be long before the situation can be changed, but I'm not ready."

She leaned back in his arms and gave a full laugh when he continued in a whining voice, "I will leave you alone, if you will leave me alone."

They sat at the table and made small talk about the adventures of the past few days until she said, "When I saw you at the check-in counter, I almost fainted and then I became frightened that I had exposed you with my actions. Jake, you saved my life. I had already decided that I would not go to trial in their court."

He covered her hands on the table and said, "I'm glad I came along when I did."

The next morning at breakfast, Jake told the aircrew to be ready to take off at sunset. He said, "I don't want to be exposed very often on the way back home. Laila and I are going shopping and don't expect us for lunch."

Norm said, "We'll be ready," he put his arm around his co-pilot and continued, "This girl said she was going to kick me out of the airplane if I didn't buy her an engagement ring here in London. Shucks, I can't fly outside of the plane, so I guess I'll have to buy that ring."

There were some happy responses to the pilot's problems and some kisses for the co-pilot. After lunch they all split off in different directions, at least they said that was the plan, but on the way up the street Jake spied Harv and Marv following—one on each side of the street. The, somewhat surprised, he saw Mike Freeland moving slowly about a block in front.

Jake mused, "Well now, we have got our selves a parade." He didn't say anything about the parade to Laila. She was excited about the shopping trip, but said a number of times that she would be frugal on the spending. They entered the store that had been recommended by the hotel matron. When the sales agent approached, Laila indicated she only wanted a few pieces of clothing. Jake shook his head at the store attendant, and as Laila started shopping, he told the woman that she was to make up a package for a full wardrobe as the shopper selected a piece. When a skirt was selected, a week's supplies of like skirts were placed in the package; likewise when a pair of slacks was picked, they were packed with a week's supply. Laila was not aware of all the action until they shopped for bags. Her chin dropped in surprise when it took four suitcases to hold her shopping.

She said, "No, no, not that much. I wasn't planning to buy so much."

Jake chucked her under the chin and replied, "I'm sorry, once that stuff comes off the hangers, you have to buy it." The load was so heavy; a taxi was summoned to take them back to the hotel.

On the way, Laila asked, "Jake, how can I repay you for all this? You are too good to me."

He was quiet for a few moments, and replied, "This morning the pilot gave me an idea about buying a ring. Will you marry me?"

She started to cry and said, "Yes, I'll marry you. Of course, I'll marry you." He had to assure her that he was in love with her and she expressed the same emotion toward him. Jake leaned over and told the taxi driver to stop at a jewelry store. They went in and bought a ring.

The flight back to the states was silent after all the congratulatory hugs, kisses, and handshakes were over. After they had been in flight for an hour, Jake stepped into the cabin and told Norm to change his flight plan and land at one of the lesser-known airports for refueling and stop over. He made a call and in a few minutes he announced that they would be landing in Portland, Maine, at 0230. No one questioned the change in plans and they returned to their own devices. Mike Freeland was sleeping, the Whiteside twins were playing blackjack and Marv was winning and crowing about it. Then the cards turned and Harv was the one sitting on the roost crowing. Jake and Laila were involved with each other. The other passengers could only hear them as they chuckled or laughed at each other. It was apparent that they were enjoying the freedom to be together, but it was also apparent that Jake was concerned about possible recognition at the larger airports. With all the media coverage of the past couple of days, Laila would probably be recognizable. She was a beautiful woman that had been under house arrest guarded by the Gaza City police force; yet she escaped in a route controlled by the police and members of Allah's Army. One of the newscasts that had been heard before leaving London was that Allah's Army had placed a price on her head. It would be paid if she were turned over dead or alive.

The visit to Portland lasted only a few hours. They checked in at an airport motel with orders for a call at 1000. On the way back to the airport, Jake told them that the flight plan had been made to Los Angeles, but after take off Norm would change the plan for a stop in Hot Springs, Arkansas, and then to Los Angeles. The real plan was to shake anyone that may have information as to who they were.

Jake said, "These are just precautions. I don't believe anyone is aware of us. All of you watch yourselves, though, in case someone does catch on. It's likely that we will live the rest of our lives without notice of this flight."

Marv laughed and asked, "Jake, why are you going to California?"

Harv spoke to his brother, "Dumbass, who said anything about going to LA? I will lay odds that the pilot is preparing the change of plans after he leaves Arkansas." After boarding for the westward flight, the attitude was light and they were enjoying the company. Before reaching the Hot Springs controller, the plan was changed to a small Ozark Mountain airport.

As they were preparing to leave, one of the Whiteside twins said, "Friends, it's been interesting so stay in touch, in case you need to be bailed out again."

Amid the laughter, he continued, "Laila, when can we expect an invitation to a wedding?"

For the first time, a sense of humor surfaced. With a grin, she replied, "Who said any thing about a wedding? I wanted this ring and would say anything to get it."

Then, more seriously, "When a date is set you will be among the first that will be notified."

After leaving the Arkansas airspace, the plane turned northwest and headed for home. The flight plan had changed once again and they were soon on the heading that would take them into Ellensburg, Washington.

Venture, Washington soon made Laila feel at home. She became a celebrity, with Jake looking on with an approving smile. Much of their time was spent on the river. After living most of her life in or near a desert, Laila couldn't get enough of the fresh water. Jake had introduced her to floating the river at night and fishing for salmon. The first fish that she caught turned out to be a big one; it weighed in at forty-two pounds. It took almost an hour for her to land it and then she felt sorry for the fish.

She said plaintively, "Jake, it's beautiful. Will it live if we put it back into the water?"

He carefully unhooked the fish and said, "If you put it back, it will live," and handed her the fish. The catch was very much alive and while she was fighting it, her feet went out from under her and she joined the fish in the river. She came up sputtering and laughing as the salmon switched it tail and disappeared in the depths of the Columbia River.

During one of the trips down river, she came up behind Jake and put her arms around him, then softly said, "Jake, I want to marry you now." He took her in his arms and after a gentle kiss, he replied, "I've been waiting almost six months to hear you say that."

The next few weeks were taken up with wedding plans that included calling many people with invitations. A decision between them had been made not to use the mail for the plans because that would take time and they were ready to get married.

Samantha Silvers squealed with delight and said, "Navy, I am so happy for you. Would it be OK for me to come and help with the planning? Laila? What a beautiful name, Jake."

He chuckled, "You should see her—if you want to see beautiful. She is on the line, so…"

Two beautiful women interrupted him as they introduced themselves. Laila got off the line with glistening eyes and a wide smile, and said that Samantha would be in Venture the next day. The last call that Jake made was to Oklahoma City.

He said, "Governor, this is Jake Green. I would like to invite you and that gorgeous red-haired wife to my wedding."

His old friend's voice trembled and he heard, "Jake, we have talked about you many times and have been afraid that we had lost a good friend. I'll answer for the redhead, too; we will be honored and delighted to attend your wedding."

It took a long time for Jake to accept his good fortune. He had gained many friends, lost a lot of enemies, and he was going to marry the greatest, most beautiful woman in the world. Their backgrounds and lives did not match, but he felt that she would be with him for the rest of his life. Laila said later that she had many of the same feelings about marrying Jake Green.

They were on the boat a couple of days before the ceremony and Laila said, "Jake, I'm so happy. You have given me another world and I love all my new friends, but there is one thing I fear. Your life frightens me. You have never said, but from what I've seen, you live in danger all the time. Jake, we both are in danger so lets run away from any black operations that may be offered in the future."

Jake didn't answer for a while, and then said, " I have lived this way many years and have lost some friends and have gained many more, but now I have you. My black ops days are over."

They didn't mention this conversation to anyone. Jake had told his friends many times not to talk too much, and in this case, he felt that an enemy might recognize Laila sometime in the future. They would have to be on guard at all times. He smiled and mused, "Well, Venture will be a good place for our home. Not many people come through this part of the United States."

Wedding day dawned calm, with the sun promising to shine. The guest had begun arriving. The men went to the boat landing while the women attended Laila. Jake was getting some good-natured ribbing about his loss of freedom. Everyone was enjoying the time that contact had been established. Jake looked out over the faces of his old comrades. John and Samantha Silvers had arrived with the other friends from the Korean War. Many of the people from Detachment X-Ray had come in. There were two who were missing—the two marine generals—Tolliver and Sheffield. He was disappointed, but knew that they could be on some secret operations and with a smile he said that he was probably lucky that they weren't here. Even with the conversation with Laila he knew that the general could be very persuasive. Jake shrugged his shoulders and turned his attention back to his friends.

At 1000, Samantha walked down the path and called, "OK, it's time to get dressed. We will soon have a wedding if you can keep control of the groom to be. The bride is jaw-droppingly beautiful, so stay away from her room." She grinned and pointed to Jake, and turned back toward the house. The guests who were in the motel left and promised that they would be back to cheer the bride and groom. Jake led his Korean buddies—Silvers, Jacobs, Joseph and Carpenter—back to the house.

Everyone had made it back by 1300. The minister who was to perform the ceremony asked who the best man was and found that one hadn't been selected.

They roared when Jake said, "I didn't even think about a best man. But thinking about it, I don't want a best man." He paused and there were some surprised looks, then he continued, "What I would like—instead of a best man—I want best men and you guys are the best men that I know. I want all of you to stand with me."

There were some cheers and applause that brought some of the women out. They laughed with delight when they were told about the best men. In a few moments they joined the men and all nervously waited for the bride to arrive. The door opened and Jake told them later that the two most beautiful women in the world came out—Samantha Silvers escorted the bride to the altar area that had been constructed in the family room. Jake turned toward the sliding door and saw most of his neighbors standing on the patio. He reached a hand for Laila and they went to the door and both opened it and then the wedding began. All of the guests responded when the question, "Who gives this woman?"

In unison they said, "We do."

When the ceremony was completed, the bride and groom went to greet their neighbors, and that was the first time they had seen the serving tables and the catered spread. The town's people had made that plan without letting the others know. The wedding day of Jake Green and Laila Shawa would be the talk of Venture for days to come.

Then it happened. About two weeks after the wedding, a late night knock was heard, and they became nervous because the neighbors would have rang the bell. Jake slipped out of the back door and walked quietly around the house. There were two men and he chuckled because he recognized two marine generals. He led them into the house and introduced them to Laila.

He said, "These two men caused all of the help in getting us in and out of Gaza City." Then he turned and started to continue, General I have…"

General Sheffield, the general, interrupted and said, "We know, Jake. You are quitting the business—well, I'm quitting, too."

He pointed to Tolliver and continued, "This guy is my relief, so help him as much as you can by recommending people to work with him."

Then he dropped the bomb, "Jake, I am sorry to have to tell you, but your cover has been blown and people also know you and Laila are married. We don't know who broke the cover, but it may have been your friend, the policeman."

Jake responded, "Thanks for the warning, General. Can you take us out of here tonight?"

The people in Venture still shake their heads and wonder about a good neighbor who disappeared one night with his new bride. Since that night, no one has heard from Jake and Laila Green.

Epilogue

The boat floated in and gently nestled into its mooring. All of the children and many of the grown-ups greeted him with a welcome only they could show. Further back, the boatman could see a tall, beautiful woman, with long black hair, holding a small boy. After he had unloaded the treats for the children and the men had unloaded the ordered supplies, he made his way up the beach.

He took the beautiful lady in his arms and said gently, "Hello, Mrs. Blue, I'm glad to be home." She laughed and answered, "Hello, Mr. Blue. We are glad to have you back. Since you have been gone I have named our boy—so Mr. Blue, greet your son, Jacob Blue."

Mr. Blue kissed his wife and child and led them off the beach. Their friends on the beach serenaded them with songs and greetings until they disappeared into one of the houses of the island village.

The Curse of Jacob Green
by
Jess Parker

A curse on you and all your line,
Jacob Green will appear another time.
Beware the year of seven,
The one who pays will not reach Heaven.
When the finger goes to the right,
There is no cause for you to fight.
But if the pendulum reverses its turn,
Jacob Green is looking for one to burn.

Jacob Green was a traveling man, and it was said that he could turn the head of any woman. He appeared on regular rounds. One time he may have been a traveling salesman, but the next time he would come with a Bible in his hand preaching to those who would listen. The next trip, he may have been a mule trader. On each of the trips, at least one woman would fall to his evil influence.

One year the word reached Southport, North Carolina, that Jacob Green was on his way. This caused a community meeting of all the men. The year was 1857, and in October, Charlie Gause, Wilson Mintz, Abraham White, Harvey Swain, Solomon Willets, and Obediah Sellers hanged Jacob Green. A ghostly voice sounded the curse as the body of Jacob Green swung from the oak limb. Twice, as the rope unwound counter-clockwise, the left arm stiffened and the finger pointed at Charlie Gause—then to Wilson Mintz.

Later that year (1857) Charlie Gause died in a house fire. Wilson Mintz was found burned to death at his Green Swamp tar kiln in 1867. Mary Simmons refused to run away with a peddler in 1887, and then died in a mysterious fire. The peddler's name was Jacob Wilson, and Mary was the granddaughter of Abraham White. Al Swan burned to death in a car wreck in 1937. He was the great-great-grandson of Harvey Swain. Just before the crash, Swan had fought with a mule trader by the name of Jake Lewis. The two traveling men, Wilson and Lewis, were direct descendants of Jacob Green. There is no known evidence that the families of Solomon Willets or Obediah Sellers have suffered any tragedy that could be construed as part of the curse. People who believe in curses say that until one is fulfilled it can be extended in all directions—even changed to other families. Any changes will have to be made by a direct descendant of the one making the curse.

My grandmother told me this story, and according to her, Jacob Green was her great-great grandfather. I have traveled the world over and my middle name is Jacob, a direct descendant of Jacob Green. So is your name Willets or Sellers, or are there ones out there who are my enemies?

Praise for books in the Jake Green saga

Detachment X-Ray

Move over, Rambo…I have a new commando hero.

Modest, unassuming Jake Green has outdone, outrun, outgunned the infamous Sly in Jess Parker's no-nonsense action thriller *Detachment X-Ray*. The first person narrative is so unadorned that you feel as though this innocent southern boy, who becomes a part of an elite killing squad, is sitting next to you, saying, "Well, it was like this, ma'am…" as he proceeds to give you the inside view of a modern day, peacetime "dirty dozen." It is an enjoyable read.

C.J. Morace, reviewer and author of *Cocodrie*

Survival of the Toughest Kind

With all the current rage over the popular *Survivor* on TV, *Detachment X-Ray* delivers over 100% on the lifestyles of "real" survivors of the military kind. This novel is fast-paced, readable, humorous, disgusting, and heartwarming. Not a book for just service people, it has much to give to any and all readers who value the freedoms most take for granted. *Detachment X-Ray* goes behind the scenes of a man's life and all he "survived." Barbecued rats, turnips, and raw rabbit are just a few of the tasty meals included in this amazing tale of true grit, for sure. Two thumbs way up.

Lynn Barry, reviewer and author of *Puddles*.

Covert Avengers

In the previous book (*Detachment X-Ray*) Jake Green had told Major Long Ball Kwong that the next time Jake would gut him. Surprise, surprise, when Long Ball Kwong appeared with a trade delegation from the People's Republic of China as Mr. Dong Ping (future Premier).

Jake, his new staff and comrades from the Korean War got together to deal with a mountain feud, stop a drug running operation (via sea), and make plans for Long Ball.

Very few sequels to books and movies are as good as the original. Yet, Jess Parker has succeeded in doing it here. It was fast-paced and non-stop all the way through the novel with a climatic ending that left me laughing and begging for more! I can only hope the author is considering a third for Jake Green. I am so happy to be able to highly recommend this book and its author to everyone I meet! *****

Detra Fitch
Huntress Reviews

Jess Parker will make a secret agent fan out of me yet! First, *Detachment X-Ray* captured this reader (whose literary preferences have never strayed to the "macho action" kingdom) and then I found myself enthralled with yet another adventure of Jake Green in *Covert Avengers*. Same down-home humanity with a sterling new cast of believable and endearing characters as an older Navy (alias, Leader, aka my hero) returns to action to avenge brutal injustices of the Korean War. I keep asking myself how Jess Parker does it…the narrative is as trim as fatless sirloin but the satisfying rich taste (suspense, humor, and good-old rooting for the good guys) comes through without embellishment. And there is only one word for me now—I'm hooked! As everyone should be if they read these books!

C.J. Morace, reviewer and author of *Cocodrie* and *Applachia.*